T0171534

BEYOND FEAR

BEYOND FEAR

Vernell Everett

iUniverse, Inc.
New York   Bloomington

Beyond Fear

This is a work of fiction. All of the characters, names, incidents, organizations, and dialogue in this novel are either the products of the author's imagination or are used fictitiously.

iUniverse books may be ordered through booksellers or by contacting:

iUniverse
1663 Liberty Drive
Bloomington, IN 47403
www.iuniverse.com
1-800-Authors (1-800-288-4677)

Because of the dynamic nature of the Internet, any Web addresses or links contained in this book may have changed since publication and may no longer be valid. The views expressed in this work are solely those of the author and do not necessarily reflect the views of the publisher, and the publisher hereby disclaims any responsibility for them.

ISBN: 978-1-4401-9941-7 (sc)
ISBN: 978-1-4401-9939-4 (dj)
ISBN: 978-1-4401-9940-0 (ebk)

Printed in the United States of America

iUniverse rev. date: 1/14/2010

CHAPTER ONE

▼

Sunday mornings in Mississippi were times for church going, playing, eating good or just resting up for Monday. Everybody in this part of the world had to work five and a half days a week. Nobody was exempt, not even the small children between the ages of five and ten. There was always enough work for everybody. Now, Sunday was different. Sunday was the Lord's Day. The God-fearing people of Mississippi never claimed to work six days and rest the seventh day like the creator did; they made do with five and one-half days of working before they rested or took a break from the work they mostly hated. The other half day was set aside to unwind from a hard week and to get ready for praising the Lord on Sunday. Some of these people didn't have church on their minds on Saturday nights, they were too busy sinning. They would ask the Lord for forgiveness on Sunday, along with tithing a small offering from the monies that was left over from a hot Saturday night of paying for their sins. It cost money to serve two or more gods, a fact that the night owls knew well.

The church was the community center where all community members could get together and catch up on the local news. The local juke joints were not places that all the citizens would go, like children, ladies, and high ranking men of the church. This left the church as the single meeting place where all citizens were smiled upon. They all didn't go to church to get saved from the devil, which was understood by everybody.

Serving the Lord was almost as expensive as serving the devil, but not nearly as much fun. These old hypocrites were never glad to see the end of Saturday night but they had a hard time lasting until the long-winded preacher finished delivering the word. These fellows and some of the ladies too, needed to get back to sinning as soon as possible no matter what the cost. The Saturday-night booze guzzlers could charge Sunday's eye-opener half pints of rotgut until the next payday, most was shy of cash on Sundays. First they would pay their respect to their God on the Sabbath anyway, and then off to the joints.

J D sits on the porch tying the strings of his one-and-only pair of dress shoes. He used a spoon of bacon grease on them to give them a bit of a shine. He knew that by the time he walked to church, which was three miles down the dusty road, the shoes would be dirty again. He was wasting his time sprucing up them cotton-picking shoes, something that he knew, but he chose to ignore. Looking clean was an impossibility, but he would do his best with what he had. His mother taught him to be thankful for what little he had. His mother had a strong belief in the philosophy of making do with what one has and J D believed in the same philosophy.

J D went to church nearly every Sunday, but not only to give his heart to God, but to give his heart to his girlfriend and his friends too. He could also appreciate the spiritual benefits of belonging to the church. J D felt safer at church than he did at home. There were many at the church to share his confusions and doubts with. At church he felt that he was among his kind. He felt safe in big crowds.

The weather looked good for the walk to church, no rain in sight. The dust was always better than the mud. The roads in this part of Mississippi would become hard to travel on when they were wet. The mud would suck the shoes right off your feet. After a downpour the motor vehicles had to be pushed up most of the muddy hills. The best way to travel on these country roads after a rain was to pull off your shoes and walk barefooted. Horse-drawn wagons were the surest transportation for the old folks and the tots during the rainy season.

The old hound lay underneath the steps where he always lay, where it was cool and safe from the feet of nearly a dozen people tracking all over the place on Sundays. Sunday was one day of the week when nobody envied the old half-bread hound who had nothing much to do except lay in the shade every day. J D would often think of the whole world as being a better place for animals than it was for human beings, especially poor, blacks and hardworking folks. The old half-breed dog had it easy seven days a week. The old fleabag was good for absolutely nothing except eating what he could get and making himself as comfortable as possible. There seldom was anything to bark at or watch out for anyway. There wasn't much work for an old lazy-ass dog; no strangers, no hunting and no loose stock to chase; he had no responsibilities.

J D could still smell the scents from the girls' straightening combs. It took the girls a long while to fry their hair in order to make it as straight as possible. The straighter the better. The kitchen was the only room in the house where this hot-combing the hair could take place because that's where the stove was. Anybody from another culture might be led to believe that some special food was cooking, believing that colored folks ate mostly anything that grew, crawled or walked anyway. The girls were always the time-machines determining what time the march to church would start. The long three-mile walk to church began when the girls finished their hair. The time it took the ladies to get their hair ready dictated when the march got started. When Ann, the second cousin, spent Saturday night at the Banks, the giggling and primping took a lot longer. This was one of those times.

J D sometimes wondered just what was the purpose of all the useless activities that his people wasted their time doing. He never liked the answers that he came up with. Why things were as they were? He only got confused when he tried to answer his own questions. Most of the people whom he knew either never asked the questions or had long ago given up on making sense of the answers and accepted things as they were. Even if they could think about change, they had no idea what the changes should be to.

The boys were very much in tune with these rituals taken place before the march started on the road to church. Marching to the church where they could praise the Lord on Sunday mornings.

One could see through the house from the front poach to the kitchen, the kitchen was in the back of the house. The house consist of two sides, both had three rooms each. The only difference was on one side was a kitchen and a dining room and the big bedroom. The big bedroom was Mr. and Mrs. Banks. The other three bedrooms were on the opposite side of the house. There was no living room or sitting room. The big bedroom and the dining room were where the family hung out. The house had two front doors; one entered the big combination bedroom and sitting room, the dinning room and the kitchen. A ball could be thrown through the house on the kitchen side without hitting a single thing, if the back and front doors were opened. The other side had no back door, just a front doors and doors to the dinning room and kitchen. The third bedroom was used for company or, for Grandma Ida.

Now, Mr. Bank's' momma; Grandma Ida; was one mean woman. She had not one grand child who liked having her around; they were too scared of her. It was a good thing that she had lots of children to divide her days among. She lived a few weeks here and a few weeks there since her own house burned down. You could tell that the old lady was not here this week by the noise the girls were making while they got ready for the big day of the week.

"Ah-ite chilens, las hur up ah we be late fuh Sunday School." Momma Banks order was the signal to speed up the girl's last minutes hair touchups, slips adjustments, vanilla-flavoring their under arms and making sure their smiles were pretty enough to get the attentions of their most sought after young fellows. Everybody seemed to get a bit excited when the order to move out was given, except the old half-breed mutt.

Old flaps seemed to realize that these actions had nothing at all to do with him. He didn't move a muscle, not one. He just lay where he could watch the actions that made no sense to him at all. The old dog didn't bother to scratch the itches caused by the blood-sucking fleas. He had gotten use to itching a long time ago. The half-dead mutt didn't bother with scratching itches if at all possible.

Bud and John came out of the boy's room arguing as usual about how things should be. Neither knew up from down about how things should be...

"Is daddy outta brew yit?" Asked John.

"Nawh" Bud snapped at John.

Bud knew that his daddy had passed out last night long before he had enough time to empty the full quart jar of corn whiskey. The Saturday nights when Daddy Banks had help drinking up his stash of whiskey he might run out soon enough to sober up by Sunday morning and attend church. He had his whiskey all to himself this time and had plenty left to keep him happy all day. Yes sir, even though the old man loved to sing and pray to his God, he was not about to leave his whiskey just to attend church. He took that much after his daddy before him, who was a connoisseur of good stump juice. He was a member of a small number of old-timers who didn't take their boozing lightly. Rotgut provided a more comfortable hiding place from a butt-kicking life than the church did for this bunch.

John called the old man daddy the same as J D and Bud even though john was a second cousin who managed to stay with the Banks most of the time. John was Ann's brother. Their parents cared less about what time John and Ann came home as long as they were over at their great uncle's house. Nobody had any objections to this arrangement, or none objected loud enough to be heard anyway.

John had no objections to anything that anybody could recall, except work. He could be extremely creative when it came to avoiding labor of any kind. His extreme dislike for doing chores kept him away from his own home and other places where work was done. John was a perfect sidekick for the loafing crowd.

"Daddy loves de Lawd wid all his hart, but he love his whiskey wid all his hart and soul," J D said as h   e headed out of the door.

J D never stopped worrying about his daddy's physical safety here on earth and his soul in the next life.

"Daddy got de ida dat he kin serv mo den one gawd."

Old Flaps sort of cracked open one eye just to see if the dressed-up masters and misses were headed in the right direction. A direction that he knew his company would not be appreciated. Flaps changed his position just enough to shift his weight to his other side. He winked the eye that a fly had lit on. The fly moved on. Flapps and daddy Jessie Banks had the place to themselves for awhile. The sorry-ass flea-bag slowly rose to his feet and went off looking for his sleeping partner He liked to stick close to his sleeping buddy; Daddy Banks.

The marching church-going groups were as common in this part of the county as grazing stock in the pastures. The watch dogs at the homes that these groups marched by rarely made a sound. Sunday was by far the best day of the week, especially during the farming season. The children, adults, dogs, cats and all the other animals on the farms got alone very well on Sunday.

Momma Banks was leading the pack without saying a mumbling word. She never said anything about her husband staying home drunk as a homebrew-drinking dog, but she showed her anger by walking too fast and with an iron silent mood. A drunkard for a husband and her children's father gave her a holy cause for going to church. Mother Banks was extremely self-righteous during times like this. Daddy Banks had been the same every since Momma Banks first saw him. He had been drunk when he had asked her to marry him. She thought he needed the bottled courage to give him the nerves to ask her the big question. She learned over the years that she had been wrong. Momma once held the notion that prayer could change things, but they sure hadn't changed her children's daddy. That was her second big wrong about what she thought would be.

Grandma Ida was usually with Momma Banks to share the shame with when Mr. Banks was having Christmas. That's what Momma Banks called his drinking spells. Grandma Banks said that Jess's daddy was the same way even though he was a jack-leg preacher. He preached when he was clear-headed enough to attend church.

Everybody was hoping a ride would just happen by even though the day was perfect for a three-mile walk. They had to walk every step of the way. Shoes got dirty and sweat streaked through the girl's oily faces, but they kept the hair around the edges behind the head, called kitchens, dry to prevent it from going back kinky. The boys usually beat the dust from their pants cuffs before gong into the church house. This attempting to clean up a bit before entering the House of God was nothing to fidget about. Most of the members had to do the same clean-up job even if they rode on the back of trucks. The girls headed for the girl's outhouse for a quick makeover. This attention to their clothing was not for the benefits of the Lord

The two outhouses were fifty feet apart but that did not stop the boys from going visiting the
girl's outhouse once in a while. The frequently- used path between the toilets was not made by 'coons.

The young, and maybe some of the old for that matter, used the path to have a moment of privacy with some person who might be instrumental in fulfilling some wishful thoughts. One of the reasons that many went to church was to answer the call for lust gratification. The church was the social watering hole for satisfying the thirst for the opposite sex.

People practicing in forbidden love was a common social problem in this part of Mississippi. A few serious church members came to church on Sundays just to try to relieve a bit of guilt resulting from the practice of eating from the trees of forbidden fruits. According to the Gospel nearly all physical love that is enjoyed is forbidden love. The preacher's most soul-searching sermons were usually about the sins of sex other than sex to procreate. This meant that everybody in the county and maybe the whole world was living in sin as far as sex was concerned. The young never paid much attention to these hell-fire and brimstone sermons; they loved just thinking about the girls too much. Half of the young were scared to death of a real physical relationship. They were just practicing for times to come.

Before the Sunday school leaders could corral the young folks, the young'uns had gathered underneath the old oak tree, which had shaded unlimited generations of young people for as long as anybody could remember and then some. All the generations before this one had the same thing in mind; forbidden contacts between girls and boys. When called to get inside the church, the whispering, giggling, gang of youths was a little reluctant to give up their outside shade-tree party which made coming to Sunday school tolerable in the first place. With a few last glances at their chosen puppy loves, the children self-conscientiously marched stiff-legged into the church to be taught how to be good soldiers in the army of the Lord.

The church was the axis around which the local societies revolved and all the clans could connect as one in the name of the Lord. The church received the newborn into this world and sent the dead out of this world into the great beyond. The young had a good chance of meeting their future wives and husbands at church. The schools were meeting grounds too, but the school children were not usually old enough to get serious about their future and whom they want to share it with. The children were usually finished with school by the time they reached fifteen or sixteen years of age. Anyway school only lasted six months of the year, the church continued all year.

Aunt Sal was one good Sunday school teacher. She never missed one Sunday teaching her class, no sir, not one. Nobody could recollect Aunt Sal missing attending church even when she was down with the miseries. Ailing or not, she was the best at explaining the meanings of the Ten Commandments.

The rumor was that Aunt Sal was not as dedicated as she seemed to be to doing the Lord's work, but more committed to keeping an eye on Rev. Mayfield. The common belief is that the good Preacher may have been the father of Aunt Sal's two younger children. All three, Rev. Mayfield and both the young boys had those huge funny looking ears. They sure had something in common. Aunt Sal was also into other spiritual practices too. She was known to have made trips a-plenty to Mobile and New Orleans.

J D did not remember a time when he was not reminded of the importance of obeying the teachings of the Ten Commandment. This Sunday was no exception. He was fifteen years old this past May. This was about the time he began having feelings and thoughts that were in direct conflict with the commandments taught here. No matter, he was unable to pay much attention to Aunt Sal. He knew what she was saying without thinking about it. He had heard this same teaching all his fifteen years. The new experience in his life was Wilma. He glanced in Wilma's direction every half second, and she returned the glances. She sure looked pretty to the young buck. He could feel and hear his own heart beating every time he got near Wilma.

"Whad's adultey"? Tommy asked, leaning over and whispering in J D's ear.

"Ah donno," J D whispered back at Tommy.

There was no break between the Sunday school class and the regular service. Those benches got mighty hard after about two hours. Once Rev. Mayfield got started there was no telling how long he would go. The church usually had to hear prayers by Uncle Joe, Uncle Bill and a few selections by the choir.

" Ah knowed it, heah is Uncle Joe n he got a heap uf sins ta unload today." Tommy whispered.

Uncle Joe was normally a low-down bastard all week, afterward he would come to church and try to clean himself up in the sights of his Lord. He worked extra hard at church trying to fool God into believing nothing sinful happened during the week. J D and everybody else knew better, but nobody had the guts to say so or felt a need to. Uncle Joe had five different personalities and could switch to whichever one the occasion called for.

Uncle Joe was known to partake in anything that would yield a profit, or anything that he could enjoy with no cost to himself. The old fellow had no problems with short-changing anybody doing business with him. White, black, or any ethnic group of people were fair game for him. This fellow was whomever and whatever he needed to be at any given time. He was just as good at getting things done for the church as he was at getting his way in the community. He kept God's house in order. Uncle Joe was a valuable asset to the house of God. He was all things to the up-keep of the church house and the grounds. He was in charge of the building, grounds and grave diggings. He earned a bit of a right to breaking a few of the holy rules.

Finally the old man had squared himself with his maker and went silent. Wiping sweat from his forehead, he raised himself from his knees and made his way back to his deacon's chair. The service moved on.

Reverend Mayfield had his work cut out if he wanted his sermon to get more shouts, moans and amends than Uncle Joe's prayer did. The Reverend had to reach into his bag of sermons for the heavies. He would outdo Uncle Joe if he had to keep these folks here all afternoon. The congregation knew how to play the game, they would let go with their best shouting, dancing, falling out and what ever else they had to do to satisfy the good preacher. Once he worked up a heavy sweat and had the church in an emotional uproar he could safely close with a feeling of joy. Sermons on the sins of lusting after the flesh always brought out the guilt and shame. The total congregation was guilty of this one. The Reverend couldn't miss. The riding on the guilt of his flock didn't do any harm to the collection plate either.

J D never felt as guilty as he did after the sermon. It sure looked like the preacher was talking directly to the J D who had been having all those immoral thoughts about Wilma, and other girls too. J D had visions of going straight to hell if something was not done about his dirty mind. No sir, it didn't look too good. He even thought about asking Uncle Joe to plug in a few words on his behalf. It stands to reason if Uncle Joe could square himself with the Heavenly Father after the kind of things he did all week, except Sundays, it would not hurt to have the old man add a few powerful words for his sins too.

The guilt feelings did not last beyond the edge of the graveyard fence. J D forgot all about his doubts and struggles with his inner self when he saw Wilma walk out of the church door. He was beginning to enjoy these sinful thoughts about Wilma. His heart was thumping so hard that he stood at a distance from Bud and Tommy so they couldn't hear his heart. He sure liked Wilma and he thought she might like him a little too. He sure hoped so.

"She's lookin at me en smilin.' 'Is she laughin at me?' or is dat an Ah-like-u grin?'

J D sensed a change in his physical self and decided to shuffle over by the Graveyard fence until he regains control of things.

"Boy! She sho gits me agoin."

The church crowd was just wandering around like a leaderless flock of chickens. Most of these people only saw each other at church which gave very little time for gathering all the latest dirt on everybody. It takes skills to spread the latest on folks within such a narrow space and without offending somebody. These people were very skilled at just this sort of thing, spreading the news. Not only do they have to listen to, and spread news, but also have to watch who is might be talking about them too. While the old folks whispered behind each other's backs, the young were learning what it were like to be teenagers in heat.

While the people regrouped for the trek home J D waited by the fence hoping to make eye contact with Wilma just one more time before she climbed into her dad's old truck and rattled down the road in front of a cloud of dust. He wanted to make a bit more than eye contact. He was not always looking into Wilma's eyes either. This young fellow saw more than her eyes.

J D stood by the fence even after most of the people had gone on their way. He was one crazy dreamer today. He had never paid too much attention to the cemetery before, until now.

"God! Whad ah lonely place to spen all eternity, dat is til all is called tah be jud and sent ta de appropit places." He said to himself. He looked over to where his granddaddy was buried and wondered if maybe, just maybe this was the end of the line for everybody.

"Dar Ah go agin wid dese crazy notions." "Ah' ain't a chil now which means dat Ah kin go ta hell fer mah sins jus lak gron folks."

Walking faster than usual, J D rushed to catch up to the other boys. He knew they all would go home and change clothes and meets at the swimming hole in Turkey Creek.

"Hey y'all!! Wait fuh me."

"Ya betta come ohn, ya slo pok." Tommy yield back at J D.

Except for a few night chores, Sundays were fun days for the roaming boys. Their daily lives during the week were anything but exciting. Working hard all day was the order of their lives, but that never stopped them from plugging a few fun times into their otherwise dull lives.

"Whad wuz ya doin so long?" Tommy asked

"Chasin atta Wilma lak a broke-dick dog." Bud said before J D could answer for himself.

"Dat's a ball-face lie." J D said restoring his status with boys.

Chapter Two

▼

It didn't take the boys much time to cover the three miles back home. There were good reasons for the speed, the boys were in a big hurry to get to the creek where they could have fun and escape the heat as well. Getting dusty and sweaty were pluses in this case. The funkier, the better. J D, Bud, Joe and John ran far ahead of the freshly purged-of-sin group that was strolling at a leisurely pace toward home. The women were not rushing to get in the hot kitchen to prepare the mid-afternoon meal.

Sundays were not a day of rest for the women folk. The young and old were expected to help prepare a good preacher-loving dinner on Sundays. Preparing a full-course Sunday meal was a long hard job, plus it was a good time to train the young ladies in the ways of being country ladies. The food had to be gathered, cleaned, washed and seasoned before cooking. Wood for the fire had to be fired up and water brought in for washing the ingredients before the actual cooking. The women's work was never done, it seemed like. Some of the food for the evening meal was usually gathered before church so that the cooking would not take forever. Now ringing the chicken's necks had to be done as close to the cooking as possible. They had no icebox in which to store fresh meat.

The men, boys and the other farm animals had Sundays off from any hard work. The men sat on the porch and swapped lies, chewed tobacco, smoked and sometimes drank a few snorts of homebrew until it was time to eat. They didn't mind the wait though. The little boys were looking forward to a day of roaming the countryside looking for fun things to do the same as their big brothers were doing.

Flaps came crawling from beneath the steps after the boys got within hearing distance to the dog. Old Flaps would lead the swimming crew to the creek just the same as he had done for the past few years. The mixed breed mutt had always enjoyed Sunday afternoons by just laying in the cool sands at the water's edge and watching the boys play in the water. Maybe he will scare up a rabbit or something and get the innards like he had always got after wild game was slaughtered. Shit! The old dog wouldn't catch a rabbit if it ran through his mouth. The only rabbit's innards the dog ever got were from rabbits that he had nothing to do with catching.

The old hound was a symbol of the wished for life that most of the hardworking country folks prayed for. Old Flaps had an easy life.

When the boys swooped across the porch, Daddy turned over, saw who was making so much racket and turns over onto his back and continued to sleep.

"The old man hasta be gittin ta de bottom uv dat fruit jar by now." J D shared.

What the boys didn't know was that the old man was in pretty good shape with his supply of whiskey. He had been sleeping all morning, not drinking. Yes sir, he had enough to make himself happy for quite a spell yet.

"De las one in is ah rotten aig". Bud yield as they got near the swimming hole.

J D, John, Tommy, T J, Joe, Bud and Allen made a quick dash for the cool water, undressing as they ran. Undressing was easy due to the fact that none of the pack wore underwear, shoes or anything else requiring time to take off. They had left their Sunday dress clothes at home.

Everybody could swim well enough to swim out into the deeper water and make it back to safety, which was only a distance of about twenty feet. Everybody except Willie, that is. Willie could not be taught much of any thing. He never learned to swim. Willie being unable to swim was the reason that he had the job of watching for company. After all, everybody was buck naked.

Willie was the last to arrive at the creek. One reason was Willie never went to church. His adopted parents were not often seen inside the house of God either. They insisted on Willie working from sun to sun six days a week, but they cared less what he did with the rest of his time. Willie didn't go to school either until all the crops were gathered. He went sometimes when the weather turned too nasty for working in the fields. Many of the Mississippi boys and girls didn't go to school when they were needed in the fields. Willie showed up at school on those occasions simply because all the other boys and girls were there. The other boys kind of felt sorry for Willie. His mother gave him to old man Davis when he was about ten years old. He had been working in the fields, around the house and the barn every since.

Poor dumb Willie gave the warning that somebody was coming, almost too late though for the naked water bugs to take cover. The gang just had enough time to slip into their breeches before the five white boys came down the path to the river. All the fellows knew the dangers of these chance encounters with a bunch of bored whites looking for amusement at anybody's expense except their own. Nobody said a word for what seemed like an awful long time.

The boys had no way out from the swimming hole but to walk, or run, by the bored-to-death white boys. The creek made a ninety degree turn here which created a swimming hole deep enough for diving and dog paddling. The other side of the creek had a fifteen feet high bank;

no escape that way. The only ways out was down stream, up stream or by the white boys.

Both the groups of young men knew each other and usually got along quite well. Sundays were a different story; the Grays had cousins, uncles, aunts etc. over on the weekends. These local whites had to show their superior status to blacks when they were with others of their own kind. They also got a great boost to their self-worth while doing it.

The white boys were doing the same thing as the black boys were doing; looking for a break from their bleak and empty lives. If they could switch races so that blacks became whites and whites became blacks, nothing would've change; the game would've been played the same...

Howard was the oldest of the five fun-seekers, but Mac was the nigger hater. If trouble started, it would be Mac's doings. Mac lived with his daddy and his mother on old man Frank Well's place. These Shelleys were no kin to the Grays. Howard, Ralph and Tony were Grays. Tony was Howard's and Ralph's cousin. Mac was a Shelleys.

Mac's daddy was a drunkard like his daddy was before him. Mr. Shelley did odd jobs for Mr. Wells and sometime he would build a barn or repair an existing building or shed. Mr. Shelley had many skills, but he loved his booze above his wife, three kids and loyalty to his handyman career. Yes, he was extremely fond of his rotgut. The saying is that his laying out all times of the week drinking and having little concerns for his family was what drove Mrs. Shelley cuckoo. Boy, Mac's mother was crazy as a bat. Some say she never had a grain of common sense even before she married Mr. Shelley.

J D began to feel that old nagging fear that was never too far away under these kinds of circumstances. He knew the right words had to be said, the submissive attitudes had to be displayed and with a strong I-will-if-I-have-to attitude. This combination of character traits was never easy to manage. J loved all that this part of the country had to offer except the positions in the social arrangement assigned to colored folks. The other colored boys followed J D's leads.

J D had to make sure Mac was not given an opportunity to vent his frustrations on them and at the same time, to keep Allen quite. Allen was the black troublemaker. Allen was the other side of Mac, or maybe Mac was the other side of Allen.

Neither of these boys would have a happy future here in these parts under the Jim Crow system.

J D broke the silence. "Hi Howard, Ya'll goin swimmin?"

"Naw, Ah don't reckon so"

"We wuz jes comin out, ya kin go in if y'all wunt to." J D said.

Mac started to strut around Howard and move closer to the edge of the creek. He wanted to get an idea of what they would be up against if trouble started. Mac spotted Allen who was behind the others by the creek's edge. Mac didn't want to make a change of mind obvious, but he thought Allen was crazy enough to be a problem. He was probably right. Everybody knew that Allen love for white folks was a negative eleven on a scale from negative ten to a positive ten.

"Howdy boy!" Mac said to Allen.

"Who is ya callin boy?"

"Ah is sorry Mr. Boy."

"Y'all sho ya ain't goin fer a swim." J D quickly asked.

Fear was a safety tool to hold the behaviors in check on both sides of the racial dividing line. Without rigorous training in the many ways of handling fears the system had no chance of functioning at all. The teaching started from the cradle and ended at the grave. It was believed by some of the people that it might extend beyond the last breath.

"Nawh, we don wanta swim, we jes stopped by ta see what yew darkies wuz up ta." Mac said.

J D sensing that the crisis was over, began to breathe a little easier. J D had enough man-power and skills to beat hell out these five whites here and now. He also knew the fallout from such actions. Blacks had no civil rights here in Eastern Mississippi. Blacks only kicked the daylights out of whites when there was no other way around it, like saving a life, and sometime not even then. The boy was learning to make the best out of whatever came his way.

"Les go boys. Les go by de stoe" J D yelled over his shoulder while still giving Howard and company their unearned respect.

J D and company had to walk close to the edge of the bushes to avoid making contact with any of Howard's bunch. Howard's crew had to maintain their make-believe superior human status by standing in the middle of the narrow path that didn't belong to them anyway. The blacks were on their own land, but did not dare exercise owner's rights against these socially vain kings.

The boys headed for the Britton store. The Britton's store was approximately two miles away, which was no distance for these youngsters who had their minds on a cold royal crown cola and a stage plant. Yes sir, life was not as bad as it might seem to an outsider here in the red-clay country. Not only did they have treats at the store, but also supper was waiting at their homes. Yep, except for a few misguided white folks and black folks, life could be very happy here in these great lands of Mississippi. J D had all these kinds of thoughts rambling through his head. He had never lived anywhere else except the one time that he stayed with his aunt a few weeks in Alabama. That didn't count much toward outside-of-Mississippi experience. He had zero experience to qualify him as an expert on life styles in different parts of the country, none at all. He did not believe that any other part of the world could make him feel like he was part of the total life cycle like Mississippi did. He was at home here in the country. J D and the other colored boys had a place in the community, even though it might be at a lower level than they wanted. None of the members of this peculiar system were ignored.

Due to the negative experiences the gang of boys just had, they had to become as close to being hooligans as possible, short of committing a crime, just to restore a bit of dignity into their lives. There were very little socially approved activities for a bunch of colored boys to take advantage of simply for fun.

Bud sent the half-breed hound home because the brittons had some mean well-fed and highly trained killer dogs. Old Flaps didn't stand a chance in hell of kicking just one of the Britton's dog's ass much less all three. The old dog had tangled with them bastards before, but back then he was a younger mutt and could out run the pack. Old Flaps obeyed Bud and just sniffed his way back home and to his favorite waiting place under the front steps.

Allen let out a little bit of his pinup frasturation. "Ah bet Ah kin beat any uf yu nigguhs fahm heah ta dat simmon tree."

"Whatta ya bettin." Joe questioned.

"Yunamit."

"R.C. cola?"

"Y'all heah dat?" Joe said loudly so everybody would pay attention.

"Willie, ya go up ta de old 'summon tree so ya kin see which one gits thar fust." Joe instructed.

"Git set y'all. Go!" T J said smiling. He was too slow himself for racing but, he loved to watch others race.

Joe won the race just as all knew he would, including Allen. They all felt a tad better now that they had done something to take their minds off the white boys. They needed a bit of ego building actions just to reinstate some balance to their self esteem. It was always hard for the boys to switch from one expression of self-value to another without some help. They made character switching easier by competing with one another. Their social character depended on where they were and to whom they were relating to.

CHAPTER THREE

▼

The Britton's store was built across the road from the main house. Why they put the store on the other side of the road is anybody's guess. It could've been so that anybody entering or leaving the store would be visible from just about anywhere in the main house, even from the barn. The barn was on the south side and slightly behind the house.

The store was a shotgun built structure with only two doors, one in the front and one in the back. One could see straight through both doors of the store from the front of the main house. This was a good thing when all was on the up and up, but it sure was no good for any hanky-panky happenings. Sometimes there might be a car or truck gassing up at the one gas pump, which hid the front door from the prying eyes over at the big house.

There being no work on Sundays for most people, therefore there was very little traffic on the gravel road that separated the store and the main house. Nobody was in the store which meant that one had to ring the cowbell that hung over the door to rouse someone from the house. If the first ring didn't summon some action from the main house, you rang again a bit harder the second time. Now this second time had to be ranged with a noticeable degree of respect from the blacks. Colored folks had to do what they had to do without agitating the whites. Colored would ring the bell with a bright smile, no matter how many times they had to jerk the string. White folks did not stop what they happened to be doing at the time just to serves colored. Even though they stood to make a bigger profit from sales to colored. Whites had to make sure they never missed an opportunity to inflate their assumed importance over the assumed unimportance of the colored population. No sir, they never dreamed of downplaying themselves and uplifting the egos of the colored customers. Here in Mississippi the colored customer was never right unless he somehow added to the already over inflated self-value of the white race. The colored were very skilled at doing just this. They had done it so many times until it became second nature. It just was not right the way colored folk lied to white folk, some of the Christians colored sometimes thought. The whites loved to be fooled, though.

Right and wrong, just and unjust, fair and unfair treatment between the races had next to nothing to do with the everyday interactions in the social arena. These high-minded notions would render the Jim Crow system unworkable. It was about survival without giving up some social advantages or making life harder than it was already. Equal and fair treatment was not thought of as being necessary to have good relationships between the races.

The eight boys had no more than a dollar and a half among them. J D probably had an extra dollar hid somewhere, but getting him to spend it was harder than convincing a colored man to be glad he was a Negro. Cold drinks were seven cents, stage plants and moon pies were eight cents each, which meant that all would get plenty of something out of the one dollar and fifty cents. They had to share with Willie because he was the same as he always was, broke.

Bud rang the old cowbell once, and then waited. The boys knew if the Brittons were eating dinner or entertaining cousins or something it would take a while to get someone out to the store. The boys made sure they did not appear agitated or impatient; because if you wanted to be treated well you better not show any displeasure which would be a normal response by whites to unnecessary delays in services.

"Rang agin". Allen told Bud.

Bud jerked the string once more. After what seemed to the boys to be much too long, Jennie glided out the door with keys in hand. J D's stomach did a back-over flip when he saw who came out. He believed that this blond girl had the entire makings needed to get every nigger in Mississippi hanged by the neck until dead. There were a limited number of safe ways for a black male to relate to white women. J D knew one sure way to get by while doing business with the white females, reduce yourself to a nobody or a complete nut case.

The boys stood aside to let the young lady through. The boys wore their most unconcerned blank faces. Every one of them acted as if the girl was invisible; they never looked directly at her at all. This pretending that the white woman didn't exist as a sex object was learned by every colored boy over six years old.

J D and the rest of the crew did not have to be told how to handle situations such as this. They all would stick together. No one would be caught alone with this bomb waiting to explore. It was not that the girl put boys in danger deliberately, but being the prettiest white girl in the area drew the eyeballs of every redneck within a fifteen-mile radius. The rednecks fought for her attention and The boys knew for sure that these crackers would not hesitate one moment to hang a colored man whom they thought might be the receiver of her sought after attention. They would use any opportunity to get her attention.

Jenny had always showed affection for J D even though he tried never to get close enough to her for her to reach out and lay hands on him. She had played with him every since they had been small kids but now either she had grown too much or he had become aware of something. Either way this closeness between the two was scaring the guts right out of him. They were no longer small kids.

As usual all her attention was for J D. He tried to get what he came for and make his get-away before some Negro-hating cracker walked in. When he dipped his arm down into the ice-cold water for his RC cola, he was thinking of how to get his moon pie and escape out the door. That was not to be because when he offered to pay the fifteen cents, she said.

"That's okay, and that's my present to you."

J D felt his heart bouncing from one side of his chest to the other. He had problems breathing to the point that he was barely able to walk out the door. Jennie's giving Him fifteen cents worth of nothing was enough to set off half the population's tongues wagging, both black's and white's.

"Dat gull don kno whad she doin n whad kin come uf dis."

J D was saying to nobody in particular. He walked on out near the road before waiting for the rest of the gang to join him. He was not about to give Jennie a chance to call him back into the store after the others came out. She had done just that in the past. Up until two years ago that was all right because both were thought of as being little kids. Now is a different time. He didn't have to be told what lay in store for him if he let this friendship be seen by the wrong people, white or black. Jennie would suffer irreparable harm from what people would think about their friendship. There was no way for a white girl and a black boy to be close friends. It mattered none if the relationship was platonic or not.

Their flirting may be just that and nothing else, but that depends on who was looking. Mississippi had white women who would play the flirting game just to see the poor colored boys and men squirm. Most colored men caught in that kind of situation didn't know if they should shit or go blind.

J D had moseyed down the road apiece before the others caught up with him.

"Hey J. Ah thought we wuz gonna eat unda de tree at de stoe?" Willie stated.

"Yu kin ifn ya wanna." J D had a safe distance between him and possible troubles. His innards were almost back where they were supposed to be now that he was at a safe distant. He could now swallow.

Old man Britton's father, Luther Britton, was said to have been a great womanizer with both white and black women. This was more a common truth of many of these leading citizens than people wanted to admit. It always was much safer for the colored women and the white men than it was for the colored men and the white women. There were no records or rumors about a white man being hung for crossing the color line, or records of colored women being hung for crossing the color line either, at least in this part of the world. Old man Britton, who had long been dead, had a reputation of taking part in many flogging, one-way bus tickets out of town and a few lynching, so the stories go. One could not hold this against him because he was a product of his environment the same as everybody else. Most colored thought highly of the old man. Mr. Britton was a Mississippi natural good redneck.

All those who preach against those that take the advantage of others are none other than the ones who would if they could do the same thing and get away with it. Some have tried and failed and are out there pointing fingers at those who succeeded at getting over on their fellow men and women. Old man Britton was fortunate enough to have done what most men of his day wish they could have done, but didn't have the nerve to do or didn't have the means.

Jennie might have gotten that flirting behavior naturally. After all she was the grand daughter of one who believed in ignoring the governing social rules that were there to keep order and protect those who may not know any better. J D thought maybe he had to appear indifferent to Jennie's friendliness toward him. He was not a stupid young black boy.

"Jennie sho could make thangs hard jus cuz she friendly." J said under his breath.

The road ran between fields of cotton, corn, hay, beans, etc. The shade did not exist for the first mile because there were no trees. The boys wanted to consume their goodies there at the store where there was unlimited shade. J D did not think that was such a good idea; Jennie would not have gone back to the house with them still there.

"Com on ya road lizads, we'll stop unda de walnut tree at de edge of de woods."

"Ah don know howcome we had tah come all dis fah. My drink will be wahm," said Allen.

"J D is scared uh Jennie, dat's why he flew outta de stoe so fast." John mumbled.

"Ah wish ah had a white gull who's daddy owned a stoe and Ah could git thangs fer free." Willie plugged in. Willie was not known for his rational thinking.

"Yu'd mess 'round and git yo self hung, dat's wha yu'd do." Tommy said. Tommy made out pretty good due to his knowing where the lines were drawn and being guided by this knowledge.

The boys finally reached the edge of the woods where they sat down to enjoy their treats. All knew that it was getting late and they or most of them anyway, had to be home before dark. They needed light enough to get their night work done. The night got pretty dark before the moon lit up the night. Their night work included feeding the stock, getting enough stove wood for momma to cook breakfast and hauling water from the pump, which was located a few hundred yards from the house. The pump was placed in the old well that was at the long abandoned house that nobody could remember who lived there, none of the young folks anyway. The boys knew the old saying that screams could be heard coming from the house late at night when the moon was full. The old house was located over a hundred yards from the newer house where the Banks lived. At times voices could be heard, lights seen and doors banging at the old house. White people lived there until the husband shot his wife and then hanged himself. Nobody went to the well after dark, not even on moonlit nights.

J D told the boys that they were going by Wilma's house on their way home. He became excited every time he thought about her. Wilma was prettier than Jennie and much safer.

"Yussuh, Ah lak mah own. Ah'll leave dem otta folks ta dey ohn." "Ah can't see why some fool will take chances wid a white gal and git hissef kilt."

"Me nedda." Tom said. Tommy agreed with most anything that promoted safety.

Wilma had two nice looking sisters, but she was the best looking by far, J D was thinking. One sister was older than J D, and one younger. He thought about being at school where he could see Wilma every day. Their brother was the oldest of all, but he didn't seem to care much one way or the other about what his sisters did. J D's mind went out of control when he got to dreaming about Wilma.

"Hea comes a truck!" Yelled Willie.

All the boys ducked into the bushes so they would not be seen by whoever was coming. It never was too safe for a bunch of black kids marching down the road on Sunday afternoons. The truck was coming from the direction of the store. The gang knew that it was most unlikely to be colored folks.

"It looks lak dem old McCrays." Said john.

Yep, it was their old jalopy of a truck all right. The boys knew all four of the teenagers stacked in the cab of the truck. The two McCray brothers and the two cousins from town were in the cab.

"Shucks, a man can't wak de roads witout jumpin inta de woods eva tiahm a car load uf crackas take a notion ta drive down de road." J D whimpered.

"J D, ya just mad cause yu mite not git t see Wilma."

"Shut yo mouf Bud. Wilma ain't got nothin t do wid dis."

"Howcome we hav ta be so rabbit-jumpin fraid uf everythang in de wold? " Allen said to nobody in particular.

The truck disappeared from sight ahead of its own dust. One could always tell when a car or truck had passed through, especially during the dry months. The weather was hotter than hell itself and had been for the past month. Working in the cotton fields did nothing to make the week days something to look forward to. Those cotton-chopping days were the days when most of the field workers would gladly exchange places with old Flaps. Comparing life style of the cotton fields to the life of a catfish, the catfish's life style would win, especially at two o'clock in the afternoon. Now when these poor hardworking kids get a chance to enjoy a snack from the store, they sometimes had to run from folks who think a little fun and peace were too much for these poor bastards. The underprivileged were not entiled.

CHAPTER FOUR

▼

J D, Bud and John had night duties to carry out before it got dark. They didn't have to do much of a good job as long as daddy was on one of his Christmases and didn't give a doo doo about what got done today. Therefore, the brothers were not in any almighty hurry to pass Wilma's house. Daddy's drinking binges were given the nice sounding name Christmases. That's the name Momma Banks gave daddy's little retreats from the here and now. The boys had a little more freedom at times like these.

J D had it bad for little Wilma; just the thought of seeing her again today got his old heart going like this was a frightening situation. His girl-experience was near zero on a scale from 0 to ten, ten being the highest rating. He might have forgotten about the nightly chores even if the old man had been as sober as Christ himself. J D was a bit crazy when he got within forty miles of Wilma.

"Do ya thank we kin find a melon out dar in old Jack Boone's field? " HEY!!!"

"Heah gos Allen agin wid his troba-makin ides." Bud said.

"De las tiahm we tried dat dis tiahm uf de evenin, yu know wha hapen."

"Yeah Bud, we 'member." J D snapped.

J D did not have melons on his mind at all when he passed Wilma's. He was near enough to get a peek at the star of his most wonderful dream. The barnyard where the animals were kept was on the west side of the house and was blocking the boy's views for a moment until he reached the edge of the crib. Being this close to his dream made him feel warm, even though he'd have no idea what to do if she popped out of the bushes and grabbed him right there.

"Hey ya'll, dar is de gulls comin outta de chicken hous." Tommy blabbed out.

"Heahs's yo chance J" Bud said mockingly.

"Look ah, Bud, ah, know wha my ah, oh shut yo mouf." J D starts stuttering when he gets near his one and only.

Suddenly there she was, just standing there, looking beautiful. Poor J D stopped breathing, thinking and just about everything else that animals normally do to continue living. His leg stiffened up, he made jerking moves while walking.

"Wha is de matter wid me?" J was trying to regain control of himself.

He was a straight "A" student in school, was the unofficial leader of his siblings, but when he got near Wilma he turned into one awkward fool.

When Wilma waved at J, but he could not remember if he waved back or not. He was as nervious as a goat at slaughtering time. Wilma was the calm one, the one that seems to know what to do and how to do it. J D wondered how girls always seemed to know at the age of ten things that a boy may never learn or learn much later.

"Wilma act lak she wuz too learned fer her age. " J thought.

The sun was almost down when the brothers and friends arrived at the Banks's house. T J, Joe and Allen had chores to do at their house, but three boys had nothing pressing at home to do, Tommy, John and Willie. These three boys made no attemps to go on home from the Banks yet.

"Comon heah John, ya kin lend me a hand wid waten de mules and dat old bull in de stall and Tommy kin give Bud a hand wid de wood." J D ordered.

Nobody paid Willie much attention due to the fact that he was sooo clumsy.

The saying was that the boy was as green as a goose turd. A term often used when people described Willie's mental abilities. Somebody once said. Willie moved about like he was put together somewhat loosely. What little sense Willie once had had been beat out of him a long time back by the family that took him in. His mother was not the mothering type so she gave Willie and his brother James away. The surrogate parents only wanted them for working in the fields.

Bud's job was feeding and watering the two hogs in the hog pen and hauling the wood in which he did pretty well. The hogs were easy to care for because they gave less than a damn what they ate or drank. Bud felt kinship to the hogs; they too seemed to be hungry all the time. It was a tradition around here to be short of food all the time, therefore the family took lessons from the pigs; eat whatever was available. Bud tried his best never to take things too seriously.

The first thing the boys did was to haul the water from the well at the long-ago abandoned house. They were in no mood to hear voices, see lights and hear banging doors from a long dead past. There seemed to always be warm air blowing from the old house the minute the sun went down. The boys could sense the presence of something from the dead past still hanging around the old house.

After the work was done, the five boys headed for the kitchen to share what was left for their supper. There was enough for all the boys because momma knew which boys would be guests for supper and which boys would go home where their own suppers were waiting.

Daddy was in the bed now, which meant that he had run out of booze and was too sick to go after more. He always ended his binges with two or three days of being too sick to do much but lie around until he felt like working again. Daddy Jessie was known to get drunk and remain drunk for days at a time, or until his beverages ran out. A whole lot of the local community leaders forgave Jessie for being somewhat neglectful of his head-of-house-hold duties because of a popular local consensus that the man had been fixed, or voodoo, that is. Once the spell wore off he returned to being a hard-working church-going husband and father. Everybody didn't buy into that voodoo business though.

Grandma Louisa was one who didn't believe that voodoo crap a tal. She was Jessis's mother-in-law so she was not expected to excuse her son-in-law for mistreating her daughter and grandchildren.

"No suh, he is xactly like his daddy wuz.' 'His daddy drank hisself t death n Jessie is doin de same thang.' Voodoo mah foot." she use to say.

The truth depended more on who was doing the doing and who was doing the watching more than on what the real facts might be. These woodsmen and farmers needed few motives to take a vacation from their everyday condition and with a bit of help from the mason jar full of homemade brew, they could escape, if for no more than a moment.

The rattling of pans in the kitchen brought out the old half-breed mutt. Two separate supper hours gave the old fellow two chances to beg upon enough scraps to fill a small section of his belly. None of the boys felt confortable eating and looking in the face of that tail-waging dog without pitching it a tidbit of grub. The dog instinctively sat near the person that felt the highest level of compassion for animals. Flaps usually got more food when using this technique; this night proved his system worked again. J D was always sharing his food with the half-breed bag of bones. J D felt some weird kinship to the old good-for-nothing hound. They might have had the same destiny in life; a bumpy road ahead.

Finally it was getting close to bedtime at the Bank's because Monday was a workday and nobody will be exempt from working to the limits of his or her abilities, except the old man and the half-breed dog.

"Well ya'll, Ah guess its tiahm fuh me t mosey ohn home." Tommy said to no one in particular. Tommy lived over past the church and the graveyard. This was always the case with Tommy; staying past dark and then being scared to go home.

"Gon Mr. Scaddy-cat, nobody is holdin ya!" Bud said.

The same friends played this same game just about every Sunday at this time of the evening, and. Tommy never thought much about changing his going-home time so his playmates wouldn't have to walk him hone, or to walk him half way passed the graveyard, at least.

J D, Bud, Willie and John didn't mind the mile walk because this extra time together was appreciated more than any of the boys were willing to admit. The old half-breed dog didn't mind going along with these masters either. It was much cooler at night anyway. The night was at its quite time due to the daytime critters bedding down for the night and the night critters hadn't come out for their shift of feeding and play. The boys started talking about the ghosts that are believed to roam around after dark. This was a bad time of the evening for traveling pass a graveyard for the boys. The question now was how far was far enough to walk with Tommy to make sure he didn't get scared and start running and hurt himself. J D, Bud, and John were not too afraid for themselves because it was three of them and an old dog.

"Uncle Barlow said dat a hant won't cross water." John broke the silence.

"How do Uncle Barlow know dat?" Asked Tommy.

"He said dat he kin see em. He sees em all de tiahm, even in de day tiahm." John answered.

The ghost phobia was creeping throughout the brains of all the boys like crazy. Every bush took on live ghoulish shapes and appeared to move all over the place. As they started by the old Jones place everybody was silence. The only sound was four sets of dirt-crushing feet on the sandy and clay road. The Jones place had been vacant for many years, vacant since Mr. Jones's death.

The grown folks often talk about how many men Mr. Jones had killed in his lifetime. They say Mr. Jones suffered before he died, suffered for all the men he had killed. Some even say that you could hear him yelling out the dead men names and threatening to kill them again and again. He died in that house alone. Some say that at times when the night is warm and the wind is calm you can still hear him calling out for death and peace. Nobody knew where Mr. Jones came from and nobody knews where he went. These boys believed that maybe he hadn't gone anywhere. The folks in this part of Mississippi believed more in the dead than they believed in the living. In the minds of the locals the dead had a knack of not being all the way dead.

The barn, half standing and half down, stood as a memorial of yesterday's lives that had ceased to exist except their wandering spirits. The young men talked in whispers as they hurred away from the haunted home site. They acted as if their passing by quietly would somehow not attract the attention of these rambling human leftovers.

"Uncle Barlow said dat a colored fellow wuz hung right dar ohn dat big red oak'. 'He said dat wuz when white folks lived hea." John added a little more terror to the boys' already large inventories of fears. "Uncle Barlow said dat old oak neva growed one mo inch til all dem crackers dat helped hang dat colored man wuz dead."

"What did dey hang hin fuh?" Asked Willie.

"Uncle Barlow said de po guy wuz caught stealing suga cane, but ran off afta pushin dem cracker down who caught him."

"John, do ya blieve everthang dat uncle Barlow tell you?"

J D and gang knew the story from memory, but they never got tired of hearing it anew. J D didn't take all he heard to heart no matter from whom he heard it.

"Look J D, De man is gittin ohn in age, but he still hav a putty good mind, ya kno."

"Well, Tommy, heah we is." John called an end to Tommy's escorting guards.

"We'll wait til yu git passed de church, k?" John was not too eager to hang around graveyards at night either.

They had already passed the cemetery. Tommy would never pass the graveyard alone at night, not in a million years. Now it looks like Tommy might falter even this close to safety. They could blame John for this shit and his own fears. After them ghost stories, nobody wanted to travel alone, not even a short distance.

To add to this difficult departure a warm breeze began to blow from the direction of the graveyard side of the road.

"Do ya'll feel dat?" John uttered.

"Dat's nothin, I feel dem hot winds all de tiahm." Tommy uttered back at John. "

"Dat don't mean a ghost is close by." Added J D.

The five young men experienced the same feeling of discomfort as they had a while ago when they were passing the old Jones's place.

"Yep, thar had to be somthin to whad dey say bout hants still livin in and round places lak dis huh?" J D mumbled.

J D thought to himself about the whys for things being the way they were. Were there things that man could do that would guarantee a better ending to this life than the endings that the old folks talked about? He heard nothing postive about dying. He heard very little positive stuff about living from the old folks and it stood to reason that dying was even more pessimistic.

He walked along with the boys wondering if this was all there was to look forward to. An old sinner dying in agony for a life of doing the best he could, a good Christian dying a horrible death due to a lack of proper food. It looked like you lose no matter which way you jumped.

The boys, lost in their own thoughts, felt their way through the dark night toward home. John needed no hand-holding to get home.

He did not have any scary spots to pass, plus he lived less than six hundred feet from Bud and J D. The boys wondered how many boys before them had walked this same road, thinking these same thoughts and looking forward to the same tomorrows and then winding up a haunt looking for a final resting place.

CHAPTER FIVE

▼

A trip to the city was one of the high point in the lives of these small-time farm owners, share croppers, sawmill workers, crosstie cutters and pulpwood workers. They all eargely anticipated an enjoyable time at the county seat while spending their hard-earned dollars. Even the little children went to town with their mommies and daddies at the end of the cotton-picking season. This was the settling-up time of the year for the farmers. Usually nobody had made any money above what they owed, but they could borrow on the next year's crops. These hard-working country folks never spent their own money; they never had any. They lived on borrowed money, which made breaking the poverty cycle almost impossible. They were milking as much good time from the left-over money as they could. The sharecroppers seldom had moneys enough left over for more than one good weekend. They made the best of that one weekend.

All the colored and a few of the poor whites parked their cars, trucks, wagons and themselves in the alley behind the main front street. The one main street had stores on one side and the railroad on the other side. The alley behind the stores was the main street for those who were not welcome on the front street. This arrangement worked right well for a people who could never be quite comfortable socializing with people who thought of themselves as too good, or not good enough to mix with people of another race, religion or another class. The colored and the poor white folks had a lot more in common than their different colors led them to believe. White trash weren't invited to share the front streets with the high class folks either.

Knowing Wilma was sure to be in town today, J D could feel the slow buildup of excitement and the nervousness that he experienced every time he got near her. The folks from J D's neck of the woods were easy to find; they all hung together in or near the alley, except when they went to the movies. J D found some shade near the hamburger stand and waited. The hamburger stand was the popular hangout for the colored folks. Everybody showed up for one of those hamburgers sooner or later. Member of the high class even dropped back in the alley for a greese burger once in a while. These burgers were a must-have for all the visitors from the countryside.

"Heah dey comes." J D said to no one in particular when he saw the truck turn into the alley.

J D wanted to walk right over to the truck and help Wilma down, but he didn't. He didn't want her to know how eager he was to get her away from the others and into a movie house. Suddenly one of the McCray brothers walked over to the truck and starting talking to Wilma. He didn't offer her a hand getting down from the truck though.

"Wha is dat bastad sayin ta Wilma?" 'How kin dey be so friendly wid colored gals when we can't even speak ta white gals in public unless dey speak to us?"

The playful teasing between Wilma and McCray confused J D. Wilma was turning colors.

"What is dat called?" J D was trying to remember.

Wilma was blushing, as much as a brown-skinned person could, laughing and talking back to the white boy. J D stopped walking toward the people unloading from the tailgate of the pickup truck. He had never hated anybody in his life until now. The combination of sexual attraction for his girl, fear of trouble in an unwinable situation and extreme jealousy paralyzed him. This jealousy was a brand new emotion for him, especially being jealousy of his girl. He had never liked a girl this much before in his young life. The poor boy didn't have the freedom and courage needed to get in the way of a mean white boy who was flirting with his colored girl.

J D had no idea how to express what he was feeling right then. He had seen Wilma flirt with boys of her own race, but not with a white boy. He could handle her flirting with colored boys and men. She didn't see J D leave the alley and head for the movie, disappointed and alone. He didn't have the courage to do otherwise; he didn't know of any colored that had, except maybe old man Barlow.

J D didn't see Bee until he was standing at the ticket window of the movie house. Bee was Wilma's sister, one year older than Wilma and nine months older than J D. Bee was a little more filled out than Wilma was; more womanly looking. J D thought he had gone crazy as a road lizard when Bee purchased her ticket and followed him upstairs and into the far corner of the balcony. The boy went to the dark side of the colored gallery because he didn't want to be seen in the movie without Wilma. There were no rational ways to explain what happened, or how he reacted to it.

The first words came from Bee.

"Do ya mind if I set next to ya?"

"Help yo self." J D replied.

"Want some pop corn?" Asked J D.

"Yea, if you don't mind."

Bee didn't have a movie escort either. She was glad for a make-believe boyfriend even if it was just for fun.

J D was glad to go after the snacks for the simple reason the trip gave him time to make some sense out of what this had become.

"Ah thought ah wanted to be by maself but ah ain't. ' Now wha if some of dem othas see us up heah togetha?"

J was talking to himself about this mess he was getting himself into. The strange part of all this shit was nobody seemed to notice anything unusal, at least J D didn't notice anybody paying much attention to his confound state of affairs. J D was glad when the lights went out and the movie started. Now the chance of his being seen with Bee was less likely. Just as the projector started to roll, Bee leaned over and kissed J D smack dab in the mouth. She kissed with tongue and all, the same as Wilma. For a minute J thought Bee was Wilma especially when his body started to react the same as it reacted to Wilma's kisses. Now he had no idea what direction was the correct one any more than the man in the moon. Bee kept up the heavy petting for what must have been an hour, J D thought. By this time the boy sure was not interesting in eating pop corn.

While Bee sat as close as it was possible to sit in the single seats, J D thought about his uncle Abe. Uncle Abe must have young'uns scattered all over the county, even some by his own kin.

"Am ah like dat old hypocrite?" He thought.

Uncle Abe had never been known to favor much work. While others were at work uncle Abe was notorious for visiting housewifes left home alone during the day.

"Boy! He sho is a bastard.' 'No wonda he's seldom seen in church."

"Do ya want some ice cream?" Asked Bee as she got up to go to the concession stand at the entrance to the theater.

The keyed up boy was glad that Bee had sense enough not to ask him to fetch the ice cream. His pants were not made to hide the kind of excitement that he felt at the moment. He wondered how these two sisters learned so much about kissing and other things at their ages. They sure were helping him grow up in a hurry. Girls and boys pleasuring one another was one of the few enjoyable natural behaviors that were not allowed without the threats of hellfire and damnation. Even this normal physical relationship between boys and girls was wholly forbidden by the community and the church. Nobody seemed to follow these rules though.

"Is you goin to the Star and see nother cowboy picture?" Asked Bee.

"Naw, ah think Ah'll catch a ride home." J D said in a low voice.

They kissed and felt each other again and again before the lights came on at the end of the show. The others must have gone to the Star first which explains why none of them were here. J D had always gone to the Strand first when all the others usually went to the Star first. Bee knew which movie house the others were going to. That's why she did not have to worry about being seen kissing and making out with J D.

These two left the movie house together. They went by the hamburger stand and J D bought two burgers and two RC colas. They stood in the shade of the stores making small talk until the refreshments were gone.

"Ah'm goin lookin fer mommy. She is gonna buy me a par uf shoes'. Ah'll see ya tomor at church".

"Kay" J D mumbled.

Still avoiding the other kids, J D walked the alley looking for somebody who was headed back to within walking distance of home. He just wanted to get back to where he could make sense out of the world. Nothing in his past learning could explain what he experienced today. As soon as he got a fix on reality, boom, reality changed. Nothing stayed the same; nothing made sense all the time; nothing was real, nothing at all. J D was still looking to see what had happened to Wilma. He assumed that she must have been still in the moveis. He needed time to sort this out anyway.

Chapter Six

▼

The police station was at the south end of the alley. Just north of the police station is where the colored citizens unloaded, after pulling into the alley, and loaded their people for the trip back to the country. As J D got near the station he noticed something was going on. He saw a crowd of what sounded like angry white folks out in front of the small city jail. The paralyzing fears that J D knew so well begin to build up in his guts. Just as he got within hearing distance he heard one white man say,

"We should hang dat dar nigger."

That statement coming from a white man was what colored folks feared more than anything except maybe being condemned to hell for all eternity, and that's a big maybe. At least that hell was way in the future; most hoped it was anyway. J D's mouth went dry. He could barely swallow small bites of the hamburger that was left between his teeth. He kept inching closer to the crowd that had begun to assemble at the jailhouse. The whites were in front and close to the entrance; the colored were to the side and slightly to the rear of the jailhouse. J D saw Allen standing closer than any of the other colored dared to stand.

Allen never did have real good sense. One saying was that he would not live to get grown. Courage was the most dangerous characteristic a young colored man could have in Mississippi. Some say that Allen has no courage; he was just crazy as a bat. They said the same thing about his father too. Allen just loved the taste in his mouth that came from exercising the freedom of speech. Freedom was one thing that felt good to the ones who dared to claim it, Allen believed. Courage and good common sense had to work as a team for the Negroes in the deep south or life would always be at risk. Allen was short on good common sense.

"Hey Allen!"

"Yeah!"

"Whad's goin on?"

"Dey 'rested Mark a while ago.' ' De deputies had a time keeping de McCray boys and dey friends fahm strangin em up".

"Whad'd he do?" J D asked.

"Tommy tol me dat somebody saw dat Britton Gal flirtin wid em".

"Ah had a hunch dat gal was gonna cause trouble." J D mumbled.

Mark is one of the coloreds that is more white than black. He even has curly brown hair. He is the color that most white folks and colored folks too, wished they were. Both colored and white girls fell all over themselves trying to get him to pay some attention to them. But Mark seemed to be always just out of the reach of the young gals. He was nearly nineteen years old, but had no girlfriend as far as anybody knew.

Mark was over six feet tall, weighs somewhere around one hundred and fifty pounds, and went clean all the time. This was part of his problem. The whites didn't trust him being near their women folks; the colored boys didn't trust him near their women either.

Mark's whole family was half white and considered good looking by most of the local folks, even if they didn't admitted it. J D's gang thought that Mark's sisters were the prettest gals in the county. They also thought that the sisters were also too high class for the darker members of the community. The white folks were not the only people blinded by skin color in Mississippi. The colored divided themselves along the color line the same as the whites separate themselves from the colored along the color line.

Mark's folks were well off, which explained the fact that he made it into town without being hung. The McCanns were better off, money wise that is, than ninety percent of the crackers here abouts. The McCanns had their own everything. They had cattle, pigs, chickens, ducks, goats, mules, and horses and land a plenty. They were what the locals call 'nigguh-rich.' They were the only Negroes who own more than one truck. Yep, were better off than most local folks and that includes both colored and whites.

As the news spread, the town's people started drifting down to the south end of town where the jailhouse was. None seems to know the whole story and the law was not talking to anybody outside the jailhouse. There was one thing for sure; these crackers were not dealing with the ordinary colored family.

Those McCanns had always banded together when one of them got in trouble. It was a big family of those folks and they didn't scare too easily. One reason they didn't scare was that they thought of themselves as being as white as any cracker and of a higher class than most Mississippi rednecks. They were too. The McCanns were the only colored family that had a few members who had been to college. Most of the other colored stayed in school through junior high before quitting so they could work fulltime on the farm or do public work. There was no demand for educated Negroes in Mississippi.

J D and Allen stood and watched the colored round up their family members and begin getting out of town. The older folks were going to the movie houses, the stores and up and down the ally rounding up their families and heading for the country. Maybe they did not want to be near this great legal injustice. The colored spectators did not want to provide a Negro audience for these poor crackers' to teach all coloreds a lesson in what happens to them when they cross the color line. J D and Allen knew the main reason that colored moved on to a safe distant from trouble. The cold grip of fear is hard to ignore. The colored of Mississippi got a daily dose of terror to flavor every moment of their very existence.

The Mississippi colored melted into non-existence when the white folks got mad at some poor colored person. It had been true as long as anybody could remember. When whites got mad at one Negro, they got mad at all Negroes. The possibility of trouble was much higher on Saturday when a mob was easy to assemble. The free flowing spirits added to the ease of getting a mob fired up. The colored disappeared into the invisible world at times like this.

"Wadda ya think?" Asked Allen.

"We betta git outta hea wid de othas." J D replied.

Missing the last ride back home is nothing to take lightly. The thought of walking twelve miles through the hauntiest areas of the county is enough to scare the hell out of Allen even; Allen uses extremely poor judgment at times. Today haunts were not the reason for not wanting to be on these country roads. For angry young whiskey-filled whites any colored would be a target to vent their hatred on.

The two boys walked over to where Uncle Tom's truck was parked just to make sure they had a ride. From what they were seeing with their own eyes, this city was becoming a city where they would not be safe. The town, the country, the jail, the law and everything else belong to the white folks at times like these. J D and Allen knew this fact well. They had been schooled by the best; their fathers and mothers.

"Dang dem crackas, ah hope dey burn in hell!" J D growled.

Allen added his two bits. "Ah wish Ah hada 30.30 rifle."

"Fuh whad?' 'Dey got 30.30s too."

The cold hands of fear were locking the colored folks into a paralyzing state of being. Fear caused the people to be unable to think for themselves, defend themselves or their love ones. They just wanted to crawl in a hole and wait until the storms of danger blew over.

The afternoon took on a depressing and terrified gloom. The shadows of the buildings began to stretch across the alley as the sun slid futher into the western sky. The city's normal have-a-good-time-Saturday-afternoon characteristics changed this afternoon to something nobody could explain.

The folks that the boys had known all their lives did not exist anymore.Everybody had become cold dead-eyed monsters with no humanity whatsoever. The smiles were gone; the spirited eyes were gone; the head-held-high posture was gone and all signs of love, hope, brotherhood and sisterhood were also gone.

"Whad gonna happen ta Mark?" Asked Allen.

"It won't be so bad. His folks is money folks." replied J D.

"Nobody else is gonna help em." Allen said.

As the trucks and cars crossed the main US highway and slowly creeped over the gravel road leading out of the county seat, the boys, girls, men and women sat withdrawn into a world that could not be a place where life is good. Nobody looked directly at, spoke directly to anybody, or acted like there were others present. These humans gave up their humanity and became zombies.

"Ah wonda how Mark feel 'bout now." Allen broke the silence.

"Ah sho wouldn't wanna be in his shoes." Replied J D

"If he hada 30.30 he could do somethang."

J D begins imagining what it must be like to be in Mark's kind of trouble alone. He has to be in a state of absolute panic. The terror has to be beyond human endurence. J D begins to feel that crushing wad of fear deep down in the center of his being. This brand of danger was always close at hand and was a high probability of becoming a reality for any southern colored boy or man.

"Ya thank dat Mark will be his old self if he gits outta dis mess?'

"Ah don't reckon he will." J answered.

The old truck rattled on toward the settlement, dropping off riders at their homes. J D and Allen stood up and held on to the framed body of the truck just behind the cab. They kept an eye on the low hanging tree branches to avoid getting knocked into the middle of next week. The sighs of other vehicles having gone before were shown by the dust still hanging just above the road. The usual joy ride home on the back of a truck was replaced by the dreadful gut feelings that everybody seems to be riding with. Finally the old truck coasted to a stop in front of J D's house. J D jumped down and waved good bye to the others. Nobody waved back, or acknowledged J D's departing gesture, except Allen.

CHAPTER SEVEN

▼

Walking up to the front stoops J D was expecting the old dog to meet him. The flea bag was not in his usual place under the steps. Not only was the dog missing, but everybody else was missing from their usual Saturday evening perch on the front porch. The whole place looked deserted.

The colored had performed one big disappearing act that would be impossible without years of practice. They just melted into thin air. They passed no colored the whole ten miles from town to their community which was not normal for the time of the year. The only folks that were about were whites. J wondered how a total people could vanish from sight at the first sign of trouble. This was the only kind of news that travels at the speed of the fastest horse. Trouble between whites and colored folks had an emotional and physical impact on the entire community. Many community members showed signs of insanity as a result of this white/black social dish of madness.

Bypassing the house, J went to the lot and begins to feed the stock.

"How safe is de colored folks from dese crazy crackers. Is thu colored safe in dey own homes?"

The answer to that question was a big fat no-no. An insane community offered very little security for anybody. J D was beginning to believe that both races were nuttier than peanut candy.

J D always found a simple kind of peace around the animals on the farm. There were no indications of hatred among the barnyard community, except squabbles over scarce food and a few sexual privileges. The animals did what they were programmed to do in order to survive; they did not do harm to others because of fear, or fear of reaping what they had sowed.

"Mebbe we is jess lak dese po animals." J D thought.

The sun still hung at about an hour above the tree tops giving the early evening that golden glow, which made this time of the year so beautiful. Late fall was the farmer's favorate time of year. The hot days were gone until next spring. The air was cool enough to be confortable, but not cold enough to require heavy clothes. The leaves had already stated to turn the woods into a sight to behold. Soon the trees will be a bouquet with a mixture of colors. The combination of red, crimson, yellow and scarlet forest colors was one of nature's ways of bringing beauty to all who had the sense to appreciate it. Nature delivers ugliness too, just as easily as it delivers beauty. J D wondered if mankind was a part of old Mother Nature's ugliness.

Going into the house after finishing his nightly chores, J knew what he would find inside the house. He kept wishing that the ugliness of today could somehow be erased away, prayed away, or was the results of a bad dream. Entering the house through the kitchen was the usual entrance when approaching from the barn; J D automatically followed the usual. He didn't hear the chatter that was typical for the family this time of the evening.

"Dar ain't no chit-chat dis evenin." He thought.

The fear continued to gnaw at the insides of J D's guts, the kind of fear that comes from the possibility of evil being done to people within his community without anyone being guilty of wrongdoings. The hopelessness he felt came from the fact that there is not a damn thing that he could do to change the way things were. That was his most important grievance at the moment.

"Daddy, have ya herd anythang bout dem McCanns yit?"

"Naw! And Ah ain't gonna set up all night thankin 'bout dem neither."

Nobody wanted to talk about the McCanns and their situation. They were afraid to lend their voices to this; they were in denial. Keeping a safe distance from the problems between colored folks and whites made just plain good sense. Mississippi was not the place to challenge the locals's ideas of right and wrong treatments between Negroes and whites, or the relationships between the races. Negroes didn't treat whites fairly either. Negroes told the white folks the truth about nothing.

J D didn't sleep too soundly Saturday night. He woke up at every little noise that floated through the cracks of the old walls. His mind was filled with the 'what-ifs' that might make a difference. What would it take to make life good here in this county of the great state of Mississippi?

"If whad happen ta Mark today could hapen ta any uf us, wha kin we do ta protect ourselves?" J said to himself.

Mark's safety was the thought occupying his mind all night. He had heard that Mark was taken from his home by three half-drunk crackers. Things could have gotten much nastier if the law hadn't come alone. Because it was Saturday, all the family was in town and Mark had no help at home.

"Tongues will be a wagging at church tomor.' 'We'll know somethang even ifn it be wrong." J D mumbled as he tried to go back to sleep.

Aunt Sal was one to keep up with all the bad news coming from her neighborhood, or any other neighborhood that she could get news about. How she received all the news was anybody's guess. Some say that she used voo-doo to make people bring her all the news. The community depended on the old lady for something to talk about after services and to keep tongues wagging throughout the following week.

Nobody within the church community had to be dragged out of bed that Sunday morning. The folks in these parts of the county could remember another time when something like this had happened. Most of the teenagers were too young to remember the details but they had heard the story many, many times. The old folks kept the story alive to remind the young of their place in the Mississippi society. Daddy Jessie was sober this Sunday and singing one of the two spiritual songs that he recalled all the words to. He knew that the church would be packed today with old and young hypocrites pretending to be holier than the angels until the scare blows over. Daddy Jessie was no different; he would be a good husband, father and son today. Daddy, singing as he went out into the morning sunshine, was remembering another time when his cousin got into trouble with the white folks over in Alabama years ago. Daddy Banks had long ago given up on having a good life on this side of the great divide.

"Dang crackas." He muttered into the fresh morning air.

In all his forty eight years Daddy Jessie could not remember any event as clearly as he could remember the details about what happened to his young nephew Steve. Daddy Jessie's oldest sister, Aunt Margaret, never did get back her right mind after she lost her baby. Steve was her only boy; he was her youngest child. Aunt Margaret had five girls before she had little Steve. He was named after his father that died before Steve was old enough to remember him. The family showered the little fatherless boy with enough attention to spoil hell into him. This pampering did not cause Steve to become a spoil brat, it had the opposite effect. The spoiling seemed to have made a empathetic man out of Steve.

Daddy Jessie recalled Steve as being one big joker. Life to Steve was all fun and games. He never understood the realities of life in the world of Mississippi's social mental illness. Daddy had often tried to show Steve where all people was good some of the time and bad some of the time. Steve just never was pessimistically programmed to recognize the evils that are part of all living things. Daddy could recall just how much Steve loved everybody and believed that everybody loved him a lot too. Steve carried this trusting-everybody attitude to Alabama with him that Saturday afternoon.

He had always been kind of free to go and come as it pleased him; therefore nobody worried about him when he would spend the night with a friend, male or female, without telling anybody. He had been known to walk the five miles into Alabama, the ten miles to town and even farther distances, returning home days later. Folks were use to Steve loafing all over the county. They never thought much about this.

Daddy remembered his uncle, who lived in Alabama, bringing the news about Steve early the Sunday morning after it happned. A few of the older colored citizens drove up to bring the body back to Mississippi, or what was left of it after it had been burned to a crisp. They put the burned body in a ten-foot long cotton sack for transpotation, and to hide it from the women and children. People never were positive that the burned corpse was the body of Steve at the time and some still believe until the present day that the dead person was not Steve. Aunt Margaret never believed that the cotton sack held the body of her beloved Steve. Some say that Aunt Margaret fixed and saves his food just as she did before the sad day. As the girls moved out, Aunt Margaret believed more and more that her boy would just come strolling up at any moment. She continued to await her baby's return until her dying day.

Chapter Eight

▼

The Banks followed their usual Sunday morning agenda. Momma fixed the coares grits, scrambled eggs, fat bacon, syrup and biscuits and called all to breakfast. She made light talk about everything in the world except what was really on everybody's mind.

The congregation arrived at church earlier than usual, so it seemed to J D and the gang. The boys didn't have to wait for the girls to show up this morning; they were already there when the young men arrived. Even so, nobody was in their normal mood for fooling around today. There was one family missing today, the McCanns.

J D caught Wilma's eye. She came over to where he was and behaved as if nothing unusual had happened at all yesterday. She did not appear as if she realized what went on between them in town.

"Hi J D." Wilma greeted.

"Good monin. How is it wid ya Wilma?"

"Okay. Hea any news 'bout Mark?"

"Notten yit, hav yew?" J D asked her.

"Notten but dat Mista Britton might have helped de McCanns git Mark outta de county."

The news that Mr Britton might have helped the McCanns did not surprise J D because the Brittons had a history of being as fair to colored folks as it was possible to be in Mississippi without being labeled nigger lovers, the younger Brittons that is.

"Who tol ya dat?" asked J D.

"See yew lata." Said Wilma as she headed for the outhouse with the other girls. Wilma had a bad habit of not listening to questions that she had no answers for.

"Yu gals slow up." Wilma shouted.

This was not a normal Sunday morning, J D sensed. The sun did not appear to be as bright as normal, the gossip was near zero and the kids were not their usual noisy selves. The slight breeze filtering through the leaves of the old oak tree seemed to bring real news if J D could just understand it. The breeze was just brisk enough to rip a few leaves from the old oak tree and let them float so softly to the earth. The almanac forcasted rain for today.

Bee walked passed J D slapping his arm as she walked by. She said nothing verbally but the slight touch said more than her voice ever could. J D felt exposed as if he had been buck naked. He wondered how Bee could be so casual about yesterday in the movie. All of this added to the unreal experiences of today that the boy was having trouble getting a handle on.

"Is dar anythang dat dese people take serous 'nough ta try ta make sense uf? "Is we jus makin nois ta drown out de real truth?"

J D asked the winds. If the winds answered, J D did not hear it.

Bee's gesture was nothing more than a signal that all was as it had always been. Bee's wooing and fooling around with the local boys her own age was only rehearsals. Her aim was to hone her skills and be ready for bigger fish than were swimming around in the small social tributary where the young men played. Bee didn't care diddly-squat about the boys who she practiced smooching with.

Ms Sal walked past everybody and entered the church without uttering a word beyond

"Good monin Ya'll."

The group followed her into the church realizing that Ms. Sal had told Reverand Mayfield all the news which would be the theme of his sermon. Aunt Sal did not want to take the punch out of the sermon by telling the news before the preacher had a chance to get the congregation feeling guilty and scared enough to put a few more hard-earned quarters in the collection plate.

Reverend Mayfield cleared his throat several times before greeting his congregation.

"Good monin brothrern and sistas. Ain't we blessed ta be heah in de house of tho Lord dis monin?"

A few amens could be heard coming from the flock.

"Yes, Gawd's word is always fulfilled. 'For Ah git started wid my deliverance, Ahm gonna make a couple of 'nouncements this monin."

The old Reverend let the congregation's mouths hang open while he announced the usual schedules of services before getting to the real news.

"De little Dozier girl had a baby gal last Wednesday; Aunt Mammie passed away Saturday monin just fo day, services will be at King Chapel Monday at 11:30 A.M.: blab, blab........"

Everybody knew about Aunt Mammie's passing. She had been on death's bed for quit a spell.

None of the worshippers was interested in the news that all of them could have predicted weeks ago. They were hungry for news about Mark McCann. But, the old Rev. had a full house today and he was not about to let this opportunity get away. He had not preached to a crowd of this size since the revival two years ago when Peejo had to leave town hiding under the shadows of darkness. He got caught with Mr. Well's young daughter. Nobody has heard from Peejo since. The Reverend took his good old time.

The deacons had cut short their usual long prayers just to hear the latest news about how Mark had made out with the mess that he had gotten himself into, or somebody had gotten him into.

"Ah wish ya would git ta de news dat we want ta hea, Reverand." J D mumbled.

"The lawd have ways to brin down dose who git too high in de world ta obey his commands."

The old preacher ranted on about the prices one pays for living outside the laws of God.

"Mah text today will include lessions on de high cost uf livin in sin in de sight of Gawd. We had a nea lynchin in town yesteday, as y'all may be awar uf, but Gawd intevened in de matter. Gawd lets man go jess so fuh 'fo He steps in and takes mattas inta His own hands."

The Reverend continued with his sermon, but Ms. Sal could not hold the news any longer. She whispered to Aunt Mary.

"Ah hea dat Mista. Britton and de McCanns got togethe and paid de police chief a rite smart pile uf money ta smuggle de boy outta de county. dat's whad Ah herd fahm one uf de Evans boys dis mornin."

Ms Sal had said enough. The news spreaded all over the entire church in less than two minutes. J D had suspected something like this. He had hoped that Mark had the necessary help to escape to the North where he had some relatives. J had wished that there was something that he could have done, but what could a sixteen year-old boy do. He was scared to death of troubles like this.

"Ah'll be seventeen soon and kin make muh driver's licen. With muh licen Ah'll be able ta drive Uncle Tom's truck."

J D had become a sixteen year-old boy again. His fear and confusion were laid to rest for now. He had to get his mind off Mark and Mark's predicament.

Everybody's reaction to the good news was like the relief of a herd of deer after the danger from a predator was over, especially for the ones that had escaped the claws of the predators. The gossip mill started grinding out rumors to fill in for the questions that had no answers.

The word was out that the High Sheriff was more than willing to lend a hand because the McCray boys were his kin. The McCray's were the hot heads who had gone back to the store and saw or claimed to have seen the goings on between Mark and Jennie. The Sheriff, and everybody else, knew that the McCray boys had no problem with lying for just about anything or on anybody. Racial problems had a way of becoming messy during an election year. The sheriff wanted nothing to stand in the way of his being re-elected. The colored didn't vote but a large bunch of the good Christian whites did. These voting Christian whites did not want to be reminded of any racial problems at all. The sheriff's job was to maintain peace between the races while ignoring any harmless racially-connected disturbances. He had his reasons for watering down this possible divergence from his expected smooth re-election.

After church the church-goers did not hang around in the yard like they normally did. They were relieved to know that one of their kinds had escaped the cluches of the local trouble makers.

"Maybe Gawd do help thangs be better." J D thought to himself.

The price that one paid for venturing over the invisible lines that divide the social groups was extremely high

J D and Wilma were playing lightly at courtship when Allen called out. "Hey J! Is ya goin wid dem?" Pointing toward John and the other young men.

"Naw, not today. "

"Wha is ya goin?"

"Ah'm goin by Wilma's house on muh way to de stoe. 'Yu comin wid me?"

"Let's go."

The colored had to be careful on day like these, if for no other reason than the whites might feel that they had been cheated; cheated out of the opportunity to quench their thirst for blood. The boys thought better than taking a chance of being caught in the woods far out of sight of the grown folks. They decided to stick close to home today. It would take a while for the breeze to blow away the smell of evil and terror.

J D and Allen kept a keen eye on the little traffic that was. They wanted to make sure they would have time to take any action that might be needed to avoid trouble. As they passed the Wilson's house Allen spoke in a low voice.

"Ah wonda do Mista Wilson still sees his wife dat he kilt."

"Some folks say he do."

For the next mile the only sounds that were heard were the boy's shoes crunching through dried clay and the barking of a distant dog.

"Ya gonna stop and see Wilma?"

"Ifn Ah see her on de poch or somethin."

J D was still having a rough time sorting out his thoughts about what he did in town yesterday. But, from what he could tell from the girl's actions today nothing had changed. Wilma sure acted like Bee hadn't told her a thing.

"Well if she don't tell, I won't." J D said out loud to himself.

"What wuz dat?"

"Nothin."

As the boys reached the bottom of the hill where the bluffs were lower and the tree had been cut down the boys saw the two girls. The house set on the bank of the road to their right near the bottom of the hill where the banks were a lot lower. The walkway up to the house was sloping enough to cause the boys to lean forward a bit to walk up to the front yard.

The girls were on the porch as if they had been waiting for the young men to show up. The chilly breeze had just a hint of colder weather to come. The family had begun to pile kindling in the part of the yard designated for firewood. Just for a moment the boys could forget Mark.

"Howdy." Both boys spoke at the same time.

"Hey!" Both girls replied.

The truck was no where to be seen which means that the old folk had to be gone on a Sunday visit somewhere. J D knew then that he and Allen won't make the store today. The smaller kids were out playing under the big oak tree in the swings with their cousins from Alabama.

Wilma went toward the girl's bedroom which was in the back of the house across from the kitchen. As she got through the front room she looked back and motioned J D to follow. He had no trouble with following her to the back bedroom. No siree. With Bee and Allen keeping watch J D had nothing to worry about.

J D had never gone all the way with a girl before. He had a hard time getting things right, but he finally did what he could. He felt that something was missing but he didn't know what. His dissappointment had nothing to do with Wilma's performance. She seemed to know exactly what she was doing. He thought that he had been too nervous to do what was expected of him. When they heard the kids playing on the porch they went out the back and walked around the house as if they had been outside all the time.

The four young people sat on the front porch until nearly sundown. The connection between J D and Wilma had suddenly become one union that would last for the rest of their lives. J D had a feeling of belonging that he'd never had before.

"Dis aftanoon will be special." He thought to himself.

The Sunday afternoon ended on a very positive note because Mark's escape, or good luck if you want to call it that, offered hope for the coloreds in Mississippi. Any luck, blessings, hope, or events that made life for one citizen better were appreciated by all. The big change that this day brought was the lost of J D's innocence.

"Let's cut cross de pasture."

"How come?"

"Cause it's a heap shorta distant ta our houses, Allen!!"

The two friends crawled through the barbed-wire fence and started to slow jog their way toward home. They had to keep a lookout for the old bull that would sometimes get upset at anybody crossing his territory. Each boy grabbed the first stick that he saw just to have some protection in case the old bull felt like taking his frustrations out on anything that moved.

The boys knew every fruit tree they passed as they jogged toward home. They should know them because both had fond memories of the times they had gathered fruits and nuts from these trees. The pear tree stood majestically like it had stood since time begins. None of the younger generation was old enough to remember when the broken down house was lived in much less the age of that tree. But, every colored boy who grew up within miles of these trees had for the last three generations tasted the pears from that old trees, the plums from the plum trees and all the other fruit and nut trees. The walnut trees, the plum trees, the chinquapin and the fig trees were all parts of the country kids' daily diets when in season. There were no fruits or nuts this time of the year, all had been eaten or gathered for the winter. The trees had taken on that dead-forever look. The growing season was over in the great state of Mississippi in the year of our Lord of 1943

CHAPTER NINE

▼

World War Two worked wonders for the relationships between the races in Mississippi. Everybody was nearly on the same page as for as their love for their country was concerned. There were clash but far less numerous than occurred before the War. The first three years of the war saw an improvement in the colored/white relations. Both peoples saw a common enemy and a common job to be done. A few might have been a bit confused about what they were fighting for though. They had a chance to fight somebody other than each other at last.

Some thought that the colored figured if they could prove their love for their country beyond a shadow of a doubt life would be better for all Mississippians, especially for the colored. The poor folks could prove that they were worthy citizens by joining the fight to protect freedom, only God knows whose or where, and maybe that protected freedom would somehow trickle into the great state of Mississippi to be shared with the colored folks. They did give it a good try, but failed to prove anything of the sort. When the signs of winning the war were seen, the common enemy disappeared and the same old alleged enemy was back in business. It was even thought that the races got along worst now than they did before the war.

The whites thought that the colored's place in the southern society had not changed even though some of the colored seemed to think so. The misunderstanding about the colored's place in the overall scheme of things had the county in a terrible fix. Nobody seemed to know exactly what to do about the new expectation these colored heroes brought back from their war experiences. The mothers and fathers of these young heroes had not been away to foreign lands and had a better handle on the situation here at home. The old folks knew their white folks and their colored folks too. The old folks weren't crazy enough to believe that a war fought thousands of miles away would bring about any lasting changes between the Negroes and whites in Mississippi.

The old timers knew that, war or no war, these poor crackers had not changed their minds about the coloreds and the colored hadn't changed their minds about the white either. If anything, they thought that they had a bigger job to do to keep these young heroic uppity niggers in their place. A few of the house maids and personal servants working close to the masters had heard talk of possible trouble between the races. The whites believed that the coloreds just might be foolish enough to think that he was white now, or should be treated with the same respect as white anyway. The whites didn't care where the Negroes had been, or what they had done, they were still niggers here in good old Mississippi. The mommas and daddies knew this was the attitude held by most of the ruling class. Fear for their sons and daughters was causes for many long and loud prayers in church on Sundays

A high percentage of the red-necks turned into nut cases just thinking about what they had heard, and some had even seen it with their own eyes. Darkies fraternizing with white women? Extreme care had to be used whenever a darkie came within ten feet of a white woman. It only took one yap from some poor red-neck woman to set in motion a mob action that causes the devil to feel humiliated.

J D and company were too young to be drafted into the service but they were old enough now to have a real worry for their safety. J D and Allen both would be eighteen years old their next birthday. Both boys had developed into two good looking young fellows and had drawn a few flirts from the girls. Some of the boys did go into the army though, because they had turned eighteen, or seventeen with their parents consent. They went to the army camp to be trained. J D and Allen wanted to go too. They were hoping the war would last until they were eighteen. The returning black soldiers sure made an impression with the girls, and the boys too. Those uniforms could make somebody out of nobody. Those dressed-up black soldiers made those poor crackers appear shabby. Those uniforms caused some problems for the left-behind blacks as well. The girls went for men in uniforms.

J D and Wilma had not been together as often as they had wanted to within the past two years due to the war and its impact on everybody in the country. Stamps for gas, shoes and other rationed goods made living a little tougher than normal. He stuck with Wilma because he thought that he was in love with her, plus there were a limited number of girls around that were not kin to the Banks.

Wilma aged a whole lot since her first cousin was killed in France. They shipped his body home to be given a heroes' burial. But a heroes' funeral were not for the likes of Wilma's cousin. This war was causing difficulties on both sides of the racial divide by making promises that it could not keep. This going away to fight on foreign soils and being introduced to other cultures caused some confusion within the returning boys' heads on both sides of the social line. These young men and women had common sense enough to know when to get back to business as usual, if they would use this intelligence. Now, those folks up north were packing these ignoramuses' heads with non-sense. Who ever heard of a Negro being buried in the white cemetery? Nobody in Mississippi had ever heard such a silly thing, black or white. The north may not have started the rumor, but they got the credit for starting it anyway. The north had their black and white problems too.

J D and his gang were just about to get the hang of living in a society that had peculiar notions concerning proper behavior for its citizens. The system was screwed up but it worked for most of the people most of the time. Law and order were the rule most of the time even it the law was Jim Crow. Now with these new ideas flowing into Mississippi from God knows where, caused cracks in the social fabric of the Jim Crow system. The Negroes were fighting the changes even more than the whites, or so it seemed to the boys.

"De colored folks is no mo woied bout followin de racial rules den de whites is." J D snarled.

"Dey is scared, dat's all." Whispered Allen.

This was J D's favorite time of the year; spring time. This was a special spring because this was J D's and Allen's last year in high school.

"Yes suh, we is gonna git us a job at de saw mill, earn nough money ta go up nawth". J thought out loud.

"Ah don't know bout dat J.' 'My folks wan me ta consida goin way to school".

"Whad do ya wan?"

"Ah gonna thank bout it cross de summa".

The notions of enlisting into the army were slowly taking a back seat to other more promising ideas. The young Negro men were beginning to see that serving their country was not going to change things at home much at all.

J D thought about what life would be like here without his best friend. He felt the warm spring breeze on his face. The pleasant gentle wind also bought the fragrances of the Mississippi flowering plants and blooming fruit trees to all who could appreciate this gift from God. He believed that no other place on earth offered this combination of pleasant fragrances. The odors coming from the freshly plowed earth just added to what was already an aroma coming from Heaven. J didn't think that the beauty of Mississippi would be enough without a best friend to share it with.

"Ah got folks up in Detroit. Ah thought 'bout going up dar when Ah git older." J D Said

"My folks wan me ta go ta Mobile fuh school. Dey say Ah could stay wid muh uncle fuh a while." Al replied.

"Com on boy, let's go ta Detroit and gitta job makin cars." J insisted.

"Didja know dat Pearl wuz in family way." Allen changed the subject.

"Yeah, and it's passed time fuh her. She is one fast gal." Al continued.

"Aw common yu lying dawg, yu know yu got some uv dat." J plugged in.

"Yu had Wilma all dese yeahs; Ah didn't hava steady gal and Ah had ta take whad Ah could git." Al went on the defense.

The rumor was that Pearl had broken in every young man within the three-church area. It was even believed by many that she might have gone far beyond the immediate community. At times she acted like there was nothing else in the whole world but sex.

"Dey say dat her mamma wuz de same way."

"Aw man, some say her momma is dat way now, Allen."

"But dat baby can't be mine." Al continues his defense.

"How do ya know?" J wanted to know more.

"Cause it's been ova a yeah since Ah wuz wid her.' 'Ah ain't talked ta her since W C started hangin round wid'er."

"Ah heah somethin comin!" Al was kind of glad for the noise headed their way.

"Yea, Ah heah it, Al."

The boys walked close to the ditch in order to give the pickup room to pass without having to get out of the deep ruts. The boys recognized the same crackers that were always trouble makers. The only exception was that the older McCray boy had on an army uniform; otherwise they were the same old nigger-hating crackers. The walking twosome heard the truck slow down.

J D had felt the sensation of that familiar creeping dread that usually came a-calling whenever trouble, that had roots in racism, came his way. This time there were only two of them against four whites; this was not good for the twosome.

"Hey you niggers." The soldier boy yelled.

"Are you niggers lookin fuh white women?" The soldier Asked.

Neither of the colored boys said a word. They knew that the truck could not jump the steep bank and the white boys weren't fast enough on foot to catch them. No sir, not in a million years. Evidently the white boys knew this too because they had themselves a good laugh and rode on down the road.

"Ya know Allen, momma thanks dat most white folks is good folks. Ah wonda whar she git her thankin fahm."

"Yea, my daddy says de same thang. He told me dat nine outta ten whites wantta git long wid de colored. Dis war thang done goin and run erybody crazy."

J D had started doubting the possibilities of finding happiness here in the land of his hometown. Finding contentment here before the war was a possibility, not a good one, but it was still possible. The new attitudes toward what was right and wrong, who got what, who went where and with whom were beginning to drive wages between old friends, especially friendships that crossed the big racial split. J D knew now that without Allen, Wilma, his family and friends, living here may be out of the question.

The new attitudes running rampant through the community were scaring the daylights out of the people. Nobody seemed to know where the lines between the races were drawn. The poor white folks were more jittery than the Negroes were. Well, that could be because the whites had lots more to loose than the colored did as a result of socials changes favoring the Negroes. Some of the colored were beginning to have pity on these good old boys.

There were no innocent parties in the state of Mississippi. There was enough guilt to share justly with all members of the Jim Crow systems throughout the south. Uncle Barlow was one Negro who was very adamant about his conviction that the colored had more input into promoting bigotry in the south than the whites did. He believed it was not what the colored did that made the biggest contribution to Jim-Crowism; it was what the colored did not do. The Negroes were afraid to tell the whites the truth.

J D and Allen felt the breaking down of the trust that each people had in the system. The old relationships between the black and white south had its problems. But they worked to some degree that provided a measure of security.

"Ah wonda wha bought dat on?" Allen asked J D.

"Ah guess dis war changed anybody."

That was all J D could think of to blame this craziness on.

"Member wha Uncle Barlow tol us one tiahm bout how dese white folks got to be de way dey is?"

"Naw, whad did he sa

"He said dat we let de whites go on thankin dat we is dumb as doe knobs.' ' Dis playin stupid on ar part makes de white man thank he is Gawd."

"Yew know whad dey say 'bout old man Barlow. He's crazier then a road lizard." Allen said.

"Ah know whad dey say".

After the run-in with the four fellows in the pickup, the two friends decided the shortest route home was in their best interest. This just was not a good time to be roaming around the country. The local whites and colored wanted to re-establish the old understood patterns of behaving in the neighborhood. Some of these folks felt insecure enough to use any means at hand to rebuild the old pecking order. This certainly was not a good time to be out and around.

With the passing of a little time, relationships between the colored folks and whites folks would settle back into the usual. The whites started back smiling at their Negroes and the Negroes returned the smiles. The folks went to work. Neither group could do without the other and sustain the system.

CHAPTER TEN

▼

J D and Bud were working the bottom five acres trying to turn the soil over in order to get the field ready for planting. This was the procedure that most farmers in this part of Mississippi followed every spring. Turn the soil over; plow in rows to drop the seeds in; drop a wee bit of fertilizer near the seeds; bury both seeds and the fertilizer and the work was created.

Each boy had one mule to pull what they called a turning plow. This plow turned the soil in one direction which made it necessary to plow the field in a rectangular pattern. Each plow-boy plodded slowly around the rectangle…

"Whoa". Bud commanded his mule, old Cheney.

J D and old Rock automatically stopped.

"Ah wonda whad Miz Anna wuz doin ova de Sun Light way". Bud spoke over his shoulder to J D

"She is de midwife, yu know." J D answered

Bud just assumed that the old midwife was coming from the Sun Light colored settlement. All the colored communities had church names. The church usually served as the center of the community through which news, community support, and assistance with sicknesses, deaths and other people's needs were taken care of. The church was the local school house in many of the rural colored areas. Miss Anna was part of all the nearby churches. Her arms were the avenue through which the newcomers enter the world.

The old lady knew more about the communities and the inhabitants than any other person in the county. She could make a lot of money blackmailing the Ten Commandment violators. Miss Anna had delivered ninety-nine percent of all the Negro children every since anybody could remember. She was now at the stage of her long midwifery where she was delivering the second and third generations. Of all the stories going around relative to whose baby is whose, Miss Anna would not confirm any of these rumors one way or the other.

Some of the stories coming out of Sun Light were enough to make the lowest social hypocrite embarrassed. It's said that there is a hog path leading from and to every house in the community. These hog paths are not use for normal traveling from one house to another. No sire, they are the hidden routes taken when the user do not want to be seen.

The plowboys did not want to take a chance on Miss Anna getting pass without their exchanging a few words. Going for another round of plowing might cause the boys to miss this opportunity to hear some news. There was very little traffic on the road at this time of the day or this time of the year. Any company was welcome if for no other reason than for making contact with the community.

"Howdy ya young'uns." Miss Anna hollowed.

" Hey Miz Anna". Both boys spoke in unison.

The old midwife was not in the habit of holding conversations with young folks, especially about what was on her mind at the present time.

"Who hada baby dis tiahm Miz Anna?"

"No baby dis tiahm, it wuz a miscarage.' 'Wilma and Bee have always been too womlish fuh thar ohn good." Miss Anna answered.

"Who" Bud, having nothing to fear asked?

"Wilma."

Miss Anna replied as she ambles on beyond hearing range.

J D felt as if he was going to suffocate. His heart started to hammer hard enough to break through his chest. He could not feel anything but an alarming sense of just bad luck.

"Didja heah wad Mize Anna said?" That was the only words Bud could think of right then.

J D did not answer. His only concern right now was wondering why Wilma didn't tell him. He had noticed Wilma's eagerness to have sex recently. How she seemed to throw caution to the win.

"Why n she tell me"? Bud heard his brother whisper.

"Is yu saying dat dis is de first ya herd 'bout a baby?"

Neither of the brothers spoke. They went back to turning over the rich bottom soil getting it ready for planting. Both boys were aware of what the social penalties were for this king of slip-up. This kind of chance-taking went on all over the country, but the penalty for getting caught was always the same; disgrace. A great many of the citizens never knew who their dads were. If the truth was known half the people would be at war right now because of those dad-gum hog paths.

J D had nobody to turn to that came close to knowing how to handle this kind of situation. In this part of the country people just did the good Christian thing; make it legal. There were times that the wrong person was called on to make a decent person out of an otherwise questionable character. This was one reason there was very few bastards running around the country side. Very few of the locals thought much about hypocrisy. They thought that going to church, praying, doing a few good deeds, being a good father, tiding in the church etc. more than made up for an occasional grab at small pleasures in an otherwise hard and boring life. J D had plans for his life that did not conform to the usual way of solving this kind of problem. J D and Bud were thinking about what the community gossipers would do with this. They knew it would be the same as always if the news got in the wind. There would be no baby this time though. J D felt the numbing sensation resulting from what could be expected when dealing with the unknown.

"Do yew think daddy and momma know 'bout dis baby?" Bud asked J D.

"She came right smack dab by de house". Ya herd whad she said, dey ain't no baby.' ' dey ain't no child ta think 'bout".

J was trying to get a handle on what to do, or at least find a solution that would not derail all his plans for the future. He didn't know if the same good old Christian solution was required for situations like this as was required when the baby was born. There is one thing that he did know, these community leaders apply a separate set of rules for others to follow from the ones they themselves were willing to follow. This he knew for a fact.

Bud told J D that they would make one more round before unhitching the mules. Old Chaney had given her its-tine-to-go look back at Bud. That look meant only one thing, it would not be easy to get another round out of her.

This part of the evening was the best time of the day. The sun was low in the western sky, fingers of sunlight filtering through the trees bathing the low lands with weird shadows. The sunlight filtering through the trees was prettier than any picture hanging on a wall.

Trucks with sawmill workers, log cutters and pup wood haulers were making their daily returns from a hard days work. The dayshift critters was bedding down for the night while the nocturnal crew begins to plot their courses for the night. There was no prettier country on earth than Mississippi in the mid evening. Today J D was not enjoying the beauty as usual. No sire, he had other problems on his mind. Even the flowering trees, such as the dogwoods and magnolias, did not lift J D's spirit.

"How could Wilma keep somethin lak dis fahm me?" The question continues to nag at J D.

J D knew that there is a limited degree of honesty existing between men and women, but some things are hard to keep to one's self.

"Wilma had ta be some strong te handle a problem lak dis by herself. Maybe somebody else knows bout dis.' Somebody hasta know 'bout a gal bein two or three months in family way.' 'Dis is hard ta believe."

Bud rode his mule slightly behind J D as they rode to one side of the road. Even with little to no automobile traffic it was good practice to ride the edge of the rutty road.

"Whdda ya think J?"

"Bout wha?"

"Dang it', yew know whad Ahm talkin bout."

J D did not want to talk about the problem because he knew less about it than anybody. He knew nothing. The only thing that he could do was to recognize his ignorance and wait until he knew what the story was. He sure didn't want it to be known that he didn't have sense enough to know when his own girl was in family way. Therefore he figured it was best to keep his dumb mouth shut.

The boys did not notice anything unusal going on at the house which meant that all was as usual. The mules were the first chore to be taken care of and the others animals came later. Once the animals and chickens were fed and watered. The hard-working crew washed their hands and faces before sitting down for supper. Feed time never took more than fifteen minutes to half an hour. This short time was mainly due to the Banks not having very many creatures to take care of. The Bank's farm had never been a farm that one bragged about; not by a country mile. This farm was like what must have been the condition of Job's (Biblical story) farm just before the devil finished with it. Most of the critters had to eat whatever they could find.

The level of poverty in this neck of the woods did very little to encourage the young men and women to think of making a life here. Many of the young people could not visualize themselves accepting a living similar to that of their parents. Change of the social and economic laws could not be imagine to come in time to help the present generations, if change ever came at all. The older folks were so conditioned to this kind of poverty that they could not think of a better society for them becoming a reality short of the one coming after death. With this kind of resistance to a postive change facing the colored, and the whites, positive change will be a long time coming. Most of the old folks spent half their lives thanking their gods for the poor conditions that existed. They thanked God for everything.

"A fit county is one dat's good fuh all its membas, not good fuh some and bad fuh de othas". Old man Barlow often said.

"Y'all git ready fuh suppa". Mommy called out to her family.

The whole family used the same wash pan and the same drying towel but not the same water. They used very little water anyway which resulted in having to tote less water from the well. The heavy homemade table was set with collard greens, potatoes, fried corn, cornbread and chunks of pork in the greens. The only beverages were butter milk and water. The butter from the milk was too precious to waste drinking. It was for backing etc.

The family almost never talked while eating. The old folks always taught that talking with food in your mouth was showing bad manners. Therefore supper time was a time for eating, not talking. The family usually had nothing new to say anyway. The daily work these folks did was not amonition to fuel conversation. Nobody had much to say about what he or she did for a living. They may eat in silence but the blessing of the food was an absolute necessity.

"Lawd we thank thee fuh dis food." Daddy finished blessing the food before anybody dared to grab one piece of bread.

"How did de plowin go boys?"

"We'll finish de bottom tomor." Bud answered

"Good."

J D was thinking about how and why the food was blessed. He did not believe that anybody here at the table was qualified to pray for all of them. There was too much hanky panky going on for prayers to work. J D believed in God, prayers, heaven and hell, but he thought that taking too many chances were risky. The risks were sometime downright frightening. He wondered if God listened to all prayers or if he listens to the voices of a chosen few. He certainly hoped that all requests were at least given a little

consideration.

It was impossible to know who was good or who was bad in this community. Were the whites right? Were the Negroes right? Were they both right? Were many right and a few wrong? Who knew the answer? J D decided that he had nothing to loose by taking a chance with prayer. Maybe his and Wilma's sins were the reasons behind the baby coming far too soon. There was more sinning going on than you could shake a stick at.

If the truth was known, half the citizens couldn't tell you who their real daddy was. The Ten Commandments were brokered more than any law of the land. With this being a fact, J D hoped the Lord was too busy to pay much attention to the little sins shared between him and Wilma.

CHAPTER ELEVEN

▼

J D could hardly wait until Saturday so that he could go see Wilma. But until then, he had to play like there was nothing on his mind other than the usual dreaming. He knew that Saturday was not going to be the usual. The usual Saturdays began with everyone working a half day in the fields or the woods, washing up and putting on clean clothes, waiting for the older folks to depart for an evening in town and then… J D felt guilty just thinking about those Saturday afternoons.

The closer Saturday came, the better J felt. After all he had prayed over this and if praying worked, things would be alright. He had his doubts about getting God involved in this mess and expecting a full pardon.

"Yew goin ta town today?" Bud asked J D.

"Nawh."

"Yeah, Ah know whar ya'll be dis aftenoon."

Going to town this time of the year was not for the young folks. They didn't have any money. Spring and early summer were not good times for earning money. This was a period of investing all the poor farmers had in their crops. A few of the young men worked by the day for farmers who could not do their own work themselves. These day-workers were usually from families that did very little farming for themselves. They hired themselves out to other small farmers, usually white farmers. The majority of the community was either farming for themselves or sharecropping. Either way, there was no income until the cash crops were sold in the fall of the year. A few people sold watermelons during the melon season, and sold eggs and some other foods that they had too much of throughout the year.

J D had a girl that he spent these Saturdays with rather than going into town broke. Spending time in town with no money was not J D's idea of fun. He was looking forward to seing Wilma.

Saturday morning finally came and with it came the promise of rain. It was not raining when Bud and J D left for the field but it sure looked like they had a wet morning coming their way. The clouds were sailing fast and low. The humidity was near a hundred percent. The boys thought it may be a waste of time to hook up the mules. The old man wouldn't buy that at all. The old man was right again, it didn't start raining until close to quitting time at noon.

J D never liked to be around the barn, chicken house and hog pens during wet and rainy weather. These were really icky places to be when the weather was nasty. Even though he loved the beauty of the Mississippi landscape; he hated the wet and dampness that ooze through every crack and crevice in the house and barn. The Bank's home was never completely weather proof. Rainny days were times when J D doubted that he would ever consider farming as a lifetime career. There are no grounds in the world as nasty and mushy as a rain-soaked barnyard. The soft animal dung oozed between his toes, stuck to the cuffs of his overalls making J D feel messy all over.

This was Saturday, the one day of the week when the boys took the time to get spruced up. They filled the wash tub nearly half full of water for bathing, cut each other's hair if needed and put on their freshly ironed pants and shirt. Now on rainy days like this, mud became a real problem. Not only did it stick to your shoes making walking difficult, but it made any mode of traveling hard on keeping neat and clean. You had to be careful if you wanted to be looking your best when you got where you were going.

The local county roads had no gravel to provide traction for the old cars and trucks. These old cars and trucks had tires that had very little treads and would skid easily even on dry road. The tires were usually as smooth as Uncle Barlow's head. The tires had no treads; Uncle Barlow had no hair. Many a time the boys would catch a ride on one of these vehicles and have to push the dang thing out of ditches and up some of the steep hills. Riding or walking, traveling was a problem on rainy days. In spite of the conditions of the roads boys and men went to see their girlfriends.

J D and Bud had eaten lunch, gotten all slicked up and was sitting on the porch hoping that a ride would come by. They were wishing for a car, not a log or pupwood truck. There was little protection from those mud-slinging dual wheels when riding on the back of a log truck. Getting to ride in the cab on Saturday when the men had their womenfolk with them was a small chance, if any chance at all.

"Dat sounds lak Paul's pickup comin." J D said as he got to his feet.

"It do sound lak his old Dodge." Bud agreed.

Paul's mommy did not go to town often which left Paul with transpotation. His dad was long dead. Paul was the only child which meant that he did not have to share the use of the Dodge truck. The Dodge truck had a power problem but it went where the boys wanted to go. They traveled a radius of about five miles which was where they hung out except when they rode into town. Today nobody had much money so a trip to town was pointless. The boys were happy that Paul decided to drive over and they could hang around the countryside.

J D wanted to hitch a ride to Wilma's house which was maybe a mile and a half from the juke-joint where Bud and Paul were headed. J would be within walking distance from either home or the joint. He did not know in which direction he would go from Wilma's house. After all this was the first contact between J D and Wilma since he heard the bad news.

The rain was coming down in sheets now and Paul's windshield wipers were not doing a very good job, but the road was not hard to see. There was no left or right side to drive on until you met another vehecile, which was not likely today. The ditches were filling up with clay-colored water. It would not be long before the creeks and branches will overflow with this muddy runoff.

"Do ya reckon a person could git away fahm de law or a mob of dese crazy crackas in weather lak dis?" Paul asked.

"Yea, de rain would wash out de tracks and de dogs couldn't smell his scent." Bud answered.

"How could anybody git cross dese rising creeks?" J D was looking at the fast running water heading for the creeks that drained the water out of these hills into Snake Creek.

"Nobody kin cross dese woods, not in all dis rain." Bud added.

The old Dodge just sort of slipped and slid down the narrow dirt road. The road to where the boys were going was never too slippery when wet. There were lots of sandy areas between the Banks' and the Alabama line. That fact was partly the blame for such poor crops grown in these fields. Not having enough fertilizers might have played a small part in the poor yield from these fields but nobody was about to admit that. It was the sandy soil. Sand was something these folks didn't have to be responsible for. Therefore they blamed the sand for lousy crops.

Paul pulled over at the Simons' house to let J D out.

"Ah'll wak on up to the juke-joint if Ah leave hea 'fo y'all come back by." J D said as he got out of the pickup. He ran for the front porch.

The two older boys rode on off toward the Alabama line which was no more than one and a half miles. The joint was located less than a mile past the line. Uncle Frank ran the joint. He sold bootleg liquoir, pickled pig feet, fish sandwiches, boiled eggs and soda pops.

The boys loved hanging around the joint on Saturday nights. This was the only place within walking or riding distance that offered entertainment outside of church. The older joint regulars were fun to watch and offered an opportunity for the boys to learn the roles necessary for becoming leading citizens. It was early yet, the leading jokers were still in town getting the women and children taken care of before heading out to the joint. They were also grabbing a few nips of homebrew, or something, in town. They sure would be charged up before the night was half over. Most of the heavy boozers did public work. Public work was non-farm work and paid off weekly.

Uncle Frank was one of the important figures in the community. He often gave money to worthy causes such as building churches, buring the dead, helping the sick and so on. He was always at the big church functions. That's where all his customers would be, so he would take the firewater to them. Yep, he sold the evil spirits on the outside of the church while the preacher sold the Holy spirits from the inside of the church. This arrangement worked well for everybody, even the preacher would sometimes need a little outside evil spirits to help him with the inside Holy spirits. Uncle Frank was a pillar of the community.

Uncle Frank's contribution to the church's financial health would never be fully appreciated. Many of the members of the church got their inspriration to go to church from Uncle Frank's bootlegged spirits. He provided the third major opportunity for the locals to vent their frustrations safely, or nearly safely anyway. The ruffians had a place where they could swear at, fist fight, cut each other with a knives and sometimes shoot each other and yet have a chance to survive. Venting this kind of anger in town, or against the whites would end in far more trouble for everybody. Yep, the colored could get down to taking their frustration out on each other as long as they kept the abuse in the family of the colored folks. A pair of good horses was more important than one of the colored ruffians was to the mainstream population. The law paid little attention to what the darkies did to each other.

It was not a bad position to be in when everything that you did was outside the law, the mainstream written law that is. The local colored folks could just about get away with any kind of crime as long as the crime was committed against their own kind and brought a monetary profit to the whites. The illegal booze was even sold for the High Sheriff or under his watchful eyes and protection.

Being that a Negro's word was nothing when it went against the word of a white, therefore even if a Negro charged a white with violating the law, nothing came of it, except that the old darkie might get a oneway ticket out of town if he was lucky. The whites did not have to be ethical when they dealt with the poor and ignorant ex-slaves.

This lack of legal accountability enjoyed by the lower class put them in positions of advantages more often than not. They weren't expected to deal ethically with the whites either, for different reasons than the whites had when dealing with the Negroes of course. There was nobody at the hole-in-the-wall when Paul pulled his truck into the muddy yard. Uncle Frank and his half-wit son were getting things ready for the usual Saturday night foot-stomping.

"Howdy." Bud spoke as he and Paul entered the one room shack.

"How you boys." Answered Uncle Frank. The son said nothing.

"Ya wanna RC?" Paul asked Bud.

"Recko Ah will.

Paul fished around in the ice cold water for two RC colas. When it came to drinks they had to be cold, nothing less than ice-cold would do.

The boys settled in to wait for the day to move on toward evening. They did not mind watching father and son work setting up the frying pans, the bread box and so on. They appreciated being in out of the rain, drinking soda pops and doing nothing.

Chapter Twelve

▼

J D saw that the old folks had already left for town before he got out of the pickup. He was glad because he did not think that he wanted to meet Wilma's daddy and mommy just yet. He thought that he might learn more if the old folks weren't home. He had no recollection of ever feeling this apprehensive before, especially here at Wilma's. Something had begun to eat at J D but he could not nail down a reason for this feeling. Whatever it was he hoped to hide this gut gnawing from Wilma and Bee until he knew more.

The old half bread hound did not come out to meet J D as he usually did. All dogs owned by blacks were mixed with every kind of dog within twenty miles. Nobody seemed to respect and love these mix-breed mutts.

"dat sory dog did not wanna git his feet wet. What a worthless critter" J D thought to himself.

Bee was the one to meet J D on the porch.

"Hi J."

"Hey Bee."

"Wilma'll be out in a spell.' she is a bit under de weather," Bee told J D.' 'Yew look poorly yoself J D"

Bee was searching J D's face as if she was looking for something writen in his eyes.

J D sat down in the homemade cane-bottom chairs to wait. He noticed the freshly plowed fields as far as he could see. The Smiths sure were getting ready for planting. They normally did very good with their crops. Their rich black soil didn't do any harm either. They had some bottom land which out produced the hilly lands by twice as much.

"Howdy J D" Wilma spoke as she walked out on the porch.

"How ya doin." J D spoke back as he looked her up and down.

"Ah didn't spose yew'd be comin today." Wilma said.

"How come?"

J D asked. His stomach really begins to act up when she stated that she had not expected him.

"Well, it wuz rainin tadpoles."

"Dis little old rain won't hurt nobody."

J D felt a bit better with Wilma's answer.

"Wilma wuz not her usual self and dat wuz fo sho." J D was thinking.

Wilma had always invited J D to sit with her in the swing. The swing was the only seat on the porch where two people could sit together. She finally was joined by Bee who sat in the swing. J D felt like a stranger there on the porch with the two sisters. He had been intimate, to a degree, with both girls but somehow that had no bearing on the situation at hand, by this time there was no real feelings in the lower part of his stomach at all

The two sisters knew J D better than any girl, or girls in the whole world but he began to realize that he knew nearly nothing about neither one.

"Ah speck AH'll pach some corn.' How would dat set wid ya?"

Bee said, asking the question at the same time as she went for the kitchen. Bee went to the kitchen to parch some corn because all the peanuts were for planting. They had run out of gobers for eating.

"Whar did Bud and Paul git to?" Wilma asked.

"Dey went up to De juke joint as usual." J answered.

"Why yew didn't go wid em?"

J D knew at that point that things had changed and would never be the same again. He had to wait awhile before he could collect his thoughts. He wanted to ask why the sudden change, but he was afraid of the answer. He felt himself being a little less welcome now than he did when he first set foot on the porch today. He had the feeling that what he valued most was slowly moving out of reach. Some inner voice was whispering to him that maybe what he had always thought was never true in the first place.

"Ah heah dat ya been poorly dis week." J D spoke.

"Who tol ya dat?"

Bee came out the door to anounce that the corn would be ready in a jiffy. She sat down to wait for the stove to heat up before putting the finishing touches on the corn.

J D was in such bad shape by now that he could barely breathe. He was sure that both girls could hear his heart beating and were about to crack up laughing at him. He thought the rain and the muddy road sure would feel good right now.

A few seconds after Bee went for the corn, Wilma said. "Wha hapen ta me had nothin ta do wid you J D."

Neither spoke for what seemed like a very long time. They sat in silence until they heard Bee yielding about the corn being ready.

"Heah Ah com wid de cone" Bee shouted as she left the kitchen.

J D put some of the corn on a piece of brown paper bag.

"Its still rite hot." Bee warned the two.

Hot parched corn was the last thing on J's mind at this time in his life. He was too busy growing up at the moment to think about any kind of corn, but he did not have the energy to say no to anything right then. He took his corn on the paper bag and told the girls bye and walked off the porch. Neither of the girls asked him to stay, or wait until the rain slacked up.

The boy lost his concerns for the rain. The rain was responsible for the wet clothing that he'd have to wear until they dryed. No sire, these minute environmental bothers were nothing compared to what he felt and thought at this crossroad. J D was entering the tunnel that led from childhood to adulthood. The mile-and-a-half walk in the downpour to the joint up on the hill was the best kick in the rear that he could get. He sure needed a good swift kick in the pants.

J D had the proof now that what Miss Anna had said was true. Wilma's attitude had somehow lent credibility to what J D could have been easily convenced was not true. The last thing that he wanted to know was that Wilma was not who he thought she was. Even worst than getting to know the other side of Wilma, was getting to know the other side of himself.

The rain seemed to help teach old J a good lession, it never let up. The cheap hat he had on and was proud of, flopped down around his ears. The hat too was not what he thought it was. While walking through the goo, J D wished that he had someone to share his troubles with. He could never confide in his brother and buddies. They had no experience in this kind of thing. The only fact that J D could be sure of is they sure would get a kick out of this situation. They would think it was as funny as hell. The young had no listening ear for other's troubles, absolutely none.

J D saw old man Barlow out in the crib shucking corn. This was the rainy-day chore around farms. J knew Mr Barlow had not seen him and he did not yell howdy as he usually did. Anyway, the older men and women didn't think much of discussing young'uns' problems with young'uns. They would eagerly talk among themselves about the problems of youth, but not to the children. The young returned the same level of indifference; they too did not talk to older people about older people's problems. The old man would just think that this was one more necessary step toward maturity. Nothing to worry about. He might even think it was a wee bit funny too. Mr. Barlow was better at advising the young folks than any other old person that J D knew of, but he didn't have it together enough to listen to sound advise yet.

The four boys at the pub were happy to see J D show up, wet clothes and all. Joe and Allen had ducked in out of the rain a few minutes before J dripped in. Allen and Joe had no other place to be anyway, none that they wanted to be that is.

"Yew is hea already, boy?" Paul asked.

J D saw no need to answer one way or another. Nothing that he might have said would have explained why he was here, his once-up-on-a-time girl was at home and the old folks were in town. All of the four boys would do anything to have a set-up like that. They had no way of knowing that Wilma's and J D's intimacy had become history.

Bud did not add to the silent question but changed the subject.

"Wanna RC?"

"Yea, Ah'll git it."

J D fished around in the icy water until he found the pop. He sat down on the porch to enjoy his cola. After drinking a few big swigs Allen came over and offered to put some of his stump juice in with the cola. J D drank his first sip of an alcoholic beverage for causes; he was heart-broken.

It didn't take much of that one-hundred and fifty proof booze to make the sadness he felt take a temporary back seat to this brand new non-natural feeling like all is well with the world. After another small dash of the moonshine he forgot what it was that bothered him in the first place.

The boy wanted to play records but that took money. Before they had time to discuss the music problem a truck pulled in from the direction of town. The boys knew who it was by the sound of the engine of the old log truck. Mr. Dan stopped every Saturday to get his week's supply of sipping whiskey. He claimed that he used the hooch to help him sleep. The saying was that he had not always been that way especially before a certain event in his life. From what they say about the old bugger, he will do a lot of reaping for what he has sowed. Some say that he killed a man over the man's own wife. This happened long before the boys were big enough to remember though. The preacher was always saying that you reap what you sow, maybe this was true for the old man.

"Good evenin Mista. Dan." Several of the youngsters spoke at the same time.

"Evenin." Came the reply.

"Whar is Frank?"

"Out back, Ah recollect." Answered Allen.

The truth of the matter was that Uncle Frank had gone down the hill where he kept the stash of whisky. He knew when old Dan would be coming by. Dan came by every Saturday. Old Dan kind of kept to himself most of the time. Now, if he happens to be at a church function, about the only public place he went, and had a few heavy snorts, the old boy could put on a show. There was one time at one at the annual attraction meeting of King Cahapel Medothist Church when he not only went crazy inside disrupting the services, but came outside raising hell. He turned out the whole afternoon congregational hoedown. Nobody had any problems with a shorter service knowing that the cardboard boxes of home cooked foods would get spreaded out on the tables for all to consume a lot sooner. Yes sir, old Dan's breakdown was a real treat and a welcome break in the normal boring routine of church services

Old Dan got his week's supply of whiskey, crawled into the muddy ford truck and disappeared into the rainy afternoon.

J D and the other four young men sat on the small porch, on the end where the roof was not leaking, whatching the rain and the rivulets of water runing down the hill into the ravine. Across the road inside the fenced pasture lay several cows underneath a tin covered hay ben chewing their cuds. The animals were tyring to rest where the shelter offered protection from the rain. The hay that's normally stored under the shed was long gone; the owner didn't put hay out since the new grass had started to grow.

The young men still had more than half the whisky left in the pint mason jar Allen had stashed in the pickup. They were getting ready for another sip when they heard the car coming.

"Hea comes Henry." Paul stated to nobody in particular, because everybody knew the car.

Henry, Jeff, Jack and Maggie emptied out of the car quickly trying to avoid getting wet. The four had piled in Henry's car for the ride from town. The country blacks never stayed in town after dark. A few things were going on down in the colored quarters though and if you had your own way back to the country you could stay in town in hopes of sharing a few laughs and so on. There were those crazy few who would sometime get caught in town late at night with no way back except to walk. Jeff, Jack and Maggie were not that crazy.

"Hot dawg almighty" Allen whispered.

All the boys had their eyes on Maggie as she lifted the hem of her skirt and tiptoed near the edge of the muddy yard to prevent getting her shoes any dirtier than they were. All the boys were thinking along the same lines when it came to Maggie. They weren't the only ones. If Maggie told what she knew about the men in this part of the county there would not be enough men left to fill one pickup truck, at least married men. The boys wished they could become part of Maggie's list of once-upon-a-timers. Maggie has been the local alley cat for years and still draws men like a turd draws flies. The boys were undressing Maggie one stitch at a time with their eyes and imaginations. Maggie being the only female around did not help much either.

"Let's set in de truck fuh a while." Paul headed toward the Dodge.

"K" J D said.

The boys had to squeeze into the cab. The boys were really skinny, but the cab of the truck was skinny too. Each boy had a sip of the rotgut directly from the mason jar. They had no soda pop to mix with the hundred-and fifty-proof moonshine. The young practicing drunks had to take terms crawling into the pickup.

"Go easy wid dat stuff." Bud croaked, struggling to get his voice back after the swig knocked out his voice box.

"Lawd o mercy!!!" J D said choking back tears from the butt-kicking whiskey.

Old J D was learning something new to his way of thinking. He had been introduced to the realization that there might be more to life than smooching girls. The boy was gitting high as a Georgia pine.

The boys decided to stroll back to the house of ill repute. The boys had been taught that certain lifestyles reduce their chances of going to Heaven after this life. But, under the influence of the effects of Uncle Frank's throat-cutting alcohol, they easily convinced themselves that everything was just peachy.

The juke joint was coming alive by the time the young wrongdoers entered. The hut had no furniture except a wooden bench hugging two walls, a jukebox near the front door and a soda box next to the low counter that partitioned the kitchen from the rest of the opened space. The outhouse for the main house was also the same one used by the customers of the night. One outhouse for all.

J D sat down on the bench to watch Maggie boogie around the room. He knew he was getting drunker than Cooter Brown. The bench that he sat on was nothing but two pieces of lumber for the legs and one two-by-ten feet board for the seat. The wall of the hut was the back rest. The youngster was beginning to have a hard time hanging on to the bench. He didn't have a clue of what being drunk felt like even though he had been around boozers all his life.

"Hey, hey Al, let, let's go back to de ah, ah truck fuh a mmminute."

"Naw not yit J."

"Co comon."

J D quickly learned to use a trick that he had practiced after riding on a homemade merry-go-round. When your surroundings start moving and you are not, focus on one object until things settle down.

J D was the youngest of the gang which meant that the others knew more about drinking than he did. Bud and Paul decided that J had had enough rotgut for a while. They thought about taking J out to the truck for a while until he sobered up a bit. They knew the little whiskey was enough to make J drunker than a corn-mesh eating hog.

"Come on J let's go out to de truck fer a jiffy." Bud led J to the truck.

The rain slacked off before dark, a few public drinkers drifted in. The communities had many secret drinkers, but not too many drinkers had the guts to defy those Sunday morning hell-fire and damn-nation sermons. They believed that to drink behind closed doors would be more forgiving. That was called drinking with respect. Many of the good old boys made their own in the form of homemade wines and other homebrews.

These public drinkers were talked about, prayed about, preached about and cried about by the closet drinkers. The closet drinkers felt pretty safe from being hell bound due to their beliefs that disrespectful drinkers were first in line for the fire and brimstone pit.

J D got his introduction into the hall-of-fame for drunks right there out in the public. This might be a problem when his grandmother hears about his drinking in the honky-tonk. J D woke up after about an hour of sleep. It must have been the music and loud talking. Country folks talked loud enough to wake the dead, especially behind a few sips of Mr. Frank's stuff.

"Das George." George was the first man J D saw when he woke up. "Dah will be trouble befo de night is ova." J D thought.

J D couldn't remember feeling this sick since he had the measles when he was maybe ten years old. He rushed out to the outhouse but it was occupied; he threw up behind the outhouse. Feeling much better J D headed for the hut which was now in full swing.

Head was kicking back to a record by one of the great blues singers. Head never drank alcohol and very seldom drank sodas. He was usually broke as a ghost. That stood to reasoning because he sure was not too fond of work. Head real name was Luther but because of the size of his head, yep you got it. That boy always danced all night, alone. Nobody has ever seen him dance with a woman. There weren't many women to dance with anyway. The regular hard-working women in Mississippi couldn't dance if their life depended on it.

"Ain't it tiahm ta git home?" J D asked Bud and Paul. The two boys were sitting on the wall bench watching country folks having fun.

"It's erly yit." Paul said.

"Yea, set down fuh a spell, it ain't eight o'clock yit." Bud told J D

Just as J sat down he saw Leroy come in the door. Leroy was big George's younger brother. These two didn't like anybody, least of all Jeff and Jack, the two first cousins. Nobody could remember what it was about, when it started or how it continues to be. Folks just took it for granted that they needed something or somebody to fuel a feud. These hypocrites didn't need to base their dislike for somebody on truth or facts. Any kind of information would do, even information that had been forgotten a long time ago.

"Dis might be de tiahm ta scat outta heah."

"Neva mind dem, dey ain't drunk nough yit ta fight." Paul tried to ease J D's mind.

Now that the 'shine was wearing off and J D was coming to his right mind he thought about Wilma's cold attitude toward him this afternoon. He didn't have any idea what made her seem like a different girl. There was one thing that he did know; it had nothing to do with him. The dull ache in the pit of his stomach made him want another sip of the 'shine. J must have been thinking about what went wrong for quite a spell because before he knew it, it was nearly nine o'clock. It was late at nine in the country.

"Is dar any left in de truck?"

Bud and Paul were glad to give the few drops left to J D if that would keep his mouth shut for a while longer.

"Yea, a little bit."

J D started to get out of the truck after draining the last drop of 'shine from the jar when head lights swung into the parking lot.

"Foot! Hea comes de Sheriff." He ducked down in the seat. He lay there with his heart beating loud enough to wake the dead.

"Dis is one tiahm Ah ain't scared of de dark." He listened for the Sheriff to walk past the truck.

"Ah like to check dese colored boys once in a while to make sho they ain't breaking the law too much." The sheriff said to his deputy.

"Yea."

"Ah try to keep'em from huting themselves.' they'ar bout as responsible as children."

" They sho ar."

"Let's go round and come in de side door.' That's whar Ah'll find old Frank."

J D slowly raised his head high enough to see the back of the two lawmen as they disappeared beside the joint.

"Dadgumit, we shouda gotten outta hea when Ah said ta.' 'De Sheff means bad news fuh us country nigguhs"

J was too scared to go back in after Bud and Paul. He stayed as far from the law as he could.

"How come in Gawd's name do dey come heah?"

J D grabbed the door handle to get out of the truck, but hesitated when he saw the two lawmen and Uncle Frank standing at the side door.

"Uncle Frank is givin dem mony.' 'Ah can't let dem know Ah saw em.' 'Ain't no telling wha dey'll do ta me."

J D didn't mind the dimly lit parking yard anymore.

"We don't wan no trouble out heah now, ya heah?"

"Yessuh, Sheff."

J D held his breath a moment trying to hear what was going on inside. Everything seemed to have stopped still when the lawmen went in. The jukebox was unplugged.

"See ya Tuesday Frank boy."

"Ah'll be in ta see ya sheff."

J D could hardly wait until the Sheriff's car backed into the road before getting out of the truck and hurrying inside.

"Hey Bud, wha did de Sheff wan?"

"Nothin.' 'Just checkin us po folk out and makin sho we don cut each otha ta deah."

The sheriff's visit had taken some of the spirit out of the bunch. Nothing could sober up a bunch of drunken niggers faster than a visit from the law.

"Oh Frank!!"

"Yeah Henry."

"Wha in gawd's name did dey wan?"

"Nothin, Y'all git back to yo fun."

It didn't take long for the ball to start rolling again. The honkytonkers got back to business.

J D walked around Head, who had started dancing again and sweating like a bull during mating season.

"Dancing is 'bout all dat boy kin do." J was thinking as he made his way through the other foot -shuffling country boys, and the one country girl.

"J C, you git in fust."

"Bud ya always wan me ta ride in de middle."

"It ain't rainin now; yew kin git in the back."

"Ah gotta just dat dang carburettor.' Ya have ta pump thu daylights outta it.' 'Ah don't drive dis thang 'nough."

The boys' night out was at an end. They thought so anyway.

Paul was backing the old Dodge out of the muddy parking lot when the trouble started. Henry and Leroy went hog wild. Leroy hit Henry with a half-full Royal Crown Cola bottle which sent Henry falling backward through the door.

"Ah'll kill ya; ya sun-o-bitch."

With knife in hand, Leroy went after the fallen Henry. George went after his brother, Leroy. George was trying to stop Leroy from killing Henry, so, that's what George thought. George holding Leroy gave Henry time to regain his footing and come after Leroy and George.

"Ah'll whop shit otta both uf ya."

"Henry is crazy as a betsy bug." Somebody said.

"So is de two brothes." Somebody else said

Seeing Henry coming at them, George let go of Leroy and with all the power he could muster, he landed a haymaker up side Henry's head. Henry went down for the second time.

Leroy realizing he had no need for the knife, moved in to kick in a couple of Henry's ribs. By the time Leroy got one kick in, Henry was on his feet hauling ass toward his car.

"Run! Run yew piss ass." Leroy yelled after Henry.

"Stay hea til Ah git back." Henry answered from his car.

"Ah'll bet Henry is gone ta git his gun." Paul informed the crew.

"No J, he shud know bettin dat." Bud said with very little convection.

"Let's wait n see if he comes back."

"Let's git goin 'foe it's too late." J D could see no reason to wait for what might be trouble for everybody.

"Leroy and George betta watch out fer Henry.' dey say dat Henry's daddy and his uncle Abe spent time on the road gang fuh killin somebody."

"Who tol ya dat?" Bud asked Paul.

"Dat's wha dey say."

"Dat's mo reason fuh us to be gone when he gits back."

"Ah come on J D Don be such a baby.' Ya ready Paul?"

"Naw."

The music had stopped, the dancers kind of wondered around as if waiting for some kind of revelation. Leroy and his brother George were pretending to be paying no attention to the road. They ate boiled peanuts, took swigs of RC and whiskey mix and talked big.

"Ah've been wantin to kick dat nigguh's ass."

Leroy said more to himself than to anyone else.

Nobody was paying much attention to Leroy"s mumbling. They all were thinking about what will be the outcome if Henry was fool enough to get his shotgun and come back. Nobody knew for sure how the bad blood between the men got started. Some said that the man that Henry's uncle killed was kin to Leroy and George. Those killings took place a long time ago and all the people involved are long dead.

"Dey wuz usin dey heads."

"Hush young'un." Bud mocked J D.

Jeff and Jack came with Henry but they didn't look concerned about a ride home though. Walking home was no problem though; nobody there lived farther than four miles from where they were. A few did not appreciate having to walk pass the graveyard next to the church. Maggie always seemed to have a ride waiting for her; she would have no problem catching a ride, no buddy, the men might though.

Bud and J D were still disagreeing about when would be a good time to git out of Alabama and go home when Allen said.

"Hush y'all, Ah hea Henry comin."

The whole juke joint crowd didn't make a sound until Henry was pulling into the muddy parking yard. After the party folks were sure who was coming, they scrambled for safety.

Henry was opening the car door before the car came to a complete stop. He had the twelve-gauge shotgun in his right hand as he stepped to the muddy ground.

George and Leroy were the last two to make a run for safety. Both brothers ran for the wooded side of the building thinking the trees offered more protection from the double-barrel shotgun. The others scrambled for the inside.

"Dat neguh done gone crazy." Allen yelled.

"Dammit!!" J D swore.

Henry didn't stop to aim the scattergun, he fired on the run. George and Leroy were moving to Henry's left at a breakneck speed. The buckshots from the double barrel missed both brothers but took out the one front window in the joint. Henry was trying to reload the gun when the screams came from inside the honky-tonk. When Henry heard the screams coming from inside, he made a dash for his car. The motor was still running.

"Whar is ya hit Jeff." Jeff howled a mortally-hurt howled.

Jack was trying to get Jeff to get up off the floor.

"Come on Jeff.' lawdy mussy,' 'Henry don gone and shot Jeff!!"

Everybody was trying to see how bad Jeff was hit, except George and Leroy. They were still hiding in the dark, even though Henry was running like a scared rabbit.

Willie James and several other Alabama boys were getting in each other's way trying to help Jack revive Jeff.

"Let's git em ta' town." One of the Alabama boys barked out.

"Don move em, he'll bleed ta' death." Yelled another.

The nearest hospital was approximately thirty-eight miles away over in Mississippi. The nearest doctor was in Isney, Alabama less than five miles distance. Five miles was too far to get there in time to save Jeff from bleeding to death from the neck wounds to the main artery.

J D leaned over to see if he could help but got sick when he saw the gushing blood and Jeff's walled eyes. That feeling of glum and doom, which J D was so familiar with, was growing fast.

"Stand back." Mr. Frank bellowed.

Uncle Frank had gone to the house for towels to hold to the bleeding neck wound.

Seeing Mr. Frank coming in the side door with the armful of towels and sheets, Bud stammered.

"Whar wuz Mr. Frank while ago?"

The gurgling sound had almost stopped coming from Jeff's throat and the pupils of his eyes had disappeared. The small group of party-goers began to clear out.

"Somebody hafta go tell de law." Maggie suddenly spoke up.

Mr. Frank asked one of the Alamaba boys to stop on his way home and tell Mr. Walker to call the law. Mr. Walker was the owner of the Isney store, plus he had the closest telephone.

Paul needed no encouraging to git out of Alabama as soon as he possibly could. The boys rode home without saying a word. Nobody knew what to say or how to say words about this bad experience. They didn't know how to talk about a Saturday night like this one.

"See y'all at church tomor."

"Pick us up!"

"Bout Ten." Paul said hoarsely.

"Ya think we should wake dad and tell em wha hapen?"

"Let's see if he's woke." Bud answered. He was not.

The two brothers sat on the porch, with the old hound, and just thought about what they had seen tonight.

J D was the first to mumble.

"Wha wuz so bad dat Henry had to kill fuh, specially kill someone that had nothin to do wid tonight's argament."

"He didn tend to shoot Jeff.' Accidents happen."

J D kept talking.

"Ah don know,' It don hafta be much a tal fuh dese folk ta kill each odder."

Bud continued talking too.

"Dis ain't de firs tahm, and it won'be de las tahm eitha, somethin lak dis happen

J D got up.

"Let's see if daddy is sleep."

"Yea Ah guess so."

Before they knocked on the door, they heard the old man sneeze.

"He' wake." Bud said.

Daddy! Is ya wake?' J D spoke through the door, speaking just above a whisper.

"Wha's de matta wid you boys?"

"Nothin de matta wid us, but."

"But wha?' Come on in and say wha's on y'all's minds."

The two brother didn't know where to start telling the news.

"Well?"

"We wuz ova at Uncle Frank's joint tonight."

Bud spoke up.

"Henry kilt Jeff."

"Lawd have mercy on mah soul." Momma said from under the sheet.

"It wuz bound ta happed as shore is ya born." Daddy said more to himself than to anyone else.

"He didn mean ta shot Jeff.' He wuz amin at Leroy." J D added

"It won make no nevamind.' It's all de same ta de law.' 'Y'all go on ta bed. "

J D Said to himself but loud enough for Bud to hear him.

"It sho don' take much fuh a man ta die.' 'He don' even hafta be guilty of nothin, just bein at thu wron place.' "It just ain't right."

Bud whispered.

"Wonda whar Henry went.' 'Whar did Leroy and George go at?"

"Donno, Leroy's and George's car wuz still thar when we left."

The brothers wrapped themselves in their own thoughts about the killing. Each experiencing today's events in his own unique way. Sleep came slowly for the young honky-tonkers.

Chapter Thirteen

▼

J D had never felt this dreadful at any time that he could remember on Sunday morning. He was still having problem with the feeling of sadness that he felt in the bottom of his stomach when Paul braked the old Dodge to a stop.

"Morning y'all."

"Morning Paul." Bud spoke.

"Ah neva thought 'bout dying much." J Mumbled.

"Don' keep talkin bout it."

Bud tried to get J's mind back from the grave.

"It just seems lak thar should be a betta way ta die."

"Thar is.' 'Pray dat you die in yo sleep." Paul said.

Bud was trying not to think about last night.

"Hey y'all let's git goin."

The three boys past the other church-goers near the graveyard. Nobody was acting like their old Sunday-morning selves. They could hear the hum of conversations in full swing as they pulled into the church yard. The church was supposed to make life better by offering hope for a good life. The members were searching for at least some kind of confort from their faith to help them the next day after a lost of life from what seemed to be an act of fate in the first place…

J D's search for a spiritual lift from his church was further complicated by Wilma's presence. He did not feel like being in church this Sunday morning.

The congregation drifted into the church as if each member was in some kind of a daze. Reverend Mayfield sure had his work cut out for this one. The membership was looking to the Reverend for a divine purpose behind these kinds of human tragedies.

J D saw that Miss Clendon was in her usual pew. J wondered what she must be thinking about her Son killing Jeff.

"She need ta be as close ta her Gawd as she kin git dis day." J D thought to himself. 'The church is as close as one kin git to Gawd on this side of the river of life."

J was having a pretty hard time convincing himself of the truth of his thoughts today.

The prayers from the deacon bench were short. The deacons were as eager as anybody to hear more about last night at the juke house. They knew that the Reverend was usually told when there was trouble. In this case the good Reverend was not needed for the dead, but he was called anyway. But Jeff was already dead when the preacher arrived. Maybe his presence brought some comfort to the living.

The church was nearly full today because of the trouble last night. Nothing drew members to the house of God quicker than somebody getting killed. There were none of George's and Leroy's folks at this church. They belonged to the Methodist Church down the road. Jeff and Jack hardly ever came to church, nor did their folks. None of the families were at church this Sunday neither. The families might have been avoiding what was sure to be finger pointing and blame.

The Reverend took his time getting to the pulpit. The old boy knew he had a big job to do today. He had to recharge the people's faith in the powers of prayer. Keeping his congregation faithful was never an easy job. It sometimes seems impossible when the Devil had such powerful persuaders in his favor.

"Good mornin congregation!"

"Mornin" Came from the entire congregation.

"It's good to be heah.' 'Ain't dat right?"

"Amen"

"It's a blessin t be heah dis Sunday mornin."

The folks were relieved to know that God was still on the job. The Reverend sure preached it into the membership. That was the general consensus regarding the sermon. Maybe some of this approval of the preaching came more from the congregation's need to have something to hang on to than from the contents of the sermon. The contents of the sermon didn't matter too much today.

When the church let out, the members started sharing what little information they had about the shooting. Nobody knew much, not even the boys that were there. Nobody asked them any questions about the shooting and they gave no answers.

J D's infatuation with Wilma took a back seat to the new realities that he was trying to deal with. He caught her eye as she came out of the church. She did not look like the only girl in the world anymore. She came over to him this time.

"Mornin." She said.

"Howdy." He said back to her.

She still didn't look like her old smiling self. J D thought about what she had told him Saturday afternoon which left him out of whatever went wrong with her. This will be one Sunday that the usual marauding groups of boys won't be hanging around the stores and marching up and down the roads.

The colored community was always on the verge of rushing for the cover of home under abnormal social conditions. Now with Henry hiding out, who knows where, the Alabama and the Mississippi law on the prowl and angry relatives of Jeff's folks wanting to vent their frustrations, the locals felt too insecure to carry on as usual. The colored community did what it usually did, sit and wait. Fear was the one common controlling force that made the colored community one body.

Paul, Bud and J D were in no hurry to leave the presumed safety of the church grounds.

"Anybody wan a ride?" Paul offered whoever.

"Yeah, believe we would." Came answers from every-which-way.

With the cotton-hauling body on the truck the riders could safely stand holding on to the high sides. The road was still somewhat wet making walking a bit difficult. The real reason for the eagerness to ride on the back of a truck instead of a slow walk home with boyfriends and girlfriends might have had more to do with common notion that the devil had been set loose.

J D. Bud and Paul, and the other members of the boys club, were getting their last words in with the girls and friends while waiting for everybody to get on the trucks.

"Wuz yew at de juke-joint when Jeff wuz kilt?" Wilma asked J.

"Yeah, Ah wish Ah wuzn't tho." 'Ah wanted ta leave fo de shooting.'
"Al and Bud wouldn't."

They made small talk until the folks were on the truck before saying bye.

"See ya lata Wilma."

"Bye, bye."

The usual news spreaders were quieter than normal today. They didn't have all the truth and they were afraid to plug in their own fill-ins. They weren't taking any chances of aggravating the already unstable relationships among the citizens of Southern Mississippi and Alabama.

"Lawd have mucy on ar souls." Aunt Sal said as she walked over to some other older ladies. "May the Lawd have mucy on sista Clendon, and help her thou dis mess."

"Amen, sista Sal, amen." Replied Aunt Lue

The Saturday night incident was on everybody's minds. Most was more concerned with what it meant to themselves personally than what affects it had on the victims who were directly involved.

J D had never ceased to be fascinated by how the ugliest and the most beautiful could exist within a single thing. Under these harsh realities he could yet enjoy the unique beauty of the Mississippi and Alabama country sides. The flowering plants were at their best this year. One could stand in one place and drink in the sweet smells of the magnolia blossoms, peach, plum, pear and other fruit blossoms. He could never get enough of the Southern spring times. It mattered none from which direction the wind blew. The honeysuckles were just beginning to take their place on the stage of beauty. Spring time is a bad time to die.

Tommy and John were waiting for the church folks to come home. These two didn't go to church too often, but they were always there when food was served.

"Do ya know wha happen last night at Uncle Franks?" Tommy Shouted.

"Henry kilt Jeff." John added his say.

"We saw it." Paul told the news carriers.

Wanting to forget about the accident, Bud asked the pack.

"Let's ride ova to de Clark Store?"

"Les's go." Paul answered.

Paul, J D and Bud jumped into the cab while Tommy and John vaulted over the tailgate and into the body of the truck. None of the gang wanted to go anywhere near the Alabama line. The Clark Store was four miles in the opposite direction. Tommy and John began making small talk about food and girls. These two were not known for their deep thinking, they didn't ask too many questions about much of anything.

"How much money ya got Tommy?"

"Foty-five cents, how much ya got?"

"Ah got nough."

The Clark Store was open when the boys rode up. Mr. Clark and old man Grey were talking about the prices of this year's fertilizers and seeds. This concern was discussed throughout the white communities, but was seldom mentioned throughout the colored communities. The colored either thought that these kinds of concerns made very little differences or there was nothing that they could do about the cost of farming anyway. Most of the sharecroppers were too poor to plan a whole crop ahead. There was a small group that did pretty good, but that didn't apply to the vast majority.

The two white men stopped conversing when the five colored boys entered the store. This was what they always did when Negroes invaded their space. Was this lack of involving the colored in their business talk due to respect or sympathy for the assumed ignorance of the colored people, or was it due to the absence of respect and empathy for them.

"How ar you boys today?" Mr. Clark asked.

Mr. Grey said nothing.

"Prudy good, Mista Clark." Some of the boys spoke.

Mr. Clark didn't ask the boys if he could help them because he knew what they usually wanted was on the counter and in the soda pop box. The two whites just watched the boys grab their goodies. The boys didn't ask any questions, or do any talking either.

All the boys paid for their snacks before any one of them went out of the door. This was a habit of the Negroes especially when they could easily be accused of stealing. It was safety in numbers.

"Thank y'all, be careful now."

"Yessuh."

The boys hadn't seen any body, riding or walking on the road when they came ,but this didn't mean that trouble wasn't waiting in the bushes.. This absence of people, black or white, put a blanket of uneasiness over the entire community.

"Do ya thank dem white folks knowed 'bout las night."

"Sho is ya bon." Bud and Paul kept trying to make small talk.

"Dey wouldn' say nothin even if dey did." J D said.

J D was glad to head toward home. Paul pulled over into the yard of the old Jones' place so the boys would have time to enjoy their treats. At least this was within yelling distance of home and their one hundred and twenty acres of farm land.

"Yew would hafta t stop heah wouldn't ya?"

"Aw J D" Bud grumbled.

Tommy and John hopped off the back of the truck and came around to the front where the others were.

"Dey say dis wuz once some house." John said.

"Yea, when white folks lived init" Answered Tommy.

"Givme a piece of dat moon pie."

"Aw come ohn Tommy."

"Dey say Mark is back." J D said.

"Whar did dat come from?" Paul asked.

J D frowned in thought trying to remember who had said that.

"Ah believe it wuz Jack who said he saw Mark in town yestaday."

"Whar has he been all dese yeahs?" asked Bud.

J D was still trying to recall more details of what Jack said. Information that had been filtered through several sips of Uncle Frank's stump juice had to be analyzed carefully.

"Ah think Ah herd em say dat Mark had ohn a army unifom."

"He sho didn't seem ta have a hankering fuh girls, white or black." Came from Tommy.

"Dat's de reason nobody took dat gal's word fuh de gospel." J D tried to add some common sense to what happened.

"Ah know de McCray boys ain't got a lick uf sense; dey liable ta say anythang.' 'Dey's the peckawoods dat started dat lie bout Mark and Jennie.' 'Jennie had notin ta do wid de lie, 'cause she didn even know wha de fuss wuz all 'bout." J D continued his version of what must have been the case.

"Yeah, we know how Jennie is, don we J D?" Bud said teasingly.

"Yep, we sho do." Paul joined the discussion.

"She ain't a bad gal and y'all know it."

"Lease ya know it J." Paul saw a chance to get one in.

"Jennie sho laks herself some old J D alrite"

J D didn't answer to the last remark because he could see this conversation leading him deeper and deeper into a forbidden landscape. Now he was at the point of defending a white gal who didn't need defending, especially from the likes of this bunch. It didn't make good sense for a black boy to defend a white person when he couldn't defend himself. The only defense a colored person had in the eyes of the law was through some white person.

"Dem white folks knowed better,' 'Mark told dem he didn do nothing to dat gal." John stammered.

"Shucks, dem white folks don't think a niguh is capable of telling de truth' 'Dey say a niguhs will clim a tree ta tell a lie when he kin stay ohn de ground and tell de truth."

J D was glad to turn the conversation to white folks in general instead of discussing stuff about Jennie and himself.

Today it was hard to avoid mentioning white folks. The shadows of white folks dominated the serious discussions within the colored communities. The black and white debates will be ringing loudly in all Negros' ears far a smart while. What happened Saturday night was not the kind of incident that would create danger for all the colored, just the ones directly involved.

The sheriffs and their deputies might use this opportunity to push a few black boys around for proof of their authority. That's about all the whites want out of blacks-killing-blacks type of crimes. Yes, and maybe the few dollars saved up in the Negro's neighborhoods for paying the white lawyers.

"Git in Y'all, let's git." yelled Paul as he started the old Dodge pickup.

Chapter Fourteen

▼

The weekend drifted slowly and gloomily by on the breezes of despair. There was very little news pertaining to the law catching up to Henry. The tongus were beginning to wag. When the folks had no actual news about something of common interest, tongue wagged and told half trues mixed with a massive batch of downright lies. This habit could be understood if one realized the people's needs for something to talk about.

The Alabama sheriff sent word to the Mississippi sheriff telling him to see what he could do to get Henry to turn himself in. The locals knew the law went easier on the criminals if they just walked into the jailhouse and locked themselves up, especially when the crime was black against black. The law in this part of the country was very lazy; they didn't like tramping all over the county looking for the wanted. The law tolerated nothing less than law-and-order out of their colored citizens. Now if Henry had killed a peckerwood, things would be totally different. Every white big enough to carry a gun would be out to make a name for himself by killing Henry.

A few of the colored thought it was proper for Henry to turn himself in to the Mississippi sheriff. They thought he might get a fairer trail and sentencing if he remained in the state of his birth and place of residence. After all this was an accident. Henry and Jeff were best of friends. Others held the opposite view. They thought that he would come closer to getting what he had coming if he was tried and did time in the state where the crime was committed. Henry was not only guilty of killing a man, but that man was his best friend. This in itself was enough punishment without his doing a single day on the workgang, so went some lines of thought. The commoners knew very little about the law. The crime was committed in Alabama and the laws of Alabama dictated the outcome of the charges. Most of the local country folks had a hard time understanding this fact of the law.

Everybody kind of figured that Mrs. Clendon knew exactly where her son was. There was nowhere to hide in this desolated countryside. The only place somebody on the run could go was back home to your love ones or leave town and go to relatives or friends living in other parts of the country. Henry had reasons other than fear of the law to remain in hiding. Jeff had love-ones who were not thinking too clearly at the present time. A few relatives going around thinking that an accidents is somehow caused by somebody and that somebody has to pay. That somebody was Henry in this case.

Uncle Barlow was pretty close to the Clendons since Henry's daddy passed away years ago. The law was aware of the possibility of the old man getting his advice heard. They also knew that Uncle (is what they sometimes called Uncle Barlow) would have sense enough to advise Henry and Mrs. Clendon to do the right thing and at the right time. The Sheriff already knew one of the best times to step from cover is after the funeral. The funeral is where the final letting go takes place for the majority and it is where the last emotional out-of-control behavior takes place. The sheriff had plenty of time, and after all these Negroes do shoot one another once in a while. Violence was expected to happen between the colored folks. They had low boiling points when it came to friction between each other.

Uncle Barlow had supported the here-and-now philosophy for a long time as far as the Negroes' survival possibilities were concerned. The old man had seen many dead-end roads followed by his people. He had long ago resigned from hoping for a better future for himself and his kind. The ways of this part of the south were good to both races as long as the members on each side remembered where they were and who they were. The whites had no problem with their convictions that Negroes were inferior human beings and deserved exactly what they were getting. By the same convictions the Negroes were absolutely sure that the whites had too much and the Negroes had too little. Uncle

Barlow was pretty sure neither side was about to change, not in his lifetime anyway,

Uncle Barlow walked wherever he went, that is if he didn't catch a ride. He had never owned an automobile in his life. There were few times when he didn't catch a ride, at least part of the way. It was nearly five miles from Mrs. Clendon's to the Gains' farm. The body needed to be ready for burial tomorrow morning. In warm weather bodies were not kept out of the ground for long. Uncle had to see if things were coming along fast enough for an eleven o'clock burial tomorrow. He thought he'd stay the night because he had no intentions of coming back home and have to go right back. He usually spent the night wherever he wound up at when night came, or when he got tired of walking, whichever came first.

Uncle Barlow stepped to the side of the road to let the old pulpwood truck pass. The truck slowed down and stopped. It didn't have much slowing down to do because its speed was not much faster than a fast trotting mule.

"Wanta ride Uncle?"

"Thank ya Suh."

"Where ya bound fuh Uncle?"

This old Alabama white boy wanted company as much as Uncle Barlow wanted a ride. That was alright with Uncle Barlow. He believed everything had a price, even though some paid a higher price than others for the same goods. Uncle Barlow came to the conclusion a long time ago that there was no earthly fairness walking among men.

"Just ova to thu Gains."

"Yea, I know them.' 'Too bad 'bout Jeff.' 'He worked fer me a while back, he sho did."

They rode for a while without saying much. They saw a few farmers fixing fences and doing other wet-weather chores. The low lands were not dry enough to plow. Both men withdrew into his own world because conversation between a white man and a colored man just didn't amount to very much. There were not many life experiences that they could talk about to each other.

"That's de house ?"

"Thanks fuh de ride Mista Dozier."

Uncle Barlow could see that the Gains had company. Everybody was glad to see Uncle Barlow. Maybe this was because he was the oldest colored person within miles. Uncle Barlow didn't have to knock because these country folks left their doors open at all times, if the weather permitted.

"Come on in Uncle Barlow!" Mark told Uncle.

"Ah didn know yew wuz home."

"Yes sir, ahm on furlough."

"Glad ta see ya.

Uncle made his way to the kitchen area where the activities were going on. Reverend Mayfield was reading the Bible and mumbling something but Uncle Barlow couldn't make out what.

"It must have somethin ta do wid comfortin de grievin love ones."

Uncle thought. He waited a moment until the Reverend came up for air before speaking to the grieving mother and other relatives and friends.

"Good evenin y'all."

"Good evenin Uncle Barlow." was the greetings from at least half a dozen voices.

Uncle Barlow saw that all the work had been done, or there were people enough to do what needed doing. His duty now became that of a friend, community elder and a comforter.

One of the few ways of obtaining news on Mondays was to go get it yourself. Mr. Barlow knew this; of course he was too old to work. People like him were the news carriers but this kind of news was urgent and nobody felt like waiting for home delivering.

Allen suggested that they ride over to the Gains's and see what plans had been made about the burial. If the burial was to be tomorrow or Wednesday, the wake has to be tonight or tomorrow night. The weather being what it was, there was no plowing to be done.

"Ah thank we aughta ride upta de Gains and see when de wake will be." Allen blurted out what was on all the boys minds, except J D's.

"Somebody' be alon wid de news." J told the crew.

"It may be too late by den." Allen answered J D's summation.

"Y'all go ohn if ya wanna, Ahm staying heah."

The three young men piled into the old Dodge and headed for the Gains's in Alabama. One reason that they were eager to go over to the Gains's home was there was very little else to do.

J D watched the pickup disappear around the curve bound for Alabama. He needed a little time to make sense out of this mess. He had no doubts regarding God's devine plans for running the world, but there seemed to be missing information at times. He had always been told that all things happen for the best. This was hard to accept in times like these.

J D and the old half-breed dog were on their way down the road for a walk when they heard momma calling.

"Come heah J!"

The two turned back for the house. When they were in hearing distance, momma said.

"Make a far unda de wash pot so we kin do a little washin"

J and the dog didn't have to answer, just do. Starting a fire was not a big thing because there was usually plenty of wood and fat pine this time of year. The only kindling that was used was for cooking and washing clothes. The everyday clothes had to be boiled in the big black wash pot. The pot was also used for cooking the lard out of pork. Some times it was used to make hominy. The country would be in trouble without the washpot. The old stiff-ledged mutt sat at a safe distance and watched J D the whole time.

"Wha do ya make otta dis mess, yew flea bag."

The dog just wagged his tail and looked like he was glad to be.

J D and his old mangie dog lit out for the edge of the woods where they often went when they wanted to get a little peace of mind. The beautiy of the blooming plum trees were there, the flowering dogwoods were there and all that made life good had not changed. But, there hung a mist between the clear joy of yesterdays and the cloudy peace of today. The warm moist air held the promise of more rain to come. There were layers of rain clouds sailing high and fast toward the East. The two entered the woods on an old wagon road leading to areas where logs, cross ties and fire wood were cut. The bone yard where they dragged dead animals were located off the old wagon road.

The half-breed hound took this opportunity to sniff, trot and trigger up memories of the past. J D noticed that the old dog was nothing like he use to be. He was just too old. J D got off the wagon road and went through the middle of the bone yard. It had been some time since a dead animal had been dragged to the yard, but there were plenty of bones scattered across the area. The most recent skeleton was that of old Joe. Old Joe had been with the family since J D could remember. Old Joe did nothing much the last couple of years of his life here on earth. The kids would ride the old mule sometimes when Old Joe felt like letting them. If he was not in the mood, he would rub against fence post, walk underneath low branches or just reach back and grab hold of your pant leg and off you went. Old Joe's skeleton was still in one place.

While standing there looking at the skeleton of old Joe, J D thought about Jeff. Jeff was not much older than this old mule was. One lived to be an old critter and the other died young. What separate one thing from the other was a big question to answer.

"Is dar a difference betwwn Jeff and dat old mule?"

J asked the old hound. The two friends circled around and moseyed back toward the county road.

J D and the dog got in the road a few hundred feet below the house. They raced the rest of the way home. Upon entering the yard, J D saw his Daddy and Uncle Charlie on the front porch. As soon as J got close enough to hear what they were talking about, he heard Uncle Charlie taking the news of the killing to be some kind of sign from God.

"De Bible speaks of tahms lak dese. Uncle Charlie said.

"And dat is de Gospel." Daddy almost shouted.

"Any man dat lives by de sord, shall die by de sord."

J D didn't remember any time when Uncle Charlie lived by the laws written in the Bible. The old whoremonger was known to use the holy book to gain entrence into somebody's confidence. Women were not excluded either. Uncle Charlie acted as if his supporting the church with money and making sure his family attended church services exempted him from having to obey the Golden Rules. Maybe Uncle Charlie was right, after all he was one the a few successful colored men in this neck of the woods.

J D didn't realize what Uncle Charlie was doing here on the porch until the old Dodge came sputtering down the road.

"Dat old hypocrite is hea waitin fuh news bout de burial." J thought.

The old truck came to a rattling stop; the boys took their time getting out. Daddy and Uncle Charlie waited patiently for the news that they knew the boys had.

"Well now, Y'all back kinda early ain't ya?" daddy uttered.

Uncle Charlie bellowed. "When's de burial?"

"Tomor at one o-clock." Bud answered.

The boys went on in the house because young folks didn't mix well with the old folks. The old hypocrites might be on the porch all evening.

"Everybody who passes heah will stop if dey see dem two settin out dah." J D knew they had lost the use of the porch for the rest of the day. He didn't want to be near Uncle Charlie for long.

"Lighten is gonna straight dat old liar one of dese days." J told the crew.

"How come you say dat." asked Paul.

"'Cause Gawd gonna get tied of de old man's shuckin and jivin."

Bud added his token's worth

"He's been gitting way wid it fuh quite a spell if ya ax me."

J D didn't argue with Bud's summation of Uncle Charlie's escape from having to reap-what-you-sow scales. But he was wondering how that could be.

"Some folk deserves ta have bad thangs hapen ta dem for the bad thangs dey don, and at de same taihm bad thangs happen ta good folk." He said to no one in particular.

J D had to agree with Revernd Mayfield's preaching about the need for faith. Having faith without questioning is the only way one can be a true believer. Some of the ways of God might not make sense to him because he hadn't read enough of the Bible.

As the afternoon slowly passed, the cloud thickened, the wind increased in velocity bringing a mist to the quiet Mississippi afternoon. The quietness was broken by the sound of the Grey's truck laboring up the hill. Now these old peckerwoods didn't much care which directions the racial winds blew; they were content to just be part of whatever. There were several families of Greys but these two were the blacksheeps of the Greys.

The Greys pulled into the yard, got out of the truck with beer in hand, walked up and sat on the edge of the porch.

"Howdy do." Herb spoke.

"Evenin Mista Grey." Daddy spoke back.

"We reckon the time has been set fer old Jeff's burial."

"Yesuh, tomor evenin at one o'clock."

"He wuz a good old boy, good worker too." Tony Grey spoke for the first time.

"Yea, we shared many a jugs of homebrew ova at old Frank's."

The two Grey brothers were talking more to themselves than to the others on the porch. Conversations beteen the two races were hardly ever direct. They talked in a round-a-bout way to each other.

"Reckon we'll be gitting." Said Herb more to his brother than to the porch sitters.

The Greys started the old muffle-less truck and went up the road. These Greys could fix or build a truck, but they would not fix their own. They were often referred to as white trash which was not true. They just had no love for working and a great love for homemade brew.

"Who wuz ova at de Gains?" Asked J D.

"Mark wuz thar wid his army uniform ohn." Allen was glad to share this bit of bright news.

"Whar did he go when he left heah?" J wanted to know more.

"He wen ta his uncle's up dar in Chicago." Allen had the floor now." He said dat de colored wuz free as a bird up dar.' 'He even seen colored men n white women walkin hand-in-hand down de midle of de street and nobody said nothin."

"Now ain't dat somethin." Grunted J D.

"Dat show muss be some feelin, huh?"

"Look Allen, colored folks aught to know betta.' 'Dey can't brin dem white women back home wid em even though dey be marred." 'So wha good do it do?' 'None, Ah tell Ya." J warned the porch crows.

J D had never felt safe talking about these kinds of things at all. He felt as if he would be in violation of some sacred laws or something. White women brought out his worst fears.

"It musta been mo than Mark ova dar." J D changed the subject.

"Mr. Barlow, Revernd Mayfield, Jack, Maggie and several mo.' Jack had nothing ta say atal."

"Wha did it matta who wuz dar, nobody, not even de Revernd could make no difference now.' 'Death wuz a one way thang and nothin changed dat.' 'Jeff wuz worth no mo now than de bones of de old mule ova in de woods."

J D had to make sense out of this birth, life and death thing. He had to talk to somebody who knew some answers to his questions. He went out on the porch in hopes of learning something from the older folks. There was nothing to learn from Allen and the rest of them morons.

Momma had joined the old folks on the porch listening for some hope and instructions to come from the exchanging of opinions among the men. J was seeking the same. The older men offered nothing new, or anything that was not already common beliefs; 'Leave destiny to the lawd' was their philosophy.

"We'll neva undastand how de devine woks.' 'It wuzn't meant fuh man ta know as much as Gawd.' 'No suh, not nealy."

Uncle Charlie was in the pulpit preaching his understanding of the way things were.

"Man's taihm ta be born and his tiahm ta die wuz already written in de book uf life fo man wuz ohn dis oith.' 'Ain't nothing he kin do bout it eitha."

"Amen" Came from momma and daddy.

"When de Lawd gits ready fuh you, yo tiahm has come."

"Amen"

"No matta how good yew been, or how bad yew been when yo tiahm comes, dat's it."

This front porch preaching didn't offer much hope for mankind. J D thought.

"Livin like de good book tells ya got ta make a difference."

J D just had to break into the one-way conversation.

"No suh, not from wha I read.' 'Gawd writes down yo birth date and yo death date at de same time, lone foe yu is born.' 'His writin can't be changed."

"Amen."

"Ah reckon I betta git back down in de bottom.' 'Ah got wha I come fuh."

"Ya kin stay fuh suppa' 'Its purdy nea ready."

"No, thanks ya.' 'De old woman will have suppa awaitin when Ah git home."

"Yew is welcome ta wha we got."

"Thank ya."

The old man got up, stretched his legs, put a pinch of snuff in his mouth and picked up his walking stick and waved bye. Everybody knew why he left before supper. He wanted to tell the news to the bottom folks as he passed their homes before dark.

J D thought that the gun fire, the blood and the death of Jeff seems to bother him more than they did the other people, especially the young men.

"Maybe dey is somethin wron wid me." He thought while he was doing the night-work, and during supper too.

The weather didn't look good for the burial on Tuesday. The constant drizzling rain gave the country side a gloomy surreal reality. The liveliness and energies were trickling into the wet and soggy earth. The pending burial did nothing to help this mood of hopelessness. It was a known truth that burials and sickness were determinants of negative moods that sucked the energies from just about everybody in the settlements.

The church was full to standing-room-only capacity. Every tom, dick and harry was at the church. This was the norm for the burials of the really old, but not for the young men and women. Due to the weather not being fit for work, everybody that was physically able was at the church. Many were not there because of the poor soul that was the guest of hornor, but to enjoy the company of the entire communities. There were some in attendence that didn't even like the deceased at all. They all came so as to be part of a milestone in the history of the settlements. Events for years to come will be talked about and be chronologically measured relative to before or after this killing. These horrible markers-of-time were what gave the already half-dead people a sense of being alive and that time was important in spite of their dull existence.

Burials were times when the attendees dressed in their finest dark-colored and white clothes. They dressed according to handed down rituals from god-knows where or when. They almost never questioned what came to them from some forgotten times in the past. Anyway, they came dressed in their best. Dressed as if the gods of the dead would be affended if they came dressed in casual clothings. Except for the mud on their shoes, they looked fine,

J D and his gang didn't have the proper dress-wear for burials. They hardly ever thought about dying. They didn't think too much about living either. Therefore they never thought about buying costumes for grave occasions such as funerals. They had on the only dress-up clothes that they had. J D was pretty sure Jeff and who, or what was in charge of the dead didn't give a diddly-squat what the young men were wearing.

The burials attendees were too wrapped up in their own webs of gloom and despair to pay much attention to the young men clothings.

Part of the services included some family member, or friend getting up and giving a short speech about the life lived by the deceased. This was totally unnecessary here because all had known Jeff forever. A few lies were told anyway.

The dark clouds still hung low and were moving easterly at high speeds bringing the promise of a wet and soggy day. The owners of the few motor vehicles had to be extremely careful on the slick roads just to stay out of the ditches. There were no chirping birds or grasshoppers making music the day they buried Jeff. The sound of a moaning dove could be heard coming from overhead but sound as if the cooing came from far away.

Reverend Mayfield did his best to make the family and friends feel better about their losses. The Reverend attempted to make human death a blessing rather than one of the worst things that could happen to one like most human beings thought it was. He touched on the possibilities of the hereafter being what the here-and-now was all about. As much as he wanted to make this a beautiful send off with the promise of the deceased going to a better place, he couldn't resist this opportunity to scare up more Sunday turnout.

"De lawd called Brotha Jeff home, de same will hapen to de rest uf us.' 'Nobody knows when his tiahm will come. We havta git perpard fuh dis day.' 'Don't wait til it's too late, 'cept de lawd now while ya got tiahm."

"Amen!" rang out all over the church.

J D nudged Paul. "Jeff must wuzn't hit in de face lak it looked."

"Dey cleaned him up good."

"Ah wonda did dey primp him up at the mogue." J D whispered.

J D had a hard time finding saying good bye easy, especially to a man that he had known all his life. Looking down into the pine box at Jeff was like looking down into the pine boxes of all mankind. He saw that the neck wound was hidden by a scarf wrapped around Jeff's neck. He also had on the one suit that he wore to all church related functions. He wore the suit into eternity.

Jeff's cousins, including Jack, and two friends carried the pine box to the graveyard which was located less than twenty-five yards from the front of the church door. The drizzling had stopped; the cover had been removed from the grave. The grave digger (Mr Williams) had covered the grave hole to prevent it from filling with water; He had also covered the refill dirt as well so that he could fill the grave with dry dirt rather than having to shovel mud.

The usual gossip swapping among the adults, the giggling among the young folks and the hand-shaking among the older men were absent today.

J D, Bud, Paul, John, Tommy and an army of other young men gathered on the outside of the main body of people.

"He looked lak he wuz sleepin." J spoke quietly to the nearst boys."

Allen waded through the crowd to where the boys were.

"Dey still hadn caught Henry yit."

"Ah'll betcha he turn hisself in 'fo tomor." Tommy whispered.

The Reverend was saying the ash-to ash, dust-to-dust part of the service. Everybody stood still and quiet until the "Amen." The people started making their way back to the church yard as if they didn't want to hear the dirt falling on the pine box.

J D noticed the blank eyes, the staring eyes that saw nothing and the aimless walking here and there without saying much. He and Wilma stared into each others eyes but said nothing.

Chapter Fifteen

▼

Sure enough, Henry turned himself in the next day after they buried Jeff. The families of both Jeff's and Henry's became the best of friends. J D could not figure out what made these folks do the things they did. Henry gets off with a small fine for recklessly firing a gun. He gave up trying to figure out what these people were thinking about. Anyway, the killing was past now and everybody seems to have put it in the past where it belongs. One colored killing another colored was not a major concern of the law in this part of the country. The social winds continued to blow the same as it had blown since time began.

"Boy, its gonna be a scorcha today."

Bud added his thoughts.

"Dis is de last week finishin up wid de hoein."

The crops were laid by, or all the cultivating was finished. The young men made extra spending money during this time by helping slower farmers finish their work, or hiring themselves out to do public work. Working at sawmills, cutting crossties for the railroads, and many other works that were not directly connected to farming were called public works.

"If we git done today, we kin see if we kin start workin at de sawmill tomor." Bud said.

"We kin see." J responded.

J D had never liked working for the Greys. These poor rednecks were as broke as the people were who worked for them. They couldn't pay their help until they got paid. There were times when they didn't get paid at all because they owed all of the money to their own kind. The white folks usually got paid long before the colored folks did, which meant that if money ran out, the last may not get paid until much later, if at all. .

The day wore on into the morning, getting hotter and hotter as the cotton-choppers chopped the minutes away. Chopping cotton was the only field work that the whole family did together before gathering time. Everybody was needed for the slowest work of the year, before cotton picking which was even slower. J D and momma always led the pack until momma went home to cook dinner. J led the field after she left. Bud was never one to trust to stick with this mind-numbing work.

The only sound that was heard this time of the day was the hoes hitting the dry dirt and grass. Cotton was the only cash crop the small farmers grew for the market. All the other crops were consumed by the humans, or the other farm critters. The cotton market seemed to crash every year just about the time the small-time farmers got their cotton to the gin. Being short of money and all, they took what the market offered. J D thought that growing cotton was a waste of time for the Negro farmers anyway.

Cotton required more labor from the entire family than all the other crops require together. Cotton was a good cash crop for the whites who had enough money to buy up the Negroes cotton, hold it until the price went back up, and then sell it at a higher price than what they paid the poor and the blacks for it. Raising cotton tied up the whole family for most of the growing season. Cotton was the main reason that young people saw no future in farming, Especially J D and Bud.

The front porch was the family room in the evening when the heat of the day made staying indoors unbearable. The evening was foot-washing time, entertaining time, telling ghost stories and exchanging gossip time. This was the best part of the day.

J D often wished these times would last forever. Laying here listening to the bats dive for mosquitos, or whatever they dove for, listening to the night songs of the Mississippi whip-poor-wills and swatting a mosquito once in a while.

"Why'd we grow cotton anyhow?" J D asked nobody in particular.

"Cawse we need money ta pay fuh de fertliz use to grow de othea crops.' 'Dat's why." Daddy answered.

He had to do better than that to satisfy J D and Bud.

"We kin do public work n make nough money ta pay fuh de fertlizers n end up wid money lef over." Bud added to the discussion.

The porch was quiet with only the sound of the night and the barking of a distant dog. The whole family had thought about this many a time. They knew people who did just that, worked for other farmers and whoever wanted to hire help. They seemed to be doing as good as, if not better than, the folks trying to grow cotton. But family members didn't disagree with the head of the house and make headway.

"It's hard ta bar money widout a cash crop in de makin." Daddy mumbled.

"We wouldn't need ta bor money if one or two uf us hada public job." Bud shot in.

Bud was good enough at cutting cross ties to earn fertilize money and food money working alone. Food didn't cost much because if they paid more attention to working for themselves instead of the cheating crackers. They could grow most of their food. The lands now used for cotton would be used to plant hay, soy beans and so on.

The family knew, including daddy, that Bud and J D were working their last year as cotton farmers. Neither of the boys was going to school this coming year, not in their home community anyway. Jeff's death helped to push the young men futher and futher from the traditional ways of living in the country. Other factors contributing to this frame of minds in the young men were the returning colored soldiers, a little better education and a hankering for a better life than the older generation had.

Bud and J D walked up to the Greys before the sun was up good. They wanted to see if the Greys had any work to be hired out. J D was a bit hesitant about Bud's idea of working for these poor crackers just because they lived nearby. These beer drinking rednecks had a real bad reputation for not paying their help, but they were easy to work for. These poor whites had not a dime in cash, but own many acres of land, plus they were white trash.

Most colored people thought of them as poor nigger-loving crackers. The white folks thought of the Greys as white trash. These thoughts were not too far from the truth because there was a thin line between the richest and the poorest in this neck of the woods. The upper, middle and low class colored folks have more economic problem in common than some wanted to admit. The same was true of the whites. None of the locals, colored or white, had enough to make them go around boasting about. Necessities were all that could be bought with money. A man was considered blessed if he could satisfy his and his family's daily needs.

The Grey's land was loaded with dogwood trees. The Greys did very little farming which left plenty wooded acreage for dogwood. The dogwood was becoming a popular furniture building material. Bud and J D got the job of cutting the small trees. It will take nearly a week to cut one truck load of these small trees which meant that Bud and J D will ride into town with the load on Saturday.

"We got three days ta git a load out."

"Dat can't be too hard ta do." J D knew how hard Bud worked for money.

They gathered their ax, crosscut saw and lunch bucket and off they went to make a few dollars. Spring and early summer farm work paid nothing, unless you worked for someone other than your own family. The young people remained away from the county seat until they had money to spend. The white ruling class didn't hold to broke colored boys hanging around anyway. The colored didn't trust broke, lazy and loafing young colored men either, and a man didn't have to have much sense to know that white folks didn't want broke colored hanging around, unless they were working.

Neither peoples thought much of those who loafed too much and worked too little. Neither group had to think about these social ways because they were lived over and over, generation after generation. Even T C knew not to be in town broke as green as he was. T C didn't have sense enough to come in out of the rain.

J D made sure he was never in town without a dollar in his pocket. He believed that a broke white man wasn't much of a man, but a broke colored man wasn't a man at all.

"Let's git as much cut today as possible." Bud had started already with his break-neck speed.

"Ah don know wha's yo hurry. Money don las ya no tahm noway."

"Just yew don be a slowpoke."

Bud could out work all the boys his age and most of the men in the community. He usually out spent everybody the same as he outworked them. Money was as good as spent long before it landed in Bud's breeches. Bud enjoyed working almost as much as he enjoyed spending money on the girls.

The week went by and they got their first load of dogwood to town. They had done pretty good too. They had about ten dollars apiece which wasn't bad for three days work. The small logs were loaded by hand eliminating the need for mules to draw the logs out to the log road. Large logs had to be pulled out to the road and loaded by mules. Dogwood trees didn't grow that big in Mississippi.

"It sho smell good ta be in town agin." Bud said.

"Ain't too many out hea yit."

"Look J D, ovea by de burger window.' 'Ain't that Henry?"

"Sho as yo bone."

The two brothers headed over to have a word with Henry. They had not seen him since that terrible night at the juke-joint. The saying was that Henry never went far from home and hardly ever said anything. They say that if you didn't know him so well, you wouldn't recognize him. He was not the same young man he was before.

"Hey Henry." Bud spoke to him.

"Doin purdy good, how y'all."

"We been doin good."

With that said, Henry turned and walked away. The two brothers understood and left the man alone.

J D was shocked by what he saw in Henry's eyes; nothing. There was no hate, no angry and no hope and no light at all shinning from the man's eyes. J D had never seemed that level of despair in anybody. It was hard for anybody colored in Mississippi to have a bright future during the best of times much less under the particular circumstances that Henry had to deal with.

"Bud, do ya thank he'll eva git ovy it? 'It show don' look lakit."

"Some folks is sayin dat dey see him ova at de Gains' all de tiahm."

"Dat's wha AH heah too.' 'even de two mommas don become church-going friends since de accident.' 'Let's go down ta de south end fuh a spell, J."

"Let's go."

They would have to keep an eye on the people going back to the country. Ten miles is a long ways to walk late at night. The few loggers, pulpwood haulers and the small group of farmers in town will all be getting out of town before dark.

All the colored lived on the south side of town. The small shotgun houses lined the one five hundred feet street. The one and only barber shop, the one café and the funeral home were the colored run businesses in the quarters. The café had a juke-box, cold drinks and sandwiches, and bootlegged liquor of course. Some of the local colored lived near, or outside the city limits, but close to the quarters. They had their small church to soothe the pains of guilt floating around in the consciousness of the sinners.

"It's so nice n shady down hea in de quartas." J D spoke as they went in the café.

"Wha do ya wannna eat?" Asked Bud.

"Nothin."

"Ahm gonna git me something ta eat n a glass uf homebrew.' 'Wan one?"

"Yeah."

The brothers finished their homemade beer, went back up town and caught a ride with the Greys back home. They did not mention going to the Alabama juke-joint. They hadn't been back since the accident.

The hot weather was beginning to take a bit out of the little life the people had in them. Workers were slow to move out of the shade to go back to work. Country folks' ambitions were almost non-existence in the best of time, with the hot and dry dusty days slowly marching by making it seem like night would never come, people had no desire to move except to find a cool place to sit. The only living things that were out during mid-day were working colored folks, mules, poor white trash and high flying buzzards. The high-flying buzzards were up there because it was easy this time of the day due to the updrafts. Negroes were out working in this hot weather because of stupidity.

J D would never be convinced that it took this much hard work to be gully-dirt poor. He knew cash crops are too hard to sell for the small farmers to make money, but crops for consumption were different.

Chapter Sixteen

▼

The summer was turning out to be one of the hottest that anybody could remember. There hadn't been nearly enough rain to produce the kind of harvest that these small farmers needed to break even. The fields were turning into dust. This was one problem with farming that the boys didn't like; too much depended on the generosity of Mother Nature. The roadside bushes were loaded down with dust kicked up by passing trucks. The normal deep creek below the house had become a small stream.

Bud and J D were getting serious about looking for some roads out of this working-for-nothing way of life. Bud and J D were like all the others who were a bit scared to wish for much due to the belief that God frowned on those who may not be thankful enough for what they had.

"The Lord Is My Shepherd and I Shall Not Want."

"Old man Britton offed me de job of drivin truck fuh em.' Whada bout dat?"

"Sounds beta den dis.' Whada ya gonna do 'bout Jennie?"

"Shut yo mouth nigguh!"

They both laughed about the possibility of Jennie being a problem with the people who didn't understand her.

"Ah ain't seen dat gal dis yea."

"Ya know how crazy dese crackers git when dey thank dey smell somethin goin ohn tween a Niggah man and a white woman."

"Yessuh, ah do."

J D vented a few of his Wishes.

"Sho wish we could learn ta respect each otha mo and mebe we kin den live togetha widout trouble."

Bud gave his opinion of what he thought the future held for the races.

"Shoot! Not til half dese rednecks is departed dis life,' 'and half of us too."

"Dey say Henry went back ta Chicago wid Mark, or whareva Mark shiped out from."

Bud changed the conversation to what happened to Henry.

"Wouldn yew too if yew had de chance?"

"Show nough would." Bud was wishful thinking.

J D had to give the last answer some more thought. He had nothing against living here in Mississippi except he held no love for the few trouble makers. One of the reasons for his love for this part of the country is he knew nothing about anywhere else, plus Mississippi was his home.Now this time of the year might make one think of moving to a cooler country, but this hot and dusty weather will pass.

"Let's save nough money ta go down ta Mobile n find work dis fall." Bud suggested.

"We kin go down ta Uncle Dave's fuh a week n see if we kin find work."

J D did not want to give up on his home yet. He knew his hometown and knew how to live in it. He wasn't too keen on going to a strange town just yet. He was scared to death of the unknown.

"Mobile is a big city, Bud."

"So wha."

"Dese army boys comin back hea wid tails uf good livin in de cities just might not be all it's cracked up ta be.' 'Ah know Mark comes back ta see his folks evry chance he gits, but Mark has folks in Chicago too."

"Aw we won be dat fur away.' Mobile is most lak walkin distance."

"Let's wait fo makin up ar minds.' 'We still got ta git ar gatherin done, if we have any, and Ah don't know how workin fuh de Brittons will turn out."

"Ah wuz just thankin bout wha we gonna do,' 'dat's all."

The two brothers were not the only ones looking into the future and seeing only hopelessness. This was the usual group-thinking when the crops didn't look promising, the daytime temperature reaching over one hundred degrees. It was too hot to sleep before midnight and money was in short supply. These small farmers had all their saved money, and that which they could borrow, invested in their farms. The heat, lack of money and a poor crop were not pills for sleeping.

The old timers sat around a lot during these times renewing their faith and making promises to their Gods that they had no intentions of keeping. They even had time to revive old dreams of one day leaving Mississippi and moving somewhere else where a hard-working man could provide for his family. This had been an age old conversation among the Negroes every time making ends meet got hard, or harder than usual. These old folks never left. They had nowhere to go and no way to get there if they did find some other place to move to. It took money to relocate. Most of the old fathers and uncles had no skills other than farming and sawing log. Changing life styles in middle age would be more than these poor country folks could do.

J D had heard this kind of talk from the grownups all his life. They were always praying for a better life; they were always working their brains out for a better life and wishing and hoping for their just rewards; what they thought was their just rewards.

J D and Bud were in their room listening to the slow words of hope drifting across the winds.

"Do ya wanna be lak dem?" Bud saw his chance.

"Ah won't be lak dem even if Ah stayed heah."

"How come ya wouldn't?"

"Ah just won become a po hopeless Nigguh, dat's all.' 'We know Negroes dat's doin good hea in Mississippi; we kin too."

"Mor'n yu hav thought lak dat."

J D had thought about this for as long as he could remember. He still believed in the possibilities of a black man making good here in the state of Mississippi.

"Wonda whar Paul is today." J said to Bud.

"Let's head down his way, we might meet em."

J D wanted a ride over to the Britton's store to see if Mr. Britton was still interested in giving him the job starting next week. He sure hoped so. This working two or three days a week was not enough for what the brothers had to do.

The air was not moving enough to blow the dust to the side of the road that the borthers kicked up while walking. The dust just hung there for a moment and settled back to where it was kicked up from. Even the dust didn't move more than necessary under the mid-day sun. The boys walked on without talking. It was too hot to talk and walk at the same time.

They found Paul sitting under the old oak tree eating a small watermelon. He was busy fanning flies and eating his melon. Paul has no sisters or brothers therefore; he has to eat the whole melon himself, but not today.

"Hey dammit, don eatit all." Bud hurried under the century old tree.

"Howdy y'all."

"How ya doin." J D took time to speak; Bud just mumbled and grabbed a chunk of melon.

J D pulled his own switch blade and cut himself a slice of melon. Nothing satisfied thirst on a Mississippi hot day like watermelon.

"You musta had dis melon in de spran?" J asked.

"Yep."

Lots of folks would cool melons in the spring if the spring was close enough to the house. The melons were just now coming in. The fourth of July was usually the date when the first melons got ripe. This year the melons were late getting ready. The old seasoned know-it-all farmers said the melons were late because of the lack of rain. Everybody knew for sho that if the weather remained hot and dry, there would not be a good crop this year. The crops needed water.

"Wha ya doing dis evenin?" J asked Paul.

"Nottin, too hot."

"Let's ride ova to de Britton's."

"Aright."

Paul's old lazy redbone hound didn't move when J D and Bud walked up and he hasn't moved anything but his ears since they had been under the tree. Watermelon was not a dog's favorate foods. Now if the boys were eating hog cracklings it would be a different story. That damn hound didn't just eat cracklings; he dranked them. The hound sure was not working himself up in this heat over no watermelon.

The three men had to drive back passed J's and Bud's house on their way to the Brittons's. Daddy, Uncle Charlie and Uncle Oscar had not moved since the boys left. All waved and continued with what they were doing, or saying.

Paul and Bud talked all the way to the store without J D having to say much at all. Paul and Bud were use to J D moods and left him to them.

J D was wondering to himself about God's role in the whole scheme of thing here in this world. He thought that the way the folks lived might be part of God's plans.

"Kin we make a livin anywhar else." He had started talking to himself a lot these days.

They passed Wilma's house on their way to the Britton's store. J D had not talked to her since the accident and had no hankering to talk to her now.

"J D! when wuz de las ya seen Wilma?" Paul had to ask.

"Ah see her bout evry Sunday."

"Naw, not at church, at her house."

The only life signs that could be seen at the Simmons were the few checkens scratching in the shade. J D was relieved because he felt sad every time he saw that gal.

"Ah wouldn't know wha ta say ta her dese days.' 'She always did make me feel lak Ah don know nothin."

"Well?"

"Let de love-sick puppy be, Paul."

J D hated to loose what he and Wilma had, but somehow he felt relief. He often thought about what the Reverend said about the wages of sin. He and Wilma were acting like older couples who were able to handle trouble if it came. He and Wlima were not nearly ready for the responsibilities of daddy and mommy hood. The miscarriage thing had knocked some sense into their heads.

J D felt that there was something about Wilma that was not promising for making a life together. His last visit to her house made that clear. He could not put his mind on the reasons for what he felt, but the feeling of relief was still there. She was a good girlfriend, but nothing beyond that.

The roads were so dusty it even came inside the old Dodge. The doors and windows were not air tight by a long shot. Dust even came up through the floor.

"It looks lak de stoe is open." Paul said.

"Ah hope Mista Britton is round."

J D was not absolutely sure that he wanted to work for the Brittons. The store was a place where everybody came at one time or another. He would have to close his mind to the Britton's world, pretend that it doesn't exist. Working in the middle of the meeting place for Negroes and crackers mixing together could, at time, become a place where you wouldn't want to be. Trouble between colored and whites was never more than a word, screem or small misstake away. The colored usually paid the higher price for a confrontation gone wrong. He planned to be as invisible as possible and yet do his job.

Jennie was working in the store alone when the three went in. She continued wiping dust off the canned goods without much more than a glance at the three young colored men.

"How y'all"

"Good evenin Miss Jennie." J D spoke

He knew it was time to address Jennie as Miss. She was considered a young lady now and colored men made sure they kept a respectable distance between themselves and white ladies.

"Is Mista Britton home, Miss Jennie?"

"Whad you want with mah daddy?"

"He wan me to work fuh him."

"I'll go fetch him in one minute."

The three men fished out themselves cold RCs to quench their thirst. Bud paid for all three drinks. They went out to the old oak tree to wait in the shade. Jennie would have to close the store before going across the road to fetch her dad.

"Howdy y'all."

"Evenin Mista Britton." All the boys spoke.

"I won't needju until my melons git ready J D."

"Yessuh."

"I reckon it'll be bout another week.' 'Come back then."

"Yessuh."

The three young men cranked up the old Dodge and rattled toward home. The fields of corn and cotton dozed in the shimmering heat.

"It might be longa den a week if we don git some rain." J D. said.

"Yew gotta job though." Bud was also wondered who was going to help him cut dogwood after J starts working for the Brittons.

"How much did he promise ta pay ya?" Paul asked even though he knew no Colored dare to ask a cracker what he is paying. The pay is about the same all over as Paul knew, but teased anyway.

"If de pay ain't nough Ah kin always quit."

"Dey say de old man is good to de colored." Bud assured all.

The Brittons had a reputation for paying their help a fair wage and paying on time. This was more than could be said for most of these white folks. Many whites acted as if they thought that cheating Negroes out of money was not something that they needed to ask God's forgiveness for. J D and Bud hadn't told their daddy about this promised job yet.

Daddy and momma were still on the front poech when Paul stopped to let the two brothers out of the truck.

"Might as well tell dem now 'bout de job."

"Yew got de job, tell em."

Daddy and momma were sitting there quietly, daddy chewing his tabacco and momma enjoying her pinch of sweet snuff. Momma never dipped snuff when company was around, but she sure enjoyed the stuff when nobody other than the family was near.

"Hey y'all!"

"Hey youself." Momma spoke, daddy said nothing.

"Mista Britton might wan me to start haulin melons fuh em in a weeks or so."

"When did he tell ya dat?"

"Day."

"Is dat wha ya wanna do?"

"It's bout de only thang ta do as fur as Ah kin see.' 'Plus dey say he's a good man ta work fuh."

"Suit youself."

The family just hung out on the porch during these slow weeks, mumbling a few words once in a while, but mostly just lost in their own dreams. The girls could be found in their bedroom looking through Sears and Robuck, Water Field or some other wish book. Dreaming of better days to come was the one past-time that made life a wee bit better.

CHAPTER SEVENTEEN

▼

The rains came just in time to lively up everything that depends on water for the gift of life. It had been raing for two days when Paul came over with the news that Uncle Joe was found half dead in his house.

The older folks had a habit of remaining indoors when the weather turned windy and wet. This made it very important to look in on old folks that lived alone because of their being inside and out of sight. Uncle Joe was, some said, nearly ninety years old. Nobody knew exactly how old he was, but some of the other seniors remember when the old gentleman was a young man. The old gentleman had lived alone since his wife died five years back. His only living son had been trying to get his daddy to go north and live with his family. Uncle Joe said that all he ever loved had always been, was and always will be, right here in Mississippi, except his son. He had no plans to ever leave as long as he lived.

Uncle Joe had two boys. The older boy had refused to accept less money than was owed to him for a load of crossties. The white yard-man took the young man's refusal as a personal insult and did what the whites did under these kinds of conditions.

"Niggah you take what I give you, or you git nothing a tal!"

Connie refused to take less than he was owed and left the yard. When Connie changed his mind and came back to get what Mr. Orange said was owed to him, Mr. Orange then told Connie to git off the yard. Nobody knew exactly what was said, but a few words led to another and on and on until licks were passed.

Connie went out of his mind and came within an inch of beating Mr. Orange to death. The only reason that Connie didn't beat the life out of old man Orange was that he thought that the bastard was dead. Knowing the penalty for what he had done, Connie did what thousands of Negroes had done before him when faced with a similar perdictiment; he ran for his life. The word didn't reach Uncle Joe and Louis until the early morning just before daylight.

Uncle Joe, Mother Rachel and Louis never worried much about Connie staying out late, or even all night. They knew something was terribly wrong when the dogs made such a fuss that time of the morning. When Louis got up to see what the racket was about, what he saw nearly scared him to death. White men with guns were everywhere. The Shireff came up to the door to explan what was going on. Everybody was up and scared stiff by this time.

After the rednecks were satisfied that Connie was nowhere near his home, they scattered out over the country side looking for him. When Louis figured it was light enough for those kill-crazy crackers to see that he was not Connie, he left the house to look for his brother.

Louis walked all day in hopes that his brother would make contact somehow. The weather had turned a bone-chilling cold since the day before. The trees were almost naked now and the soggy leaves made a thick carpet even on the side of the road. Louis knew that Connie must be cold and hungry by now. Louis saw no sign of Connie all day. He returned home to grab some food and the rifle that belonged to Connie.

Connie had spent his last dollar to buy that thirty caliber deer rifle. He had never used the gun. Louis packed up the food, the rifle and all the ammunition, against the wishes of his mother and the old man. Connie and Louis had always hated all white folks just like their daddy had. Connie told the old folks, and the white man that sold him the rifle, that it was for deer hunting. Louis kept to the wooded side of the road for quick hiding when he heard somebody coming from either direction. Even with the long coat on, the shape of the rifle could still be seen. He tried not to think about what would happen if some of those crackers saw the rifle.

The cold westerly winds and the constant drizzles were nose-dripping, bone-chilling and fire-hugging weather. He knew that Connie had to be somewhere between home and town because there was no reason, that he could think of for Connie to be anywhere else. Connie catching a ride out of the county was not even a slim hope. Louise could think of only one place that Connie might be that everybody should think of but nobody probably would. Connie would have to be crazy to camp out in the obvious. Louis and Connie had played in the long-abandoned house for as long as they could remember. Louis walked through the woods to get to the old house without being seen. Connie whistled from the old barn area instead of the house.

The old farm house was located at the fork of the roads; both roads led to the county seat. The house sat back from the road more than one hundred yards from either road. The barn was sat back another twenty-five yards to near the woodline. This distant gave the brothers a clear view of their surrounds and time to dash for the woods if somebody approaches from the roads. The rednecks were not likely to come through the woods because of the difficulties of walking, plus, there were too many places for an enemy to hide.

Uncle Joe kept a constant eye on the roads and surrounding fields to make sure the boys were not near home waiting for help. Uncle Joe had no problem with hating these white folks. He had very little trouble hating black fokes even. He was not a mean man; he just believed in protecting himself and his from any threat no matter where the danger came from. Uncle Joe placed his scatter gun near the door while Mommy Rachel prayed.

Mommy Rachel was a praying woman. She believed in praying to more than one god. She was known to have placed a few spells around the community. These spells came from her requests to the other gods, the gods of voodoo and hoodoo. There were times when she placed more trust in the voodoo gods than she placed in the Biblical God. Mommy figured that the more the better when it came to locking horns with these Mississipp rulers.

Connie and Louis were as close as twins. They were only eleven months apart in age, started to school at the sane time, wore the same size clothing and usually went everywhere together. They had no other siblings; therefore, they had to stick together at all cost.

Connie heard the a whistling sound coming from the old barn that was nearly flat to the grond. Louis knew better than to set up in the house because when these stupid crackers wake up and understand that negroes were just like any other animal, he had instincts too, and they will figure it out.

"Didya see anybody on de road?"

"Naw. Ah came thro de woods. Most of the way.' 'Ah brung yu some food and yo rifle."

"Ah need both,' 'Ahm thinkin uf tryin ta git outta hea tonight."

"How ya pose ta cross de creek.' 'It is swollen fahm de heavy rains, ya know.' 'Ah'll go wid ya, maybe togetha we might make it."

"No, yew go back home n' tell de folks dat Ah gottaway."

Louses knew that Connie had a slim chance of making his way out of Mississippi alive. The deer rifle would guarantee that he would go out like a man if he got hemmed up.

"Don't let dese peckerwoods git ya live, yu know bettern dat, doncha?"

"Dat's mostly all dat yu n me talked bout fuh de lass few yeas."

The brothers sat for a while without saying much. There was nothing to say now that their faiths had been sealed. They made small talk about the yesterdays when things were good and they had fun. They had played in this same old barn, now they are hiding in it. They hovered in the only dry space in the old barn where Connie had spent the night.

"Dis will be a day ta remember fuh us."

"Yew betta git ohn back home now."

Neither boy moved. They both were lost in their own world of sadness.

"Whichaway ya goin fiahm heah?"

"Ah'll cross de creek at de bridge and den follow de woods til Ah git miles nawth uf town."

"Dey might be watchin de bridge."

"As long as dese crackers thank we is crazy, dey won't."

"See ya."

"Kay."

Louis went into the woods without looking back. The cold, the rain, nothing penetrated the lonelessness that he felt as he walked the two miles home. Mommy and daddy could not see that he had been crying when he walked through the door. He hoped the rain covered up Connie's tracks and made the whites stay indoors just a little while longer.

"Well?"

"He is goin ta git outta de county tonight."

"Phrase de Lawd." Momma muttered.

There was news of some shooting heard that night in the area where Connie was supposed to cross the creek. The rumor was that two white fellows were shot, but nobody knew wheather the shooting was done by Connie or the crazy drunk crackers shot themselves. Connie would get the blame for what ever happened. The whites put out the news that they had got the nigger; there never was a body to prove they did. They claimed that the flooded river claimed him. Nobody knew what really happened to Connie. He had not been seen since that late rainy afternoon.

Mommy Rachel didn't last long after Connie left. She was silent about her son, except her constant praying and practicing her magics. The old man never spoke about Connie even though he could be seen looking down the road as if he expected the boy to come walking up at any time.

Louise left home for the north after his mother passed away. He tried to convence the old man to come north too. Daddy Joe would not even think about leaving his home.

"Dis is whar ma daddy wuz born, lived n died. 'Dis is whar Ah wuz born, will live n will die.' 'Dis muh home."

Louis did get home in time to see his father alive one more time. Uncle Joe must have been waiting for Louis to show up because he died right after looking into his son's face.

Louis took care of the burial, boarded up the house and drove back the way he had come. He wasted no time in Mississippi.

Louis was one example of young Negroes leaving Mississippi forever when they have no reasons to make their homes in the state, or no reasons to come back. It sure was good to see Louis again anyway, people were saying.

There were people who expected Connie to show up at his parent's burials. Rumors circulated through out the areas that Connie had been seen on several occasions. These rumors have yet to be confirmed. Connie never made contact with folks about where he was, or if he was. Most of the locals believed that the muddy swollen creek had claimed Connie's body just as the white folks said it did.

Louis's showing up with an automobile, nice clothes and money in his pocket did nothing to help change the number of young black men leaving the south for the north. His appearance might have encouraged even more boys to start planning to exit the harsh living environment of the south that Negroes had to endure.

Chapter Seventeen

▼

"Louis looked as if he wuz doin good." Paul broke the silence as the boys rode from Uncle Joe's
burial.

"Yep, he seems to be ridin high on dee hawg." Bud commented.

"He also wuz all by hisself.' 'AH wonda if he has a family up dar in whateva city he lives."

"Ya know dey don have many kin heah in dis county neitha." Bud said.

J D never could get use to how little these folks knew about themselves, or their knowing nothing about where they came from.

"We finally got de rain dat we needed, now maybe we will be blessed wid a crop ta gatha dis fall." J D wanted to change the conversation.

"Ah guess de weatha wuz too much fuh de old man.' 'It wuz a rainy tiahm when Connie got hisself kilt."

"Awh, come on Bud, he just might not be dead."

"Well Mista J D, whatta ya thank might uv hapen?"

"Ah donno, Ah jess donno."

"Uncle Joe sho wuz one mean old devil."

"Paul, he just acted lak dat cause he kept ta hisself." J attempted to protect the reputation of the dead.

J D didn't know that Mr. Joe was so active in the church. The community sure said a lot of good things about the old man. You would not believe that Uncle Joe was hated by most of the community.

"Ah can figure out wha good itta do fuh de living ta petend bout de dead." He thought. "Sayin all dem good thangs bout de dead sho don help de dead none."

John and Tommy were waiting for the three young men when they rode up to the house. These two never went to church for any reason, they usually didn't have clean clothes to wear anyway.

John came up to the pickup before the boys could get out. John was eager to hear if Connie and Louis were at their daddy's burial.

"Did ya see Louis?" John wanted to know.

"Yeah, he was dah.' 'Wha did ya 'spect?" Paul said and waited for the question that he knew John was going to ask next.

J D beat John to the stupid question with an answer. "No, Connie will neva be dah; he's dead.' 'Erybody know dat."

J D could only image what it must be like to be in the position that Connie was in on that cold fall night. Having to run alone because you didn't won't to endanger your family or friends must be the worst position in the world to be in.

The penalties for helping any Negro that is in trouble with the Jim Crow law of the south are unforgiving. The helper could be anybody, black or white, who tries to lend a helping hand. The helper would suffer the full impact of unlimited racial hatred. This was the un-written law and every man and woman knew this fact.

This racial hatred came alive only when there was conflict between members from different sides of the racial divide. These conflicts almost never took place as often as one would think under the system. Each member knew what his role in the overall sheme of things was. Life could be a lot of fun as long as these invisible lines were not crossed. There were sometime the possibilities of real love and respect between members of the two races.

The Brittons were the kind of white folks that the Negroes could depend on for help at any time of the day or night. The people of the area, black or white, had next to zero automobiles and when there was a call for transporting a sick person to the doctor, the Brittons were there. They would help both races without hesitating at all. A few of the older Negroes remember the time when one of the Evans stepped on a rattler while walking home from night services at the church. Old man Britton was summoned to take the man to the doctor which was twelve miles away. He hand cranked his old model-A ford and drove the snake-bit man to town. Mr Britton had completely forgotten to put on his shirt. J D felt lucky to be getting a job over at the Brittons.

The three dressed-up men and the two shabby-dressed cousins lit out for the Britton store.

"How much money do we hav fuh gas?' 'Dis dodge don't run ohn wadda." J asked the fellows.

The Britton Store had a new shinny gas pump put in less than a week back. Everybody in the tri-church area thought a gas pump was what the farmers needed; hardly anybody had any thing that took gas to operate. They were still proud of the gas pump: the pump gave the store an important look.

"How much is de gas gonna cos?" Asked Tommy.

"Ya kin buy as much as yo money lets ya." Paul spoke with authority.

The five, relatives and friends, scrapped up fifty-nine cents among themselves. Gas was eight cents per gallon which was more than it sold for in town, but town was twelve miles away.

"Ah'll pump de gas.' 'Ah know how ta work dis thang." John grabbed for the hose handle.

Mr. Britton was in the store doing what he always did, keeping books and talking to anybody that happens to come by.

"Howdy boys."

"Evening Mista Britton." J D spoke for all the men.

"We wan three gallons uf gas, Mista Britton." John said while he pumped the gas into the glass cylinder at the top.

"J D? Why don't you come over Monday morning at 'bout ten?"

"Yessuh Mista Britton."

"Yew boys are awfully dressed up today.' 'Y'all musta been at Uncle Joe's burial."

"Yessuh."

The young men bought themselves some goodies and left the store and headed for the Alabama line. The young men had not been regular customers of the joint since Henry accidentally shot Jeff. The place was a reminder of the evil that men inflicted on each other over nothing.

"Ah still git de jittes by just coming heah as long as it has been ." J D said.

"Jeff is dead and bured; he can't hut nobody." John snarled.

J D didn't argue with John over anything. He knew John was one who questioned nothing; he made due with the way things were. John gave the least that he could get away with and usually asked for the same, which was not much. At times, J D wished he could accept the way things were without wondering why.

"John may know somethin dat de res uf dem didn know.' 'He show don seemed ta hav no problems, and dat's de truth." J D thought out loud to himself.

"Wha's you mumblin 'bout?"

"Nothin John."

The joint was the only place to go, other than church, for the colored folks. The usual men, and Maggie of course, were at the joint as if it was a Saturday night. Special events were excuses for a visit to the bootlegger's den. The wife beaters, the drunks, the liars and some with other bad habits were here celebrating a burial day for one of the old timers. It was hard for J D to believe that these men at the joint were more honest and forgiving than the ones that would never let themselves be seen at the watering hole.

The community was loaded with self-righteous sinners that will do anything that brings pleasures or profits. Half of the community had children by other men's wives, by kinfolks and anybody else that they could get undressed. There were a high percentage of scoundrels in the tri-church area.

The people that J D knew gave him faith in the teachings of the Holy Bible, because from what he could see, these folks were reaping exactly what they sow.

"Let's git on home y'all." Paul called out.

The boys decided to ride past the Simmon's place on their way to the Antioch community. There really was no need for visiting just to see somebody that you hadn't seen in a spell. Everybody was at the burial. These kinds of occasions encouraged very little actual visiting. This silence was due to fear of and respect for the dead. The young men and women didn't always agree with the ways of the elders, but they had to go along with them. The elders could show the highest level of respect for a departed one, but showed the highest level of disrespect for the same person while he had lived.

"Hey, dar's Wilma!" Bud said and elbowed J D."

"Ah ain't been back to her house since de day Jeff was kilt"

They had said very little about Wilma and J D because it was a common thing for young people to find new boyfriends or new girlfriends. Most girlfriend-boyfriend relationships were the results of opportunity, being in a certain place, availability and other facts that had nothing to do with conscientious choices. This kind of understanding was what the people were accepting without questioning.

"Ah saw Wilma at church and at de bural, but dats all."

"Hea she is now." Paul plugged in. "You wanna stop?"

"We kin." J D answered."

J D's memory kicked into high gear and some of the old feelings came charging back to his stomach. He had done his best to forget about what once was. Somehow he knew that a part of his life had come to an end and nothing that he could do would change that. The months since that Saturday afternoon he got no attention from Wilma other than a warm howdy.

"Evening y'all."

"How yu J D?" Wilma asked.

"Good! Good.' 'How is all wid yu n Bee?"

John, Tommy and Paul didn't get off or out of the truck. Bud was noisy enough to follow J D right to the front porch. Bud wanted to hear what these two had to say to each other. He knew about Wilma's sickness a few months back but had never learned what it was about. Neither he, nor J D ever found out whom and what it was all about. Wilma did not ask the brothers to come in. They sat on the side of the porch and asked about the health of the family. Wilma answered their questions but offered no additional information. After a few minutes the brothers knew why.

"We saw ya at de bural today."

"Yep, we wuz distant cousins ta Uncle Joe."

"Ah reckon everybody wuz dah.' 'The church couldn't hold'em all"

"Well, Ah gess we best be gitting along.' 'Be seein y'all."

J D and Bud climbed into the cab of the pickup and rode on toward home. Passing the farms after the rains and comparing them with what the conditions were before was unbelievable. The corn, cotton, sugar cane and gardens were blue-green. The people, animals, plants and the insects came alive when the rains came. The life-giving water was the life of the farm country.

"dis rain sho come on tiahm." J D broke the silence.

"We needed it." Paul commented.

J D made small talk about something he was not thinking about. His mind was on what he saw and felt when he saw Wilma. He saw in Wilma not the old happy girl, but a new Wilma. She had matured even more than the old Wilma. She was mature far ahead of her age. He thought that she treated him more like he was much younger than she. He felt a sliver of pity for her when he noticed the bulge of her stomach. Wilma was no longer a girl.

Bud asked quietly.

"Didja notice somethin different bout Wilma?"

"Yea, she seemed older fuh some reason."

"Older how?" Asked Paul.

"Oh! Ah donno, somethin changed."

J D wondered if somewhere there was an easier way to get through each day. He thought that being a good Christian might be the answer to some of his and these country folk's problems.

"Yew'd thank as much as dese folks go ta church, pray, use voodoo and work hard at farming dey wouldn' have so many problems."

"Dat's yo problem J D, you wan ta change dese folks." Paul informed J.

"Ya right Paul.' 'J D is always lak dat."

"Ah just believe if people would juss follow de teachin uf de Bible dey troubas would be ova.'

'Y'all know dey ain't one man or woman dat we know dat don't break some uf de Commandments ery day."

"Listen ta de preacha, now."

"J D is all de tiahm talkin lak dat."

"Ah just thank folks would fare betta if dey did wha de Good Book said ta do.' 'Some uf dese folks put spells on dey fellow church membes, some uf des men go wid each otha's wives, steal stock and even pick dey neighbo's cotton outta de fields at night."

When the pickup pulled into the yard J D headed for the lot and the company of the live stock. He felt like doing some thinking and the brothers and cousins were no help at times like these. That old familiar feeling of being out of control was back again. The old hound was the only animal that showed any interest in what he had to say during these times.

"Ah lak ta know wha ya thank bout de thangs people invent ta mess up a good life.' 'Whata ya think ya old fleabag."

The old dog that was nearly at the end of the trail seemed to enjoy J D's low moods. These were about the only times anybody paid any attention to the old half-dead dog. He just lay there, wagging his tail asking for more attention. The dog's life style was a reflection of the life styles of the human's here in the Mississippi farm country. Neither would accomplish a thing in this life.

J D turned his one-way conversation from the dog to himself. "Ah just know Wilma is big wid child.' Ah can see how she is so quite bout dis."

Today he clearly recognized the end of a beautiful time in his life. He hated to say good by forever to the sunny days that he and Wilma had shared. He could sense those good times sliding into the pool of yesterday's memories.

"Comon boy, let's tote some stove wood in de house.' 'Y'all wan breakfast in de morning, don't ya?"

Gathering wood for the stove, feeding the hogs and the mules and doing a dozen other things kept J D's mind off his dull everyday existence.

"Wonda who got Wilma in family way, Ah wonda."

CHAPTER NINETEEN

▼

The hot and dry days crawled by slower than a land tortoise looking for a lover. J D and John were pretty busy hauling melons, plus other things for the Britton. Bud and the others were working hard at trying to get the crops gathered on the home front. Nobody had to worry too much about being out of work this time of the summer. The crops that took all year to grow had to be harvest in a short time and be harvest between rains and other work stoppers. Hot and dry weather was not too good for the growing season, but it sure was good for the gathering season.

"Dis is de las of de melons dat's ready." John told J D.

"Yea, les take tiahm so de old man don't find somthin else fuh us ta do fo quiting time."

"Dis a good tiahm ta go take a do-doo." John headed for the fence.

The woods were the only cool place other than the branches and creeks. John was always good at wasting time on the job and taking a long doo-do was right down his alley. There was no bathroom for the colored anywhere but at the Negros' own homes, or the woods. Nobody ever thought much about such an arrangement; they accepted the lack of bathroom facilities as something that had always been and always would be. This arrangement bothered John more than it bothered some of the colored folks though.

The boys coming back from the Great War did more to upset the shaky relationships between the races than a hundred years of this kind of existing had done. The tales they told sure set some of the younger people's eyeballs a rolling. These returning heroes had a tendency to streach the truth a bit which didn't help matters much. Men like John were just green enough to start dreaming about the kind of freedoms that could get a young colored man in trouble in Mississippi.

John believed that the white folks were the people that stood next to God. He had always looked at the white's ways of living as being as close to heaven as it's possible to be and still be on this side of the grave. The white man's life seemed to be so easy when viewed from the positions of black men. John came back into the hot sun thinking that he would not have to work in the heat if only he was white.

"Ahm goin up nawth soon as Ah git som monny."

"Whaja been out in dem woods thankin bout.' 'Ye wuz spose ta be out dar messing."

"Ah wanna live lak white folks fo Ah die.' Live high ohn de hawg."

"Ya better wait til ya git up nawth, boy.' Now les git dese melons ta de sto."

J D had often had the same notion too except that he knew that was not always the case… He knew that whites had it easier than Negroes in many ways, but maybe not as easy in other ways. The whites had to make sure that the relationships between the two races were kept stretched tight. It was the white's responsibility to maintain the existing social system as is, in spite of the pressures to change. These pressures were coming from religions, northern politicians, and world leaders and from a few ambitiously liberal Negroes

"Ah don believe dat white folk havit as easy as ya thank.' 'We might be happer than some uf em."

"Dey don hafta ta work lak a mule lak we do jess ta put bred on de table."

"Ya don hafta ta be unhappy jess cuz ya hafta work."

The boys had about all the melons on the pickup that was safe to haul at one time. It would take a few minutes to unload a few at the store for sale this evening. The majority would remain on the truck for delivery tomorrow. There were several country stores between the Britton's and the county seat that they supplied fresh melons to.

Jennie was in the store when the boys rode up. She was helping a family of whites; the Jasons. The Negroes considered the Jasons white trash. They were poorer than the average colored.

"Hey John, how'd yew lak bein one of de Jasons?"

"Not ohn yo life."

"dat's all ahm tryin ta tell ya.' 'Bein white don mean diddly squat when it com ta bein happy."

John was not alone in his beliving that the only thing standing between Negroes and happiness was the color of their skins. The majority of the Negroes remained black because they had no choice. If they had their druthers, there would be no black folks; at least these wouldn't be black. The popular opinion among the Negroes was that even the light skinned Negroes had a better chance for a happier existence than their darker skinned brothers did. In Mississippi skin color was king.

Jennie was her usual flirty self around all men, white and black. This gal showed no preference for color when it came to people. Jennie was ignorant of the rules maintaining the social relationships between whites and blacks, or she just didn't give a hoot. Her actions said that there was nothing bad in the world that could happen to her.

John loved this unusal attention from a beautiful white girl. Jennie loved everybody; Loving everybody was a sure way of getting into trouble with everybody.

"John! Ah woun't be caught a lookin at Ms Jennie lak dat."

"Lak wha?""Les grab a drink and head home."

The two boys could walk home in less tha an hour if they didn't stop and fool around. Sometimes they caught rides with men goning home from the woods or from the fields of other farmers. That was not likely to be today because they were early and most of the workers in this part of Mississippi or Alabama worked much later. J D didn't like to have John hang around Jennie too much. "Dat boy is dumb as a jack rabbit." J D thought to himself.

"Ahm gonna save my monny so Ah kin catch de bus n' go stay in Detroit, or sommers."

"As crazy as ya is?' Yew'd be betta off stayin heah.' 'Who'd yu know up nawth anyways?"

"Ya know we got people up in Detroit and Chicage."

"Dat maybe so, but which uvem will take ya in?' 'Wha work kin ya do?"

"Ah'll find a job in no tiahm."

"Boy hush, yew ain't got de sense Gawd gava a jay bird."

"Ya jess wait n see."

J speeded up just to get a few steps ahead of John, thinking a faster pace might shut him up. He thought about John plans to get ahead. John was a cousin, but the boy sure had his head on sideways. This dreaming went on all day long; maybe it was John's way of passing time. The dream of going north and making plenty of money was rather common throughout the farm country. There were people though that just didn't buy into that easy-money thing.

"See dat durn rabbit settin dar lak he can't be in stew' 'Ya kin see dat when ya don hava a gun."

"De po boy is jes tryin ta las de night, lak yu and me, John."

It was normal for the wild vermits to fatten themselves up during this time of the growning season to get ready for the long winter ahead. They spend the frist part of the spring and summer raising their young and the last half of the summer and the fall getting themselves ready for the lean times. These poor wild animals and birds planned ahead better than many of the people did.

J D figured that the words these folks said had a different meaning than the words they lived by. The prayers prayed, the wishes wished and the promises made to themselves were unrelated to their daily habits. He could see that these people lived in one world and believed in another.

J D thought he'd try a few ideas on John; He used John as nothing more than a sounding board, or to say something out loud without appearing to be talking to himself.

"John, wha will ya say ta us buyin ar own truck and haulin fuh arselves?"

"Whar wouldja git de truck fahm?"

"Whar do people git trucks fahm?' 'Whar do dey git anythan fahm?"

"Shoot,! Ah donno."

"Boy yew is green as a gourd."

J D got what he expected out of John, a lack of seeing the big plan. He had experienced similar responses from people that he thought could understand what he was talking about. John kept most of his crackpot ideas to himself. The saying was already that he always had some cockamamie ideas swimming around in his head. An ambitious Negro was not appreciated too much by neither side of the great racial divide. A Negro letting his dreams interfere with his daily existence was not only a potential problem for himself, but could become a problem for those in whose company he might be at times.

The men and women of the fields never talked about future plans once they reach the age of about forty. Many ceased being ambitious before the age of forty if they were blessed with a wife and three or four youngsters. They had enough sense to realize the near zero chance that they'll ever have of saving enough money to move north. Some of the army boys went north, got themselves jobs and saved enough money to send for their wives, or return to the south and marry their girlfriends. The older generation gave up before giving anything a try. They knew the danger in trying to better their state of affairs.

J D thought that Mississippi had plenty of space for all its citizens, both black citizens and white citizens. Troubles between the races could be avoided by using what the local population already knew. The southern cracker was gullible enough that any old stupid Negro could fool the pants off the poor bastard. J D had sense enough to know the dangers of dealing with gullible fools too. J D could smell trouble a mile off, plus his guts told him when it was time to back off and make tracks. He knew that reasoning would not win against stupidity in a head-on confrontation. His greatest fear was to be in a no-win situation with a people who would not recognize the truth if it came up and bit them on the butt.

It was even harder for J D and some of the other young men, to accept the fact that their own people choose not to use these cracker's stupidities against them. Playing the roles of fools without profiting by this game was insulting to all Negroes. J D thought that maybe the Negroes had knowingly played the fool long enough to become victims of their own foolishness. These Negroes had become fools to the point of fulfilling the crackers' beliefs about the Negroes being niggers and subhuman and the whites being superhuman. J D wanted to live in his favorite state with a little dignity even if he had to wear this dignity under his shirt.

J D and John arrived home in time to help with pea shelling. This was the season when the women folk did a lot of canning. They would go in the fields and pick the peas during the first part of the day and do the hulling in the evening. The family would shell peas, cut okra, peal and chopup cucumbers, and a thousand other vegetables, to can after dark. They would bring the kerosene lamps to the porch to have a little light to see by. The lamps were more for keeping the ghosts away than they were for seeing by. This was the time to tell tall ghost stories. After a ghost-story telling night the younger members of the family had to be forced to go to bed without the lamp burning.

Uncle Bill, (Aunt Lou's husband) was one of the biggest liars in these parts. Nobody knew exactly where Uncle Bill came from, or how Aunt Lou happened to snag him as a husband. Some say he came to this area from prison, nobody knew for sure because he was so famous for lying. People down here in these woods enjoyed a tall tale whenever they heard one. Uncle Bill's most famous tales were about ghosts. The old boy had three favorites that he loved to tell to the youngsters and their parents too.

The story about the headless man always got the ears of all within earshot.

"One night ny de en uv Octoba ah wuz ohn mah way home fahm anotha church meetin when ah saw dis man, or wha ah took ta be a man, jes standin side de road.' 'Ohn dis heah night de moon wuz ashinnin bright as day, ah even hada shadow out in front uvme.' 'See, Ah reckoned dat Ah hadta know de man cause Ah knowed evrybody tween wha Ah stayed and wha Ah wuz acomin fahm.' 'Jess when Ah got almos close nough to speak to wha Ah though wuza man, he started walkin behead uv me.' ' Ah jes started walkin a little fasta so Ah would catch em.' 'It didn matta none how fas Ah walk, de space tween us stayed de same.' 'By dis tiahm Ah felt de har rise ohn de back uf ma head. Ah slowed down ta a crawl.' De still ahr all of a sudden turned ta a wamn puff uf ar.' 'De space tween us stayed de same.' 'Ah wuz gitting fed up wid dis game by now, so Ah pulled out ma ol snugnose thirty-eight.' 'Ah slowed down even mo, dar wuz no change in de gap tween us.' 'Now Ah sho nuff got on edge, so Ah stopped.' Dar wuz de stank uf rotten aigs in de hot ahr.' De thang neva changed its pace, but gained no mo grond.' 'Now Ah knowed full well dat no man could do dis, not dat Ah knowed uf.' 'De only thang ah could thank uf to do wuz to holla.' 'Yew know how ya holla when ya is scart outta yo mind.' 'HEY! HEY YEW DAR!!" "Dis is when de thang turned inta a big ol shaggy dawg.' "Ah didn know wheatha to mess mah britches or go blind." Ah tuned round rite den n went back bout a mile ta mah uncle Sil's house an spent de night.' 'Ah total fogot de thirty-eight in mah hand.' 'Ah'll neva fogit dat night as long as Ah live."

Uncle Bill had a way of stretching out a tale for maximum effect. He would say SOOooo, instead of so. The folks never did figured out how he could have these terrible experiences and still go where ever he wanted to at any time of the night without a backward glance. Everybody knew Uncle Bill habit of stretching the truth, but they didn't know how much was the truth or how much was lies. Therefore, they leaned toward beliving all of his fibs.

When Uncle Bills deep and heavy voice went quiet nobody said a word. All the sound made was the soft sound coming from shelling green peas. The pea-shellers could almost see the headless man standing on the side of the road. They wouldn't be going anywhere tonight.

Chapter Twenty

▼

Allen and Steve had gotten involved in the bootlegging business over in Alabama. These two boys had made up their minds to make a few fast bucks to pay their way up north. These two had always found the southern social system not to their liking. Their dreams were to move up north, make a lot of money and come back south to show off. Allen's ambition was to get out of the south as soon as possible and don't come back until he could come back riding high on the hog. Steve was just copying his buddy's dream.

Allen went and bought himself a 1941 Chevrolet to use to transport the whiskey from Mobile to the joints in Mississippi and near the state line over in Alabama. He hauled the legal sealed whiskey, from an area where it was legally sold to dry counties where the whiskey was illegal. If the two big business men could make it to the county line they had nothing to worry about. They were hauling the stump juice for the High Sheriff. They had very little troubles until near election time when the local law enforcement people had to make an impression on their constituents. All the rest of the time nobody took much notice of how alcohol got from one place to the other. Allen was his own worst enemy at times. He would deliberately provoke a confrontation with the powers.

Allen had been a daredevil all his life; he hadn't changed in all these years. He would drive out of Mobile County at sixty miles per hour for no good reason other than to see how fast he could go on the narrow and curvy roads while hauling a load of whiskey. Steve tried to hold the boy in check, but Allen never paid much attention to his mother, you know he was not about to take Steve's advice, not one bit.

"If we hava accident en bus dis hea likker we be in hot watar."

"Don wory yoself none bout us havin accidents.' Ah kin drive de piss outta dis baby."

"Dese dirt roads is nuff ta break de jugs without yew havin an rake."

The condition of the back roads was bad enough to break the glass containers while driving at high speeds. Steve tried to address the little common sense Allen might have.

"Ah don believe dar is a car dat kin keep up wid dis ol Chevy."

Allen never believed in following rules made by a few to control the many. He had never seen himself picking cotton all day for near nothing. At times it sure looked like Allen had the right idea, especially to the young who were picking cotton at two o'clock in the afternoon. Allen was always easily bored.

Steve was no coward by a long shot, but he had a sense of what was worth the cost. He didn't think it made a whole lotta sense to deliberately put one's self in a no-win situation.

"Why is ya gwine dis way fuh?"

"Gotta have some gas.' 'We kin go by de Britton's store while we be dis close."

Allen and Steve could not miss the McCray's pickup parked at the gas pump. They could see it far enough away to have continued past the store. The boys could not see who was riding with the McCray boy.

"Yew see dat?"

"Don let dem rednecks git ta ya Steve."

"Ah ain't' 'It ain't me Ahm worrd 'bout.' 'We shoulda kep goin ohn by and come back latta."

"Nobody is gonna mess wid us."

Steve knew Allen had a bad habit of not knowing when to keep his mouth shut, especially around certain people. Steve knew Allen reasons for mouthing off all the time had nothing to do with his speaking up for justice. Allen had a habit of being additive to trouble no matter where or when the opportunity presents itself. Steve on the other hand had no hankering for a fight with anybody about anything.

Allen pulled up behind the McCray's old rattletrap to within twelve inches. Allen knew that his Chevrolet would be a source of interest to the two crackers coming out of the store. The nigger-hating Mac was with the McCray boy.

"Ah hada notion we shoulda kep goin."

"Who lent y'all that dar Chevy?" Mac asked.

"Who tol ya we bard it." Allen answered.

"Cause Ah jes know it ain't yourn."

"Yew don know nothin."

McCray never said anything to Allen, he just said to Mac. "Let's git."

Mac was not satisfied leaving things as they were, but even he realized that to do otherwise could lead to a fight that the two of them had no chance of winning. Everybody knew that Allen liked nothing better than a fight and he didn't care with whom it was. Allen had a bad reputation for kicking butts.

The white boys crawled into their old pickup and took off. They had never been too fond of a fair fight when it came to locking hornes with blacks. They were much more appreciative of having the deck stacked in their favor.

"Ya know ya didn do us any good by messin wid dem crackas." Steve whined.

"Ah ain't gonna git ohn my knees and crawl fuh nobody.' Ya kin if ya want ta, Ah ain't."

Jennie was standing in the doorway watching the two men pump five gallons of gas. She didn't have any idea that there could ever be trouble between her customers, black or white, not yet.

"HI y'all!"

"Hi Miss Jennie." Steve spoke, Allen said nothing.

The two went into the store, paid for the gas and two stage-plants and two RC colas. The whites usually sat around in the store to eat their snacks, especially when the weather was either too hot or too cold for confort on the outside. The Negroes never ate their purchases inside the store. There were no sighns saying, 'Negroes aren't allowed to eat inside the store.' Most of the rules governing the social behaviors of the two races were not written down anywhere. This knowledge came through cultural training.

"Heah come J D and John." Steve informed Allen.

"Dey quit mighty early to be workin fuh de Brittons." Allen had to throw that remark in.

"Mr. Britton is a good man ta work fuh."

"Dat's wha yu say.' 'Ah ain't workin in de fields fuh nobody."

Allen promised himself everyday that he would not become like the other Negroes in Mississippi. All he wanted to do was to make enough money so he could go north in style. He had no intentions of cooking his brains out in the fields for nothing. Allen watched his mommy and daddy grow old and dry up like a cracklin working in the hot sun year in and year out. "Nosuh, dat shit ain't fuh me."

"Wha'd ya say Al?"

"Nothin, jess talkin to myself."

J D and John waved as they got out of the truck. "Hey y'all!" John said.

Allen would not miss this chance to remind the two regarding the unpleasant job they had working for the boss man. The two farmers started unloading the few melons to be left in the store.

"How many melons didya' haul today?" Allen said with a smile.

"Moen ya did." snapped John.

"He jess tryin ta git somethin started, John.' 'Pay em no neva mind."

"If y'all wait a few minutes ya kin drap us off at home.' 'Save us a long walk afta ah lon day in de fields." J D humored Allen.

"Take ya tiahm, we ain't in no hury." Allen said.

J D didn't have to worry about Allen not taking them home. The truth was Allen was glade to take the men home. Allen wasn't about to miss a chance to show off his forty-one Chevrolet. They better not try to stop him from taking them home, and the long way at that.

The four men jumped into the Chevorlet and down the road they went. The top speed was about thirty-five miles per hour on the bumpy roads. Allen did the top speed just to show his friends what the car could do and ride as smoothly as possible on the rough country roads.

"It's good ya don' meet nobody cause we'd wreck fuh sho." J D reminded Allen.

Allen cared less about any other vehicle being on the road. He was on the lookout for stray farm animals more than anything else. There were many a bent vehicle from encounters with stray cows, hogs and mules. Other dangers were running up behind a slow moving wagon or horse and riders in the middle of the road and most of all, children. Children sometime played in the middle of the public road.

"Wha'd ya thank?" Allen asked.

"It sounds good." J D answered.

"Dey is nothin dat kin outrun me tween heah n Mobile."

"If ya keep drivin lak dis nobody will have ta catch ya.' 'Dey'll find ya hung up on a tree sommers."

"Shucks, Ah kin handle dis baby."

Allen had been driving for all of six months and now he was one of the best drivers in this part of the world. He didn't have to be much of a driver to be one of the best because very few Negroes could drive at all. Allen would not have a license if he was not hauling for the Sheriff, and he would not have a car if he was not hauling for the Sheriff. He could brag about not working his hind end off in the fields, but J knew that Allen was even more a slave to the whims of the white man than the field workers were.

In Mississippi a Negro man had no other choice except to get in the back pocket of somebody that has power or leave for distant lands. The Negro man has very little political, social economical or swaying power that they could use to help themselves. If a man did not have a white man in his corner he could be victimized by any person or situation that he might run into. A Negro's money would not buy the kind of power that is needed to be in charge of his life. He had to use a different kind of power other than money to get alone within the system. Negroes had no legal powers at all in southern Mississippi, or anywhere else in the south for that matter. A few of the Negro citizens had mastered ways of getting the job done outside the legal system. Allen was slick enough to walk one of those thin lines between the two realities.

"We could save ar money and drive dis hea car ta Detroit whar ma uncle live.' 'He'll hep us gitta job out dar whar he work.' 'Allen almost begged.

"Wha work do he do?" Asked John.

"Mah uncle work fuh a place whar dey melt ion used ta make motos fuh cars.' 'Dis moto in dis heah car might be one uf 'em."

J D had been thinking about the north for a long time. He could not see too much difference between life in the country and life in the northern cities.

"Dat juss might wok boy."

"Three or fo uf us could go togetha, gitta room n start workin fuh one uf dem big factres." Allen was still trying to get to the big times. Allen had high hopes of moving up to a better life than he could image being possible in his home state. Allen was not a patient young man. He had a hard time handling the everyday boring tasks of farming as a route to the way he wanted to live. He needed more than a place to eat and sleep. Allen wanted to experience life now, not tomorrow, now.

"How much didja pay fuh dis automobile?" John asked Allen.

Ah don know xactly.' 'De sheiff bought it fuh me.' 'Ah kno it's in mah name, and dat's fo sho."

"Ya thank he'll let ya drive it up nawth?" John asked.

John was not the traveling partner that Allen was looking for. He thought John was not driving with a full set of lights. John's chances of getting a job in the factories were less than a one-legged man winning a foot race. Allen had J D or Bud targeted for accompanying him north. They might have enough sense to get a job once they get there. John didn't have enough sense to do a good job in the fields without somebody standing over him.

"Dat boy don have sense nuff ta understand doo-doo.' 'We won' ax de Sheiff if we kin driv dis car nawth." He told John.

Grandma Ida was sitting on the porch when the men drove into the yard. Grandma Ida loved to see all young folks working from sun to sun. She didn't cotton to a car load of younguns riding aroung when they could be picking cotton or something. That was all she had ever been taught.

"Evenin grandma." The men spoke.

"Wha deviment have y'all been in?"

"We been workin grandma." J D answered.

"Who lets dey hands git off dis erly?' 'Nobody dat Ah kno bout."

Proving an old person wrong was a no-no in this part of the world. You just agreed with whatever they said and continued about your business. Grandma Ida was not one to hear what the young were saying. She had to be pretty headstrong to have had twelve younguns, starting when she was just thirteen years old. She got married at the age of twelve which meant that she and her kids grew up together. She also helped raised two step children that were nearly as old as she was.

"Whars dem otha boys at?"

"Dey's still in de woods, grandma." John said as he passed grandma on his way to the boy's room.

"How much do de Sheiff pay y'all fuh gwin gittin his likker fuh em?" J D wanted to know.

"He pay us by de gallon.' 'If we brin fifty gallons, he pay us thirty cents fer each gallon.' If we brin les then fifty gallons, he will pay a little mo."

"How much do yah git outta dat?" J D wanted to know how long it would take Allen to save enough money to get out of the south.

"Som days Ah git ta kep six or seven dollas afta Ah pay Steve somethin fuh ridin wid me, buy gas n wid wha de Sheiff takes out fuh paynent on dis car."

"How many tiahm a week will ya be goin to Mobile?"

"Ah don know xactly.' Mebbe two or three tiahms if Ah'm lucky."

J D figured that Allen and Steve would never save enough money to cross Mason and Dixie line. With working only two or three days a week, they had too much time on their hands to save money. These two would use that much in gas and cold drinks while they wasted time.

"Ah'm thankin bout doin a little sellin likker myself." Allen said knowing what J D and the others were thinking. 'Ah'll pick up a gallon or two fuh myself whilist Ah'm down in Mobile."

"Don let de Sheiff catchja bootleggin hind his back." J warned.

"Ah don told em." Steve added.

Allen was planning to steal some of the corn likker from the Sheriff. He was thinking of stealing a few quarts from a batch of ten or more gallons without anybody being the wiser. The corn liquor was never sealed, therefore close to a pint could be poured out of each gallon and replaced with water. The sealed whiskey was another matter, it couldn't be tampered with. Two to three gallons a week would be his ticket out of the south, but he would not tell the others, not even J D, not yet anyway. He would make sure it would work first before telling the boys.

Allen had no guilty conscious as a result of his stealing from those who stole from him. Allen didn't feel guilty for stealing from those that didn't steal from him either. Allen had a problem trusting hypocrites; therefore he had a problem trusting anybody because he thought that most of the people here in these woods were hypocrites. Nobody that he knew spoke their minds, or said what was really on their minds. He believed that the folks around here said and did what they thought was in their best interest. They were afraid to say or do otherwise. Being honest with a bunch of thieves is like going to war with an empty rifle.

The men were back sitting in the Chevy when Daddy Banks and Uncle Barlow showed up. Neither of the older men did anything other than speak to the car-crazy young men. Uncle Barlow had told Daddy Banks about the car as soon as he saw the vehicle parked in the yard. Automobiles owned by Negroes became common transportation for the entire community, especially when there was an emergency. Folks knew who own automobiles and who they could depend on for fast rides into town. White folks were also dependable when it came to a need for fast transpotation to town due to accidents, snake bites, mule's kicks and other emergencies including injuries as the results of the fighting among relatives and friends.

Grandma Ida didn't speak to the two men until they sat down. "Dem younguns need a car like dey need anotta hol in dey head.' Y'all neva got toys lak dat ta play wid."

"Momma, dey wuz no toys lak dat when we came lon."

Chapter Twenty-one

▼

J D and John had finished hauling cotton to the cotton house when they saw the strange shinny car pull up to the store.

"Ha ha! Lookat dat car."

"Yea John, Ah kin see.' 'Les see who it is drivin sucha fiahm automobile.' Nobody dat Ah know bout."

"Me neitha."

When the men came across the road from the cotton house, they saw a familiar man starting to pump some gas.

"Well, Ah'll be a dead mule ifn dat ain't Mark.' 'Is he gon and lost his mind?" John whispered.

"How yew doin Mark?' I herd bout yo momma, but Ah didn thank yew'd come back hea though.' 'Dis oughta be de las place yew'd come." It would be if Ah wuz yu." John said quietly.

"Whoa dar, everthan is alright.' 'Ah gotta letta from Mista Britton a lon tiahm ago, he knows dar wuz nothin Ah don."

"When didja git heah?" J D asked.

"Sunday."

"How lon yew gonna be heah?"

"Ahm on mah way de fust thang in de mornin.' 'Dat's why Ah'm buyin mah gas today.' 'Ah'll be outta de state fo any of dese trouble-makas wake up."

"Ah sho would hate ta see yu wind up lak Connie did." J stated.

"Wha most folks thank happened to Connie, didn," Mark informed the two men in a low voice.

Hearing the low talking outside, Jennie came out to see what was going on. Jennie knew that Negroes never talked in a low tone unless they were gossiping. No siree, they were loud talkers. She turned a shade whiter when she saw who it was pumping gas. The young lady was really glad to see Mark.

"How are yew Mark?"

"Jes fiahn, Miss Jennie, jes fiahn."

The men wasted no time paying for their purchases and hightailing it out of there. A few of the rednecks had never forgotten the last time Mark had been at the Brittin's store and these boys were unforgiving. Citizens were guilty until proven innocent was the usual rule when it came to Negroes who were accused of breaking the un-written laws governing the relationships between the races. Now the rules were reversed when it came to whites violating the same rules that governed the links between the same two races. They were considered innocent until proven guilty. The guilt had to be proven by the people who had no civil rights and no power.

"Hop in y'all; Ah'm goin y'all's way."

The three men left the store. Jennie stood in the doorway until the shinny car disappeared in front of its own dust cloud.

"Now, bout dis thang bout Connie." J D had to know what Mark meant by what he said about Connie.

"Well, yew know Connie wuz at his momma's n his daddy's burials."

"No Ah didn see em." J replied.

"Yu jes didn know who ya wuz lookin at.' ' His own kin didn know he wuz dar, onla a few knowed.' 'He didn tell em cause of whad dey would say ta him and he felt lak dee crackas mite be watchin."

"How did he manage to scape fahm dem peckawoods?"

"Let mh tell ya how Ah herd it.' 'Ah don know how true dis wuz, but Ah got de news fahm ol man Barlow.' 'All us knows dat ol man knows jess bout evrythan."

"Yea, dat's 'cause evrybody goes ta him wid all dey question axin fer advice." J D explained.

"Anyhow, de sayin goes lak dis.' 'When Connie got to de bridge he realize dat sumpten wuz wrong.' 'As he made a mad das fuh de brige he herd de hillbilly holled, '"Heah is de niggah!"' Connie didn make it ova de deep watta foe de shootin started.' He doved ova de side in de shalla part uf de riva, loosein his hat n de bag dat Louis had given him.' He los de riffle dat he carred.' De raffle wuz drapped on de brige foe he jumped ova into de wader.' 'He said de wild shootin wuz goin on by de tiahm he hit de wader.' 'All de crackers wuz runnin from 'hind de trees wha dey had dey trucks hid.' 'Connie said dat he couldn't member swimmin, or wadin, to de foot of de brige, but he did.' 'He said dat he wuz too scard to feel anythin; his hart wuz beatin so fass n loud he thought de half-drunk crackas would heah it.' 'When he knowed anythin he wuz unda de brige whar it met de muddy bank.' 'He thought he had been caught fur sho til he hard some of dem sayin, '"Thar he goes down thu river. "' 'Dey wuz shootin at his hat and de brown bag floatin down de edge of de strong river curent."

The dark had saved Connie's life because it was hard to see what was floating down the swift and muddy river. He heard the laughter and the joking about how they had taught the niggers a lesson about hitting a white man. The ignoramuses celebrated a job well done of teaching the negroes where their place in this part of the state was. After a few swigs of brew, they left. They had to git back and report to their families about one more Negro becoming catfish food. The boys didn't say anything for a few minutes. A couple of the white half-drunks had been nearly killed by their own.

"Dat nigguh been live all dis tiahm and none afus knowed nothin."

John was talking a mile a minute. "He got clean away, hot doggit."

Mark stayed at the Bank's house for a while because all seemed to be glad to see him. Mark was an example of one of them getting out and doing good up in Chicago. Mark had lots of kin up there to help him out too. He also had family with money still living in the great state of Mississippi.

"How ya lak livin in Chicago Mark?" Daddy Banks asked."

"I like evrythin but de cold weather.' 'It gits cold nough to freeze de ears offa mule.' 'A man kin walk wid his head helt high even though he be a Negro.' 'But, de whites have de best jobs, live in de nice part uf de city and keep de nigguhs in whah we call colored section uf de city.' 'De whites don't even speak ta Negroes up nawth if dey kin help it."

"Dat's wha ahm tryin ta tell dese colored folks hea, de whites don lak ya any mo up nawth den dey lak ya heah." J D Plugged in.

Mark replied. "Dey jess put up wid de colored, plus dey don gatha togetha a tal up der.' 'Dey don live next doe to de Colored lak dey do down heah.' 'De grass ain't all ways greena on de otha side of de feace."

"J believes we kin do good heah in de south if we so mind ta." Daddy Banks said.

"He right in a way.' 'I didn leave ta look fer a betta livin, ya know."

"Ah reckon so.' 'If ah recollect, ya had trouble wid dat Britton gal."

When Mark was leaving J D followed him out to the car. J wanted to know more about how the one Negro beat the Whites at their own game.

"Is Connie livin in Chicago wid y'all?"

"No, Connie lives less then fifty miles fahm heah.' 'He won leave Missippi; he's lak his daddy wuz."

"It's de same wid me, ah don thank life would be any easer in de nawth den it is heah at home."

Mark and his shinny car melted into the evening sun. Mark's opinion of the conditions in the north for the Negroes was not the same as it would be for the average Negro. Mark was speaking like someone who was forced to leave a good life for a worst one. Mark's family owned everything the upper class whites owned. He certainly wouldn't have left an easy luxurious life, by Mississippi standards, for a life of squalor in the black slums of the north if it had been his decision.

"Do ya see wha ah have been tryin ta tell yu fools?' 'De nawth ain't nigga heaven lak half dese ignert niguhs thank."

"Look wha kind of car Mark's drivin.' 'If it's so bad up in Chicago, howda he git dat prudy car?"

"Boy yo head is hard as a rock; mark had money when he went ta Chicago."

"It's good ta know dat Connie ain't dead." J D said to change the subject.

"Ah don believe he gottaway,"

"Ah don reckon Mark would lie 'bout somethin lak dat."

Mark kept talking to John because there was nobody else around to bounce thoughts off. He said his goodbyes and took leave.

"Mark sho ain't scared uf dese crackas.' Ah woul've been scared shitless ta go by de Brittons.' 'It darn near scared de livin daylights outta me when Ah looked up and relized who he wuz.' 'Ah wouldn't be dat dad-burn crazy, nawh, nawh.' 'Dese crackers ain't nothing ta play wid.'

"J D ya always stay as fur as ya kin frahm de white folks.' Dey ain't gonna bite ya, not all uf 'em anyhow."

"Ah ain't talkin 'bout all uf 'em, Ahm talkin 'bout de trouble-makin few dat kin git yew kilt.' 'De good white folk can't help a nigguh dat's in trouble wid some otha whites widout being call ah negguh lova.' 'Ah don'blame de crackas fur not wantin ta be called ah nigguh lova.' 'Being ah nigguh lova is wost den ben ah nigguh as fur as some uf des peckawoods is concerned."

J D was trying to explain to John the dangers in hanging around some of these nutty hillbillys when Bud and Tommy came home.

"Wha is de talk bout dis tiahm?" Bud asked before he said 'evening.

"Nothin but de sam ol thang.' 'John has it in his head dat de nawh is heven fuh niguhs,"

"Naw Ah don neitha.' 'Dat's yu sayin dat, but Ah do thank its betta den hea.' 'Anyhow, Ah lak ta see fuh muhself, dat, s all."

Young men bringing good news about the north didn't help the local folks to accept their lot and be thankful. News of a better life without having to die to reach it was as welcome as a spring shower. These old dumb country boys were driven by partial trues to downright lies about the freedoms that Negroes had up north. These young men were hungry for something that they never had; the wish to feel like men. These dirt-farmers and day-workers were sitting ducks to be sucked in by tall tales about the high wages, night life and the loose white women just waiting for these ignorant country boys. These poor bastards were turning away from paying attention to Reverend Mayfield's sermons about there being heaven waiting after this life and not in this life. They wanted to catch a bus for the great north.

Chapter Twenty-two

▼

The old and the young were primping up for the big days ahead at the church. The late summer was the time of the year for the churches to have what was called attractive meetings. The whole community would come together at one local church and have services of all kinds, and all kinds of services it would be. Nobody who was able to ride in a wagon, truck, car would think about missing this shindig. The people even brought grain for the mules and horses as a tocken of appreciation for hauling their mistresses, masters and family to church. The dogs came to church on these Sundays and they too were welcome. The old sisters always brought enough for all.

Meetings like the attractive meeting, when the members brought food from homes, had a few of the sisters bringing food that most of the congregation avoided if at all possible. These sisters' food was said to be on the nasty side. The dogs didn't mind at all, and a few of the people didn't mind too much either. The custom was that everybody received a helping of food from all the sisters' cardboard boxes. There were other reasons for avoiding certain foods by certain people. Where there is love to be found, there is also hate too.

There were a couple of old gals in the community whose food was definitely avoided. The local gossip had it that these old biddies were knonw more for their spell-casting abilities than for their good cooking. The local voodoo queens had a reputation for helping the good Lord with his duties of making sure that the guilty reaped what they sowed. Some community members believed that this penalizing for wrong doing was accomplished through extra spicing in foods served to the assumed guilty. The guilty included every living soul in the community. They were all guilty at one time or another.

Many of the older community members had been swapping wives and husbands so much until everybody at the meeting was close kin. If a community member wanted to get hitched, he or she might ought to leave the local area to find a mate, or take a chance on hooking up with a half sister or brother, not to mention cousins. It was a common belief that when someone acted funny or was nuttier than a fruit cake, either they had been daddied by a kin or had been spelled by one of the hoodoo queens. The average church member was more afraid of being hoodooed , or caught doing wrong with someone else's mate than they were of going to hell after death. The fear of hell after death was the good Reverend Mayfield,s hold on the community. He never hesitated to preach on it either.

This was the big day that Allen had been waiting for. He thought that he might make a big splash in the pot of riches. He mamage to skim a few gallons of stump juice off the top of the many gallons that he was hauling for the Sheriff. Allen made sure that he was at the church early enough to get a shady spot underneath the old oak tree. Yes sir, he would be able to operate just find from here. Allen also knew that the Reverend always parked his long hearse-looking car under this same oak. Allen made sure he had a pint of shine in a store bought whiskey bottle for the Reverend. The Reverend seemed to do a better job saving souls when he felt the spirit. The spirit that didn't come from his God.

The Reverend nosed his long 1941 Ford hearse next to Allen's Chevy. The Reverend told his bunch to get on in the church for Sunday school. He didn't have to go in right now, being the preacher and all.

"How do Reverend!" Allen spoke.

"Monin in de name uf de lawd."

"It looks lak it's gonna be a scorcha, huh!" Allen said as he slid a half pint on the seat next to the Reverend.

"May Gawd bless an keep ya young man."

The good Reverend bent over and took a big belt of the easy-to-swallow corn before getting out of the car. He called himself hiding from people who knew that he drank. They forgave him. He now felt like mixing with his flock. This was the day of all days for the Reverend. He had to be ready to deliver his best sermon ever. Of all the sermons that he had written, he had one special sermon that seemed to git the congregation worked up quicker than all the rest put together. "AND DE LAWD SAID TO PHARAOH, LET MUH PEOPLE GO." The glow from the slug of whiskey began to spread through out the Reverend's guts as he headed toward the side door of the church continuing to repeat the title of his sermon.

The line of cooks came one by one with their cardboard boxes of food. The men had the make-shift tables set and waiting for the lunch boxes. Every tom, dick and harry had on their best Sunday-go-to-meeting clothes. They were one miserable bunch of cotton pickers with shoes on that didn't fit their callused feet. These folks very seldom got a chance to doll-up and this day was one of those few occasions. These country folks were going to look their best if it killed them. Some of the folks had spent their last money buying clothes just for this day.

J D brought the Britton's pickup home just for this reason, to haul the faithful to serve their God. He had to make several trips because of the number of souls wanting a ride and also because of the slow dressers. The young ladies wanted everything to be exactly right and this took a while, especially when nobody had a clue of what was exactly right. The gals had to make sure their rusty elbows and knees were polished to a shine, the kitchens hair was straightened (the kitchen was the area in back of the head where the hair was short and hard to get the straightening comb on) and all the rest of their gear was fitting right. Today they were launching an all-out assault on ugliness. The young hopefuls had worked all summer for this special time to prove to all the half-blind men how pretty they could be. The beauty queens and the muscular young men were not the only ones working hard getting ready for the day.

Uncle Frank closed his joint and moved his operation down the road from the church yard. There was no reason for him to be open at his place and miss an opportunity like this. These times were usually his best times to make money. He'd get his share of the crop money from the men while the preacher would get his from the women folks. Somebody even had something for the younguns that wanted something cold on this hot Sunday. They made ice cream to sell to the little ones.

The mothers of the church had their hands full trying to keep an eye on the young ladies and praising the Lord at one and the same time. The path leading down to the outhouse was busier than an ant hill after a mule stepped on it. The young gals couldn't get enough checking each other for flaws in their outfits; the other side of this great meeting was another force at work, the gambling men.

Not too far from the men's outhouse was the gambler's hide-away. These boys could take two dollars and shoot dice all day and come away with the same two dollars that they started with. This was where the trouble usually started from. Loosing a quarter after drinking a pint of rotgut was enough to get trouble brewing between men that didn't care for each other in the first place. These boys would get a bit loud at times until some cooler head stepped in to calm the excitement down. Someone always kept an ear and an eye turned toward the path leading to the church just in case one of the mothers of the church wondered passed the lady's outhouse. The heat and the insects didn't help the tempers much either.

The flies and the gnats were pestering everybody and everything in sight. Even the horses, mules and the dogs were fighting these armies of bugs. It was hard to believe that this many bugs could show up at one yearly eat-out for one day. Where were these things before today? These annoying bugs were just an introduction to what the congregation would get once the food is spreaded out on the plates. There will be a houndred times more ready to help everybody feast on the fresh foods. The sisters brought enough food to feed all anyway, including the gnats.

Sister Ruby Mae came to the great meeting by a mule-drawn buggy. Her grandson made sure the old lady got where she wanted to go and how she wanted to get there. The old lady was dressed in a solid black dress with a black hat trimed in red. She wore the usual necklaces and bracelets. She had all the protection from voodoo, witchery, spells, majo bags and any other evils that may be waiting in any corner of the world. Sister Ruby believed in the powers of evils with all her heart. She had dedicated her life to the practice of fighting evil with evil. Sister Ruby's habits were not criticized much by anybody, for good reasons too. Most of the country folk didn't take chances offending any of the local gods and, or devils.

Many people from the immediate area and from as far away as Mobile and New Orlean have been clients of the evil-worshiping queen. The common beliefs were that she could put a hex on someone as well as remove a hex. They came for both and sometimes wanted both done at the same time. If one of her clients had problems with a husband or boyfriend she had the love potion to straighten the mess right out. She was also a good cook.

Sister Ruby's food basket was a popular stopping place but nobody ate their helpings. The people were scared not to get her food and scared to eat it once they had it on their plate. They figured that one could not be too careful in a community where rumors got started at the drop of a hat. Many of the rumors were true but nobody knew what part Sister Ruby would be playing. She could even put the mouth on someone which was nearly as bad as giving one the evil eye. Sister Ruby had no close friends.

The dogs and gnats didn't appear to suffer from a stomach full of Sister Ruby's cooking; therefore her cooking had to be safe. The congregation was still a bit reluctant to eat her good cooking.

The harder Reverend Mayfield preached the more liquoir the drunks consumed and the louder the gamblers got. The young flirted with each other and the whoremongers blinked and smiled at each other. It sure looked liked all fronts was equal. This was the one Sunday of the year when all was welcome to participate in the affairs. One of Uncle Barlow saying was, "It took all kinds to make things work."

The Reverend knew when to speed things up a bit. He knew that wives, girlfriends, mothers, fathers and food would keep things from getting out of hand. He also was aware that if he waited too long half the men would be drunker than cooter browns.

The church was rocking when the Reverend ended his sermon and opened the door of the church to potential members which there were none. This is the same time the collection plate was passed around. The money had to be collected while the members were still in the mood. If the deacons gave the members and vistors time to cool off and come back to their right mind their pockets might become shallow. They had to get them while they were hot. Opening the doors of the church was just noise to make while the collection plate was passed from hand to hand. There wasn't anybody in there that didn't already belong to the church, or a sister church.

While the collection plate was being passed around, the sisters were still in a trance. They were moaning, rocking and fanning themselves with the funeral-home issued fans. A few of the old professional shouters were being fanned by the younger ladies. Reverend Mayfield made sure that he kept the open door policy going long enough for the collection plate to make its rounds. The now sweaty Reverend grabbed his water glass and took a swig of corn while the congregation cooled down. It was hot in the church because every pew was full. The Reverend had prayed for a full house, his prayer had been answered.

"Dis sho is a blessed day, praise de Lawd." The Reverend saw how busy the deacons were counting the bills and change; he had to say it again."Praise de Lawd, thank ya Lawd!!"

The church was in the praise-the-Lord-hallelujah-amen stage and would take a few minutes for the sisters to calm down. The sisters used the amens, hallelujahs and thank-gods to wash their sins away. Once this cleansing is done, these old lost souls will come pouring out of the church hungry enough to eat whatever they could lay their hands on while gossiping about every soul attending the big meeting.

The younger women and small boys and girls who were picked to fan the flys away from the food baskets were beginning to get fidgety. The young people were picked for such an important job because the older folks could not be trusted with looking after the cakes and stuff. Anyway, the young would get their behinds beat if they even thought about such a lowdown act of grabbing food before the Reverend blessed it. The only problem they had with the food watchers was that none wanted to stand over Sister Ruby Mae's box. They did though because they were afraid not to.

The Coker brothers were checking the well water to see if it was drinkable. Sometimes a wild animal would fall into the well. Leroy and George were not big on going to church, but they were here this Sunday the same as everyone else. They had to do some good in order to feel deserving of a full belly. They made sure the water was fit to drink. A few of the folks were praying that this was all the brothers would contribute to the festivities today.

The old open well was dug years before most of the present generation could remember, but still had the coolest water in the vicinity. Animals would fall into the well making the water unfit to drink until the dead critters were drawn out. The only times the well was used were during school days and when church service was going on. The churches doubled as the house of God and a school house. The Negroes didn't have a school building as such.

The Negroes went to school when there was nothing to do in the fields which were about five monthes out of the year. Once the boys got big enough to work in the woods and the saw mills, they usually never went back to school again. A high percentage of the white and the colored population didn't see any reasons for the Negroes to be in school in the first place. Most of the Negroe children went to school the four or five monthes anyway wheather they learned anything or not. Most did just that, went to school, but learned nothing. There was nobody to teach them.

The non-regulars were nearly always late coming to these functions that were tailored for the entire community. Maggie was no exception; she was nearly an hour late. The prayers had been prayed, the songs had been sung when Maggie showed up with her brothers. She floated across the two hundred feet of yard like she was on a cloud. Every eye out side of the church was on that honky-tonk mamma as she sauntered across the hard-packed clay yard toward the front door of the church.

Maggie causes an equal stir among the praying people inside the house of God. Every head turned as Maggie entered the door and followed her to where she sat down. She knew the women and she knew the men and some she knew too well. Now the old bidies will have to put more into their churching in order to get God's forgiveness for what they felt toward Maggie. One would think that everybody would be welcome to the house of prayer, but that just was not exactly the truth. More hatred was in one building during church service than in any other one place that you could think of. Now that the collection plate was being passed around, Maggie put more money into the plate than any other person in the

church. This kind act didn't help build love, or gain forgiveness, from the congregation. Maggie intentions were not to ask for forgiveness or love from the likes of this bunch; she was hoping to have the opposite reaction from them. Maggie figured these hypocrites needed more love and forgiveness than she did.

The Reverend slowly brought the service to a close with a big loud amen. "Amen. Let's Eat."

The oldest members struggled to their feet and put forth their best efforts to walk as fast as possible toward the church door. It was considered disrespectful for the young to walk out of the church ahead of the older people, except the very young. Any other day when there was no food involved, the young could make a mad dash to the door. It was ok. Today was different, the food was served to the oldest first, behind the preacher and his deacons, and to the next age group until the youngest' term came. The children could push and squeal like pigs and eat like pigs, it was all right.

The Reverend led the regular members, and the sometime members, through the food line. All the sisters made sure that the Pastor had a generous helping from every box. The old boy was a big eater and had no problem with a full stacked plate of vittles. The Reverend might have been one of the few who had courage enough to eat from all the sister's baskets, including the root-lady's box.

The community had a very limited number of chairs to sit in, therefore, cars, trucks, wagons and the ground were used for places to sit and eat. The insects attacked from all directions. The flies and gnats attacked from the air and the ants and other crawling critters attacked from the ground. Even a few birds showed up to share in the feasting. There was enough food for all, including every dog living within trotting distance to the church. There were two special critters that showed up for the big church picnic, the Sheriff and his deputy.

The Sheriff and his deputy were only doing their jobs by coming out to the picnic, have a healthy helping of food and checking on Uncle Frank and Uncle Frank's booze supply. The Sheriff knew the same as all the others in the community, that when the total local Negro population got together trouble is never too far away. Food may slow down the effects of the hundred and fifty proof white lightning, but only for a little while. The Sheriff and his deputy walked with their plates so they could see who, what and where of the meeting. Another reason they continued to walk was to avoid providing a stationary target for the millions of insects competing for the grub.

Uncle Barlow was in his usual spot under his favorite oak tree near the cemetery, from where he could watch the members of the community show their best and worst selves. Uncle Barlow had witnessed this same play so many time that he could write the script before hand and wouldn't miss an act. He saw the Sheriff and the deputy collect food from Sister Ruby's basket and enjoy the food without fearing her mojo powers. He saw Roy Evans drank himself into becoming a candidate for spending the night in jail; he usually did that every year. Uncle Barlow knew that nothing would change these people's journey to their own destruction; they didn't seem to want any more or less than what they already had. He had to conclude that this may be what their destinies were and they could not break the possible preordained directions of their lives.

J D and his company had their plates and were walking toward their observation perch to sit in the cool shade and enjoy all that was to be had. J D continued on to where Uncle Barlow was gumming his foods. J D never got enough of what the old man could put into words. Uncle Barlow could put in his conversation what nobody in the community could even think.

"Evening Uncle Barlow.' ' dese gnats sho is bad today."

"Yea, dye got ta eat too, same as us.' 'Have a sit-down if ya want ta."

J D kept his mouth shut while eating more out of respect for Uncle Barlow than anything to do with eating ethics. It was the local custom to let the older person lead the conversation. J D saw how tough it would be for Uncle Barlow to gum his food and talk at the same time, His false teeth were not for eating. In the meantime, J D watched the people do what they knew how to do best, shuck and jive. He saw Wilma going down the path toward the ladies outhouse.

J D still had problems with how to think about what once was between Wilma and him. He saw that she was a piece along in family way. He had not heard who the daddy was and he never asked. He had the feeling that he had lost something precious. He was still in a state of mourning for the lost of a time and experience that will always be with him; but he can never have again.

"Wha's on yo mind young fellow?"

"Nothin in particula.' 'Ah seen yu out heah by yoself and decided ta jine ya."

"Ah reckon ya got a little gal heah sommers."

"Nosuh, Ah wish Ah did."

"Ya got tiahm a plenty fo yu too old."

The Sheriff and his deputy were moseying around the edges of the church grounds looking for actions that would set well with his constituency; the whites who voted him in as their sheriff. The Sheriff's job was not to provide security for the darkes but to make sure no crazy whites came through causing trouble for the blacks. His keeping the Negroes in line had more to do with protecting the system than protecting any one or two people of either group, especially Negroes. Trouble between the races resulted in causing the good white folks problems. The white population depended heavely on the darkies being happy and willing to do good work. There was nothing more aggravating on Monday morning than having a bunch of disgruntled Negroes to deal with.

No sooner than the Shireff and the deputy got about even with the well, who pops up out of the woods but Evans, drunker than a corm-mash eating chicken feeding around a whiskey still. The fool came wobbling toward the Sheriff and the deputy wobbling worst than a bent rim wobbles on a T-Modle ford. Evans didn't spot the law until it was too late to turn back, even if he could have turned back, which was doubtful. He said nothing when the deputy led him to the Sheriff's car.

Uncle Barlow and J D watched the scenes unfold before their eyes. One observer was near the end of his journey through life and the other was at the beginning of his journey through life. Uncle Barlow had seen many lives come into existence and then disappear into the dark hole of eternity to never be again except in the memories of the ones left behind. A small number of people were Uncle Barlow's age here in the county, but he was the oldest male living here in the Antioch community.

"Uncle Barlow wuz ya dee one dat built dis church?"

"Ah wuz jess one uf de men who worked on dis old barn.' 'All de othes who help build dis church is rite out dar." He pointed toward the cemetery. Dis is de new church."

"Ya knowed all dem burred out dar?

"Most all.' 'Ya see, de old church wuz built when Ah wuz a boy and dar wuz no graveyard.' 'Ah kin recollect when dey had de first burial heah.' 'Ah wuz a small boy 'bout de size uf dat litle youngun ova yonda." Nodding his head in the direction of a boy who was about three years old.

"Wuz folks de same den as dey is now?'

"'Bout de same, dey ain't changed much.' 'All de folks at dis church today came fahm somebody who is bured heah in dis graveyard.' 'De histry uh dese folks is written on de headstones in dis graveyard.' 'Even dat cracka Sheriff got some kin bured out dar, and he knowit."

"Ya don say.' 'Ain't dat a foot stompin hallelujah."

"Yea, Ah 'spect if de dead could come back and tell wha dey know a few uh us wouldn be actin so high-and-mighty."

J D saw that the old man was ready to shuffle back to the feeding trough for some deserts. He had no space on the plate for cake and pie the first trip to the food tables.

"Son, Ah reckon Ah'll make ma way back fuh some uf de sistas' pies and cakes."

"Yessuh, Ahm ready fuh somethin sweet maself."

By this time everybody was about as miserable as they could possibly be without falling dead. It would be hard to find a more miserable bunch than this anywhere except in hell itself. They were miserably dressed, miserably full of food, miserably bugged in this miserable heat. Nobody could be as miserable as these folks and not find something or somebody to take it out on. The time was getting right for the venting of miseries. The only members of the group that didn't seem to have ill wills toward others on their minds were the children. Their innocence won't last long; the old wrongdoes will show them how to live a totally dysfunctional life style.

J D saw his crowd beginning to bunch up near the well where everybody wound up sooner or later. The young men didn't mind drawing a bucket of cool fresh water for the young ladies no matter how many time the young ladies came to the well. To keep control of the well, they had to draw water for all the others too. That was the price one had to pay in order to have an excuse to say stupid things to the girls. The girls didn't seem to know the difference, and didn't seem to care either.

Bud, Paul, Allen, Tommy, John and J D were sitting on or standing near the two pickups. Paul and J D were in charge of the trucking and would have to be ready to transport people when the gossiping, eating and lying was over. They would drive the older people home and come back for the boys. The girls would be riding with the first load out. The mothers and grandmothers made sure that the gals went with the first load. T J and Willie held on to the job of drawing water for all the thirsty congregation, but their targets were the girls. Everybody, except these two nitwits, knew that the young ladies eyes were looking in the direction of the pickup trucks and were using the well as an excuse to get near the men near the trucks.

Aunt Sal paraded up to the well with her two young'uns in tow like a proud hen with biddies. She sure knew how to fire up the wagging tongues. The old sisters weren't too interested in truth; they were more interesting in entertainment in the form of gossip. Rumors were always welcome among this collection of holy mothers of the church. It didn't really matter wheather the rumors were true or not as long as they were about acts of forbidden behaviors. Aunt Sal fulfilled all the inputs needed to make a good rumor. Aunt Sal was not the only one who had children that resembled other children in the community. There were other look-alikes and it didn't come from tribal genetics either, or did it.

The knee-bending gamblers made their way to the feeding trough after the regular tithers had their fill. The dirty-kneed boys didn't have to worry about food running out: the worry was that all the food would not be consumed. The leftovers could not be saved until another day due to the heat and the invading insects. Cooked food bagan spoiling the moment it cool enough for bacteria, air borned or other wise, to attack. A few of the old ironbelleys had no problem consuming half spoiled grub. These dice shooters appearance fueled another round of tongue wagging. Everybody including the children knew that these knee-gamblers didn't come to church to be saved from their sinning ways. No sire, they were at the meeting to practice their sinful ways.

The self-righteous congregation was not seeking good news about anybody. They were not paying much attention to members doing their Christian duties; they were probing for the whispering kind of dirt on their fellow Christian and the not-so Christians alike. The home folks had plenty good wholesome news about members of their immediate families. They wanted to enjoy bad news relative to somebody else's family other than their own. They needed to hear about sin, and the wages of sin committed by others that make their sin almost disappear completely. They wanted mouth-watering jucy dirt on somebody. The self-righteous needed to hear about really big sins in others; sins that made their own look like child's play.

The Reverend was now full as a tick and starting his rounds through the crowd to give out free blessing and praising the Lord. There were no greater rewards than being the biggest fish in a small pond.

"Bless ya Sista Ruby.' 'Dat wuz some chocolate cake yu baked."

"Would ya lak notta piece Reverend?"

"Ahm 'bout to bust, Sista."

"Ah'll put yu ah piece in dis papa bag ta take wid ya."

"'Preciate dat Sista."

"Howdy do Miss Ann?"

"Faily middlin, Reverend.' 'Faily middlin."

"Lawd have mercy, Sista."

Allen hadn't sold a drop of his stolen moonshine when

Uncle Frank left for the joint to pick up another gallon of corn and a few half pints of sealed whiskey. He had run smack dab out.

Allen saw his chance to get rid of a few half pints even if he had to sell to the younger fellows. Uncle Frank was not about to let the elders catch him selling liquoir to the young'uns. That's where Allen came in; he would sell to the boys without blinking an eye. But, it would be bad if Uncle Frank caught him selling whiskey to anybody, even the customers that he didn't dare sell to under the noses of the elders. Allan might get less butt kicking if he got caught by the Sheriff than he would get if he got caught by Uncle Frank. Uncle Frank did not cotton to Allen's arrogant smart-alecky ways. Uncle Frank hated uppity niggers almost as bad as the rednecks did.

The Negro population did more to enforce the unwritten Jim Crow laws than the southern crackers ever did. The colored had no chance of winning in a confirntation with the whites, and they knew it. Therefore, trouble hurt the colored far more than it hurt whites no matter who or what starts it. The Negroes having no protection from the law, not being allowed to defend themselves and having no civil rights put them in a loosing position when there came a showdown between the races. colored with the sense God gave an ape knew how to avoid a hanging. There was nothing more frightening to the coloreds than a bunch of bloodthirsty ignorant mad crackers. So, the colored made sure that their folks stayed in their assigned social order. One Negro getting out of order could spoil the week-end for the whole colored community.

J D was getting to the point where he was afraid to be anywhere near Allen, especially with peckerwoods around. He always felt that deep down fear nagging at his innards. At times he wished he could rid himself of that feeling like there was big trouble lurking just around the corner for him or some of his loved ones. His fears made him careful enough to do whatever necessary to avoid trouble with these Negro killers. When it came to his family, he often thought that his carefulness may not be enough to portect them. All Negroes didn't feel the same though. The insecure position Negroes occupied in the southern social order sure didn't do much for Allen; it seemed to make Allen even crazier than he already was.

Allen didn't drink or smoke which was a blessing. J D thought that Allen was a big enough fool without the added affects of a gut full of moonshine

"If dat fool got drunk he wouldn las as long as a chicken would las in a pigpin wid a chicken-eatin hawg."

Allen zeroed in on those weekend drunks who either owed Uncle Frank for booze of had other reasons for avoiding him. These non-customers of Uncle Frank's were to be Allen's regular customers. These drunks who were in need of some cheap moonshine services had a new man on the job, Allen. Allen was and had always been one of the young men who lacked the usual fears that were necessary for keeping the men safe from the expressed haterd of an unfriendly social system.

"We gittin ready ta take de old folk home.' ' We'll be back inna spell.'

"We'll be heah til de end" Allen replied, smiling all the time.

J D did not hesitate getting away from Allen and his hairbrained schemes

"Dat boy is gonna git us all kilt if we buddy round wid em."

The church set on a level few acres nestling between two hills. The slower moving caravans started for home first. This group was usually the first to leave and the last to arrive home. The walkers and buggy riders didn't hurry; it was too hot to be in a hurry. The dust raised by the departing congregation never was kicked higher than a few feet above the road bed; there was no moving air. The dust collected on the low bushes and hung there until some critter or rain shook it from its rest. Now that the big Sunday was over, the church-goers were beginning the journey back to business as usual. To the members this day is the highlight of their days in the community. The putting away of their best Sunday-go-to-meeting clothes was proof that it was over until another special day comes by.

The few good times of the year these country folks had to look forward to came on special days like this. There were no everyday goodtimes to be had. Special times that required days, if not monthes, to get ready for, were all they needed to give an old fashion hoedown. The wagons, the buggies and the walking locals fanning out in all directions toward home were the final reminders for thoses still hanging out at the church, or near by, that darkness was not too far away and the lack of light would put an end to the fun day.

Uncle Frank hauled his stock back to his joint just in case the night hounds wanted to extend their arguments, shucking and jiving and plain old juking a few hours longer. Maggie, her brothers and the regular jukers from the woods, crawled into their vehicles and headed for the Alabama line and the only honky-tonk within miles. They were full, sanctified and ready to hear some low-down blues.

Chapter Twenty-three

▼

The gang was already at the joint when J D, John and Willie pulled in. These people were hell bent to get back to everyday reality before the evening was over. Maggie and several others had actually attended the service at the church. They had gone the limits too; they put money in the collection basket. Sundays were special days for these hard working country folks and did not represent the normal everyday existence. Sundays were for dreaming of better tomorrows. Nobody in their right minds expected to see any changes for the better in their life times. They sung about, talked about and prayed about a heaven after death, but nobody seemed to be in a rush to get there. These good old boys and Maggie too, were here to charge up their nerves for what they knew will be the true reality of their being come Monday morning. The sinning would start and set the stage for the following week. The jukebox was loaded with mood-setting blues.

"Ah got some shine left if y'all want to snort." Allen offered."

Willie had to know. "Wha at?"

"Comon."

The other young men were too busy watching Maggie get back to her reality. She was doing her thing on the dance floor, alone. Maggie just didn't feel right being all cleaned up of her guilt and all. She was eager to return to her place of confort. She stuck with the things that she was good at and she knew what those things were. Pretending to be something that she was not didn't set right with her at all. She had been told enough times about the life she lived. How it will catch up to her farther down the road and on and on. Maggie did today what she always did after church when doubts started worming their way into her consciousness. She danced.

Uncle Dan interrupted the show by realing and tottering through the door."Whars Frank at." He wanted to know.

This man had consumed all his stash of sipping whiskey for the coming week and needed to restock. The old fellow had very little to keep him going and his sipping helped a lot. There was no way he was going home empty handed. Old Dan had been drinking pretty much all day and yesterday too which didn't improve his driving much. Uncle Dan's driving ability could not get much worst than it was anyway. He couldn't drive a lick.

Two brothers came in from over in Alabama on their way to the county seat in Mississippi. They stopped in for a mason jar of homebrew and to tell the news. They told about trouble up their way between a colored man and some white trash. They said that he might be headed toward Mississippi where he had family. That's what they were doing now, going to the county seat to tell his family to expect him, that was the least they could do. The two collected their brew and left.

Now J D felt a need for a swallow of the stump juice. That old sensation of danger came up from his guts where he tried to barricade it out of existence. After hearing that news, his heart changed its rhythm. He would never get used to that nagging fear every time somebody steps out of line with the unwritten customs and disturbs the peace between these shallow minded people. J D took his fears as proof that he was not as courageous as the other men. The others tended to attract troubles that could be easily avoided if they would take a second to think about what the result of their actions would be. They were either brave or stupid, maybe both.

Nobody said anything as the Alabama boys told the story. Nobody asked any questions at all. Knowing the fact behind the causes of these kinds of troubles didn't matter at all. Just being interesting in the facts alone came close to asking the parties to base their actions on the use of good sense. That was asking too much from a system that grew out of false beliefs and ignorance. Questioning the actions of certain people was considered being disloyal to the entire United States and all its citizens. The existing order of maintaining social harmony would buckle under the pressures of rationality. The citizens were hardly ever punished for breaking the written laws, but might get hung for violating one of the unwritten laws. This knowing how to live peacefully was not learned in school. Questioning the authority was definitely a no-no.

Mississippi's citizens learned the hard way to avoid trouble by keeping their mouths shut when it came to disagreeing with long held beliefs. They held on to the old ways of behaving even though the returning soldiers were bringing news from other parts of the country about different ways of doing business with people of other races. Changing the social ways of ignorant people is almost an impossibility. This mind changing might require an act of God.

The news of the troubles seemed to sober up the night owls a bit. There was no real positive interest in the news at all. The men sort of gave the news a respectful moment of silence, then got back to what they did best, nothing.

"Ah wish he'd come by heah Ahda took em to town." Allen finally spoke out.

"Dat's 'cause ya ain't got good sense." John said to nobody in particular even though Allen had spoke of helping a colored man that was in trouble.

J D again felt like getting away, far away from possible trouble. It was all he could do to wait a few minutes before suggesting to his brother and cousins to leave. He felt that anything that the men here would do to assist the colored in trouble would only make matters worst. Negroes were not allowed to help each other in defense against attacts from the white side of the racial divide. Some of his fears of coming anywhere near racial troubles were rooted in his position of being helpless to provide protection for his people. Taking a position of peacemaker between any potential conflicting people was a dangerous place to be. There was no safe position for a mediator either. The two peoples' senses of fair play across racial boundaries were thousands of miles apart. They never trusted mediators none at all. You were with them or against them, simple as that. Under the Jim Crow system of controlling the under class there was no middle ground.

"Allen, yu might be right in plannin ta go nawth."

"Ah told ya J, Ahm not plannin on spending de res uf mah life lookin up ta some dumb hillbillys."

"De dumb hillbillys is not de only problem wid dis dawg gon mess."

Reverend Mayfield's sermon was often about following biblical laws that offered a happier way to live. J D had started thinking about becoming more involved in the church. Night services ran for the entire week following the big meeting.

"J D, let's ride inta town tomor night."

"Ah thank Ah'll take de famly ta church all nex week.' 'Ya kin come and go wid us, if ya wan ta Al."

"Dat's right.' 'Dey's havin night service nex week.' 'Ah'll thank boutit."

"Ah got Mista. Britton's truck all week justa ta take de folks ta church."

Everybody was on the lookout for any strange movements along the road on their way home. There was a small chance of spotting a man on the run because he would not be able to tell who was friend or foe. Therefore, he most likely would hide when he saw a vehicle coming from any direction. One of the greatest evils of this Jim Crow system was that a Negro on the run from an angry white mob had no friends.

"De po soul would go in de otha direction if he had de sense God gave a fool." J thought. "He might head fur de way otta de county dat de mob leas pect"

J D wanted to believe that the person, who ever he was, had sense enough to not do what was expected, or what most crazy scared colored did when on the run.

Bud had been quiet all day and half the night. Bud didn't ask for something that was not already within his reach. He did what was expected of him and no more.

"Look y'all, dese thangs will hapen and ain't nothin we kin do ta stop em."

Bud didn't question the way it was, is and will be.

"Ah spect he done somthin bad, in dem crackas eyes anyhow." Willie added his opinion.

A rabbit ran across the road in front of the truck as if something was hot on its tail. Rabbits were the staple diet for every critter from man to the slithering snakes. None of the men said a word because they all were reminded by the running rabbit of a reality that none of them wanted to think about.

J D was bothered by what Willie said; the man must have done something bad. He had been trying to figure out why the system was the way it was. He had asked the question when Mark had to leave the state. He asked the same questions when Connie left on the run, if he left that is, and when Jeff was killed. The Reverend also made reference to the belief that one reaped what he sowed.

"Do y'all believe dat people deserve de thangs dat hapen ta em?"

"Dat depends ohn wha ya mean by dat." Bud tried to close this kind of talking.

"If it's a fact dat man reap wha he sow, y'all betta come and go wid us ta church evry night nex week.' 'If yu boys don change ya ways Ah hate ta thank bout wha's in stoe fur y'all."

There were about one tenth of the people at church Monday night as was at the big meeting held on Sunday. This turnout was considered good because of it being during the week and at night, not to mention the absent of food. The leaders of the church could always trust a particular group to be at church all the time. These true belivers had faith in the powers of both good and evil. Which they believed in more was a question that had to be answered carefully. The answer to this question will depend on who is involved, what is the objective and when, where and why one exercised the faith. These people had a precription for just about any ailment that might need attention. The precription would be based on what it was that you wanted done. People prayed for both good and bad things to happen to others. They went to the church, hoodoo, voodoo and other sources of power for blessings, healings and to settle up for wrongs done to them. One member of the church had to be led around like a small child because of a long ago spell casted on her by one of the local hoo-doo queens, as the saying goes.

The story was that Mrs. Evans had taken up with a lady's husband who lived down around New Jorden Baptist Church. One Sunday the wife of this man came to Antioch Baptist Church. She didn't go inside the church, but met Mrs. Evans on the outside before the services started. Nobody heard what the lady said to Mrs. Evans but Uncle Barlow was looking at the lady when she put her finger in Mrs. Evans' face. Mrs. Evans never told what the lady had said but Mrs. Evans walked into the church, sat down and stared at the back end of the church through the entire service. She lost the baby that she was carring at the time and started to slowly lose her mind. Some of the old timers say that the spell could not be broken because it was cast because of an unforgivable sin. It was thought by some that the voo doo had nothing to do with the woman going crazy; it was her own guilt that did it.

Spells are used to realize a wish, protect what one has, protection from enemies and sometimes to influence the weather to be favorable to growing crops. The spiritual worlds and their angles were always part of everybody's daily lives in Mississippi. The road to peace and success was littered with hills and swamps. It helped if the spirits were on your side at all times. You had to be extremely careful not to anger any of the spirits, the good ones nor the evil ones. The people who had an inside line to the siritual worlds were kept busier than the local preachers.

Allen and Miss Ruby Mae rode up to the church as big as you please. Allen had gotten himself a new part-time job. He was Miss Ruby's transpotation to and from Mobile, New Orleans and other near cities. Miss Ruby Mae was as much a part of the religious community as the preachers were. They all served the same group of people. People of this community belonged to all social services in this little community. Sunday shouters, drunks, preachers, bootleggers and all the others were one and the same people. The service providers went to where their customers were. Allen and Miss Ruby Mae were no exception.

Allen was slowly becoming a community maverick. The usual social rules that a colored young man had to follow offered limited choices for accomplishing any meaningful existence. Therefore, a few of the young men chose to walk the narrow roads between the two sets of rules applied to the two separate groups. This bunch of youngsters became somewhat social outcasts. The returning migrants with their tall tales of good lives waiting in distance cities made matters worse for the local system and those who were trying to get along within it.

Planning a future or making plans of any kinds was risky business. People living in the deep south very seldom made plans from within themselves. These poor folks were reactors, not initiators, in the games of life. There was no room for error within their narrow-minded realities of what it was all about. Misstakes were unforgivable and were usually punished unmercifully.

J D had plenty time to think about what it means to be alive in the world, especially the part he lived in. Working for Mr. Britton was about the best job that he could ever hope for, yet it led nowhere. How do folks make thing better for themselves and others as well? This was the big question J.D. asked himself every day.

"Allen, whadda ya thank yu is doin?"

"Tryin ta make nough money ta git outta dis hea messed up place.' 'Nottin is gonna change fuh us down heah in de South, J D"

"Jess spose ya is wrong, spose we kin make thangs betta wid de help uf de good Lawd."

"Ah don wan ta wait til it's too late, J."

"Look Allen, mabbe we kin pray harda and work though de church and brang bout some change fuh de betta fuh evrybody, both coloreds and whites."

"Let's go in de church J.' ' Dey'is preachin in dar, ya don need ta preach out heah."

The Reverend liked to start services as soon as possible due to the poor lighting in the church house. The electric company had installed the power lines as far as the Clark's store but had a ways to go before they reached the Antioch community. Lantern and lamp lights were hard to read by. The people in the church had no problems because they didn't read anyway. They had heard the same sermons and sung the same songs for as long as anybody could remember. Even the small children knew all the song and sermons by heart.

The Sermon title was "Leave "Vengence ta de Lawd." The Reverend must have picked that particular one due to it being Monday, just after the big meeting when all the hate-mongers were together in one place. He knew that most likely some old dormant grudges had been resurrected at Sunday's services. Some of the grudges went so far back until the reasons for them had been forgotten a long time ago.

J D was looking for ways to help the Negroes become each other's best friends, instead of each other's worst enemies. He knew for sure that Allen and Miss Ruby Mae brought back ways and means to do harm to other colored folks, not to the whites. J D didn't believe the Lord needed help in getting folk to reap what they sow. But there were those that figured that maybe the Lord needed their help to fulfill the prophecy of the Bible.

The Reverend announced the news about T J (everybody called him foots because of the size of his feet) being snake bitten. The latest news was that T J was in the hospital up in Meridian.

T J, Paul, George and Joe were working for Mr. Willie Grey cutting pulpwood when T J stepped on the rattler. The place where the men were working was no more than two hundred feet from where Paul's truck was parked. Paul, George and Joe wasted no time in getting Foots in the truck and hauling tail for town. Paul drove as fast as the conditions allowed which was a top speed of twenty-five to thirty-five miles per hour. The leg had started turning blue by the time they got Foots into the colored waiting area of Doctor Holyfeild's office.

The Doctor took one look at the snake bitten leg and knew that Foots should be sent to the hospital sixty-three miles to the north. The doctor did what he could for Foots and told the group to take the young man to the hospital; he'll call ahead so they will be ready to receive the boy.

Paul and the others knew exactly where the hospital was. They all had been there many times before. Now that they had good roads Paul could make some time. The hospital was a good hour away even driving far above the speed limits. There was an ambulance service in town but they didn't haul colored people. The other choice was to ask the one funeral home to use the one hearse to take the hurting and scared fellow to the hospital. Foots was frighten enough already without crawling into the back of the hearse. Paul and gang decided to drive Foots to the hospital. The trip to the hospital was made easer for Foots because of the pain killers the doctor gave him.

The hospital kept Foots more for observation than for any dangers that he would die. Foots was young, healthy and tough. He surely would not have died if he had not come to the Doctor and the hospital and just went to see Miss. Ann; the midwife. She had saved a lot of them in her day. The medical system had never been too accommodating to the Negro population.

The Negroes in the south had learned to work with herbs, roots, magic, incenses and prayers to cure just about anything that went wrong with their health. These remedies and cures took very good care of these poor ignorant folks. At least these medical practices did less harm than the doctors and hospitals did many times. If a colored really wanted to meet his maker, go to the hospital or to the doctor. These coloreds looked after their own even while in the hospital, or under the doctor's care. He might go to the doctor or hospital but he took with him his medicine from home. Most of the times the praying community and the magic workers went to the hospital, made home visits and received patients to make absolutely sure the proper powers were involved in getting the sick back on healthy feet.

Snakebite didn't elicit too many concerns for the usual evil fighters, mostly because it happened in the woods and not in somebody's home. These religious workers and sorcery people usually checked out the circumstances surrounding all unfortuants events just to make sure things were on the up and up. Not all bad lucks that happened to the members of the communities needed these healers attention.

Mr. Willie Grey was at the banks' waiting for the news that he knew would be there about T J. The old cracker worried about everybody who worked for him. His workers thought he was fairer to the colored people than most whites were.

"How is dat boy doin?"

"He be jess fine, Mista. Grey.' 'One little old snake can't hurt dat boy none Mista Grey."

"Sho glad to heah he's doing good."

Foots came home the next day from the hospital. The doctors discharged foots but had sympathy for the snake. They said that the snake might have gotten the worst end of the encouter. Foots made the best out of his moment on the community stage by pretending to be helpless a lot longer than was necessary.

The hospital was no place for a colored person to go. The number one reason was that he would not get the proper treatment that might be necessary for curing what ails him. The second reason was that he had no money to pay for the few days of rest. A few days could easily relieve the family of their year's earning. There was no such thing as insurance to cover the cost. The only insurance that anybody ever heard of was a burial insurance that might come from their membership in the brotherhood of the Masons. The returning soldiers had some veteran's benefits; none of the boys had tried taking the advantage of these alleged benefits though.

The only honorable thing to do with a permanently disabled Negro is to let him die. Friends and relatives got together at night to sit up with the sick until he took a notion to go and meet his maker. These small farming day-workers were just making it with everybody working that could walk. Having to skimp by on next to nothing was one reason these people needed all the spritual help that they could get from where ever.

J D went to church every night, taking his family and whoever else wanted a ride. He did a lot of trying to make sense out of the way his folks lived and why they lived so. There were very few folks he knew that thought beyond tomorrow. They had long ago lost the will to search for reasons for anything. J D thought maybe there were answers if only somebody would ask the right questions. J D had a notion that fear was one reason that nobody had any questions. Asking questions were showing doubt, or a lack of faith in the people, or things that were in control. There was no forgiveness for a lack of faith in those who are entrusted with the powers to provide for the children of the system.

J D was afraid to trust the trustees and he was afraid to not trust the trustees. He had no proof that trusting the trustees helped anything at all; he also had no proof that it didn't work either. His week in church without his group of young men shucking and jiving in his ear helped him to make up his mind to try giving the Lord his due and maybe the Lord will see to it that the way will be a little clearer. A lack of faith in the world that he lived in rendered him vulnerable to any sliver of hope that slid his way.

J D had never had reasons to believe in his ever finding a way around the work and hardship he saw up ahead. He was on a never-ending search for something positive to believe in. The church was the only hope he had of ever overcoming his unlimited uncertainties of the future.

CHAPTER TWENTY-FOUR

▼

The year's harvest was nearly over when Sand Field Baptist Church decided to throw its yearly shindig for the Lord. The beech, chestnut and oak trees had turned to living flames. The squirrels were busy hiding acorns in every crack and hole they could find. The many kinds of birds had begun to form their flying formations to head farther south for the winter before the cold winds begin to blow. Sand Field Church was ready to harvest its share of the leftovers after debts had been paid, or forgiven until the next harvest. All living critters were getting ready for the coming winter, except the grasshoppers and the community loafers. Now was the time to give thanks for a bountiful season. The local community leaders knew when to hit the folks up for a token of appreciation in the form of cash tithes.

The corn, sugar cane, beans and other crops still in the fields gave the landscapes a beautiful golden color in the Sunday morning sun. The half cut fields of hay gave off a sweet and pleasing scent that any old country boy could appreciate. The dead cotton stacks hung their heads in surrender to a job well done. The young calves, chicks, goats and other stock born this past Spring were nearly big enough for sale or slaughter. J D figured a man had to be crazier than a mule with a belly ache not to love Mississippi in the fall of the year.

J D drove slowly so the dust and the wind would not mess up the gals's hair and blow the boys' hats off. He would just have to stop and wait for the boys to run back a few hunderd feet to get their hats. The girls had pieces of sheets and whatever else they could get to cover their freshly ironed hair. He made sure to slow down to a crawl when he passed people walking and riding in wagons to keep from dusting up their Sunday clothes...

Daddy and mommy were in the cab, Bud and the boys were hanging on the finders and the tailgate while the girls were sitting on quilts in the bed of the truck. Nobody was talking much. Kin folks had very little to say to each other because each knew what the other knew anyway. Everybody in or on the truck was kin except Foots. He might as well had been kin due to the way he was accepted into the family. Everybody was looking forward to a day at Sand Field church just because the members of this church were not likely to be kin to the members of Antioch Baptist Church, or New Rock.

J D saw the automobiles, wagons and horses in the church yard and knew there were going to be oodles of folks here today. J D hadn't had a grilfriend for quite a spell and was on the hunt for female company. Every boy there was doning the same thing except those who had girlfriends already. The boys with steady girls will have their hands full just watching to make sure none of them outsiders got a chance to pinch their girls on their behinds. This was a big day which might offer a young man an opportunity to grab someone to share the burden of life with, at least some of it anyway. J D figured that he had a better than even chance because he had transpotation, even if he didn't own the truck. He pulled the truck as close to the shady side of the trees as he could get without spooking the horses. It was still pretty warm up in the middle of the day.

The young ladies were in no big hurry to get inside the church today because they too were searching for something more than just maintaining the lowest level of existence. The girls were too old to hang on to their mom's skirt-tails; therefore, these young women took their time going to the outhouse and coming back to the church grounds. None of the young men escaped their attention. Most of the folks, both young and old, knew each other even though they didn't see each other except on special days like these. They had to make the best of times like these if they wanted to catch the eye of somebody who can make them feel pretty.

J D didn't realize he was staring at little Eunice until she smiled at him. You could have knocked him over with a feather right then. She sure had become something since the last time he had seen her. It had been over three years since he had seen her and that was in the cotton field. He had never thought much about something going on between them, but he had always liked her since they were about seven or eight years old. He could not take his eyes off her as she went into the church. She gave him another look just before entering the church.

Eunice was next to the oldest of about five children. She had one sister older than she. The whole family was on the light brown skinned side and had wavy hair. Eunice had a line of freckles running across her face with a cluster right in the center of her nose. J D suddenly felt good about life in general and this day in particular. That will be something if he came over here and seduce the best looking girl in the whole bunch.

Bud and the rest of the Antioch and New Rock bunch were sort of keeping to themselves here at Sand Field Baptist Church. These country boys over here were very protective of their women folks. They didn't hold to outsiders coming to their church specifically looking for women. The Sand Field boys were always between the girls and the outsiders, except when the girls decided to strut down to the outhouse.

The preacher's sermon was about doing unto others as you would have then do unto you. Everybody had heard that same preaching all their lives and still didn't understand exactly what that was all about. There wasn't anybody that these people knew fitting that description. Treating others the same as you treat yourself? These old boys claimed to be God-fearing Christians but not God-fearing enough to love others as they loved themselves.

Eunice would throw a glance to the rear of the church every few minutes to where J D and the outsiders were sitting. J D's old heart remembered what it was like to be excited over a girl.

"Is Eunice givin ya de eye J?"

"Ah don thank so."

Bud and the others didn't argue the lie. They all knew what good luck was. Any of the young men would gladly trade his britches for what they could plainly see could belong to J D

The young men sit near the door which was at the front of the church and the pulpit was at the rear. They would leave one by one without destrubing the congrigation and the god they were praying to.

All the young men were out of the church long before the prayers were prayed. J D was the one and only young man not being a member of the church that remained inside until the collection was raised. He had several reasons for remaining inside and none had anything to do with his desire to tithe.

The Sand Field Church services were short like most of the folks wanted it to be, most of the young anyway. The food was being served when J D walked back to the eating area. He thought it looked better if he and his crowd waited until the locals had a go at the vituals. At least the gnats and flies weren't so bad this time of the year due to the cool westerly winds coming through. The Sand Field cooks were famous for their chicken and dumplins, collard greens and hamhocks and good old sweet potatoe pies. There were others providing services other than the preacher and the cooks.

Uncle Frank and Allen had to tip-toe with their selling sipping whiskey out here. The areas had its own hell-bound suppliers of devil's juice. The juke joint was only one hundred and fifty yards from the church. The church's joint location with other nearby conveniences made it easy for those who wanted to enjoy pure hypocrisy. The artesian well was exactly at the half-way mark between the church and the honky-tonk. Uncle Frank parked near the well because everybody came to the well. His regular customers knew where he was at all times. The local bad boys were setup at the joint where there were sandwiches, drinks, candy, and cigarettes. You name it, they had it. The shucking-and-jiving hall is the joint of the area even when there is no church services going on. These old country boys had the same needs to vent their frustration like all the other communities.

"Do ya wanna swallow uf dis feel-good stuff J D?"

"Nawh! Nawh! Ya know Ah don drank dat mess,"

J D had something else on his mind besides drinking rotgut shine. He remained close to the well and the path leading to the lady's outhouse. His heart told him to wait right there and do whatever it took to get the attention of the prettiest girl in these parts. Eunice might be a sign of better things coming for him. He had worked all summer, saved a few dollars, paid his tithes and did all the required doings for a young man to reap a few good blessings. He was dreaming so hard until he never noticed Eunice walking in his direction until he heard his name spoken like he had never heard it spoken before.

"Howdy J D!"

J D had no idea how to talk right then. He stared at the local beauty, chocked up something terrible, and promptly forgot all he ever knew. If he had been a little lighter in color he would've turned red as a beet. He had forgotten every word that he had rehersed to say to this gal.

"How yew be Mista. Banks?"

Ah, Ah'm doin jess fine.' How yu been doin?"

"How come ya don come over heah mo ofen?"

"Ah 'spect dat Ah will fahm ny ohn."

"Ya kin come ta mah house at any tahm ya wanna."

"Ah will."

At that point Eunice continued on down the path to the outhouse. J D was glad because he needed a few big glups of air to get started breathing normally again. He was sort of ashame of how he handled that meeting.

"Gawd dawgit, she must thank dat Ah don' got sense nough ta come in outta de rain." J said to himself. "She must thank Ah don' know diddly-squat 'bout nothin."

Figuring he had done enough damage for today, J D wanted to walk back to where the boys were. Then he heard the music again.

"Ah hope ta see ya Mista Banks." J D was still frozen in time and space until he heard the music.

"Ya no ya will, Eunice."

The boy finally go his locomotion cranked up; he moved on in the direction of his friends.

"We seen ya making eyes at Eunice." Bud and Paul were watching from the cab of Paul's pickup.

"Mind yo own bisness."

J D slid in the front seat of the pickup with Paul and Bud, grabbed the Mason jar and took a swig. The other two didn't have to comment, they understood.

"Let's go git us ah plate uf dem collads and hamhocks." Paul urged.

"Ah'm hongry 'nough ta eat raw aigs." Bud said as he and Paul strolled slowly toward the food tables.

J D wasn't hungry at all, but he followed anyway because he thought he might get another look at Eunice. This summer had been nothing but hard work for J D and he was grateful for any promise of his life getting better.

These hardworking farmers, or sons and daughters of farmers, had little to look forward to. They didn't have words to express contentment, comfort, beauty and happiness which were impossible within the limits of their means. Their daily philosophy was any life is better than no life. This narrow concept of life as barely getting along versus being dead is all these folks dared to hope for. If it wasn't for their religions, women and a plenty supply of sipping whiskey and maybe a pot of collard greens and hamhocks, life for colored folks in Mississippi wouldn't be worth a plugged nickle. The whites didn't have it much better than the colored did either, especially the poor white trash.

There were those whites, like the ones that sneaked by the church for a plate of colored folk's food, who were close to being worst off than the poorest colored. There was a large population of these so called white-trash people living in the Sand Field community. The one big difference between the poor whites and the poor colored was the poor whites refused to perform certain kinds of labor that was considered colored-folk's work. Therefore, the poor whites were more likely to be unemployed than the colored were. These poor slobs thought they were too good to stoop to do what was considered colored work, even when they had no food in the house.

J D, Bud and Paul watched as the white trash filled their plates that they brought from home. These people figured themselves above eating with the colored, yet they thought nothing of coming by and fixing giant plates of food to take home with them.

"Do dey really thank dey is betta n us?" J D whispered.

"Nawh, dey know betta n'dat." Bud answered the question.

"Mabbe dey jess don wanna be widout hope." Paul knew that was often the case.

J D made up his mind a long time ago that he would not let false pride stand in his way and prevent him from becoming a good God fearing man. The Bible speaks of the sins of pride. He couldn't remember exactly how it read. He promised himself that he would look up that Bible passage.

"We got moe po whites den we got po colored." Paul said with pride.

"We got mo rich whites den we got rich colored too. " J answered.

"Ah ratha be colored in dese part den ta be po white trash.' Some uf dese po crackas sho catch hell."

"All dese po whites need is money ta be sombody.' 'We need ta become white and den have money too ta become sombody." Bud told them.

"Ah gess yu is still a nigguh no matta how much money yu got." Paul mumbled.

"Lawd, ain't dat de truth." Bud grunted.

All of this was common knowledge here in the deep south. These southern Negroes had accepted their assigned station in the southern ways for so long that when one thought about moving up to a higher social level he may be thought of as being crazy as a road lizard. The majority of these church-going, whiskey drinking and whoring colored folks had no other ambitions other than being good workers for the crackers. Lots of these colored folkd had manage to make a good irresponsible life down in the land of the tall pines.

J D had a rough time thinking about anything or anybody other than Eunice. She was still small for a grown woman but pretty as ever. Eunice's father and her oldest sister died within a one-year period. She had been nursing the sick members of her family for the past couple of years. This nursing dutie was the reason nobody saw much of this beautiful young lady. Eunice's grandma, on her father's side, died only nine months before her father passed. This sickness in the family was due to a curse put on the family back fifty years ago, so the rumor went.

The saying was that it started when Eunice's grandma had taken up with a married man who left his wife and children for her. They often say that Eunice is the carbon copy of this cursed grandma when the old lady was Enice's age. The old lady had once been too pretty for her own good.

The man's wife got up in church and told the congregation that nothing good would ever come of any family member that the pretty lady would ever have. The wife promised suffering, madness and death would be the family"s curse for all times. Some say the lady was a root lady from down New Orleans way. The root lady took her children and walked out of the church never to be seen again in this part of the county. Nobody knows what happened to her or where she made off to. All anybody knows for sure is that Eunice's grandma's health begin to fail and her mind started playing tricks on her in less than a year after she married Eunice"s grandpa. She slowly went mad.

The family went to every hoo-doo, voo-doo, mojo worker, preacher people in the country trying to fine a reverse to this sickness and madness. Nothing worked to bring relief to this believed-curse put on this family. The Family even went to the devil himself for relief. They tried witchcraft, but to no avail.Most of the young folks did not remember those times and took the family"s sickness as nothing more than the workings of the Lord.

Bud thought about Eunice"s family's ugly legend that was started long before Eunice was born." Yu know wha dey say bout dat family, don ya?"

"Awh, dat's jess a bunch uf non-sense."

"Hush Bud, de boy don' wanna heah dat kind uf talk." Paul came to J D's defense.

"Ah ain't payin Bud a bit uf 'tention."

J D knew of other families in the county that seem to get more than their share of bad luck. He had no answer for this kind of family luck other than it must be God's will, otherwise it would not be. J D had very little else to believe in outside the word of God. His confidence in man's basic goodness was reduced every time he took a close look at what these people did to each other when they thought no one was watching. J D prayed to God for sense enough to see a better side of mankind and prayed for more understanding of his people. He felt that the only protection from evil man had was God's mercy. J D prayed that a strong commitment to his church and a lot of hard work would be enough to break the string of what appeared to be bad luck that has been troubling the family for as long as anyone could remember.

CHAPTER TWENTY-FIVE

▼

The early fall rains and cold winds promised the farmers a hard winter. These country folks could read the signs of their natural surroundings but most could not sign their own name. They paid attention to the migrating birds, the behaviors of the squirrels, the growing winter coats on the live stock and the aches in their old knees and elbows. The deciduous trees were dropping their leaves earlier than normal and drifting into hibernation for the winter.

The cool westerly winds made the old timers want to snuggle up to a warm fire, chew tobacco, tell lies and remember things that never happened. The fall was a good time of the year for the old folks. They could smell the parching peanuts in the oven, enjoy the roasted sweet potatoes from the ashes in the fire place and those that had teeth could chew sugar cane. The seasons came, folks got old and died, babies were born to replace the dead and the endless cycle continued without much conscientious help from anybody.

J D and the young men often tried to decuss the meaning of this intelligence of the natural world. J D argued in favor of this natural know-how coming directly from God. A few of the boys believed that all these changes were by some kind of accident that just happened. Others of the barnstormers didn't have a clue and cared less about the whys of the natural world.

The seasonal work was nearly over and J D and John were finishing up with the corn and hay. The winter time would be stock feeding time with one exception, the butchering days. The remainder of the work consists of stocking fire-wood for cooking and heating the house and the store. These were supposed to be easy days for country folks. J D and John were coming to the end of the corn pulling time and planned to start cutting and hauling hay next week. They should finish up long before the Christmas holidays. They unloaded their last load of corn and headed for the store. After all this was Friday evening which was payday here at the Brittons.

"Dis sho has been a nice day fuh pullin and haulin cone." J said to John.

The two men worked from each side of the truck, pulling the ears from the corn stalks throwing the ears directly into the truck. The truck rode astride one row while idling in low gear which lets one person pull the corn from just behind as the truck move forward. The two men worked the center together and each had a row on the side. This was J D's idea. This idea didn't work on circular rows or on steep hills. Pulling corn was easy when the weather was dry and the earth was hard so the truck would idle along without stalling. The two men worked in silence for the remainder of the afternoon.

J D put gas in the truck for use on the weekend. He kept the truck at his house and used it for his personal running around. He normally paid for five gallons and that was too much for where he had to go. He was thinking about Eunice and their plans while he and John waited for Mr. Britton to bring their pay. That was one thing about white folks, no matter how good to Negroes they were, they took their sweet time when it came to paying off their colored help. Well, he had Eunice to think about while he waited for these slow Mississippi crackers to do right by their colored workers. J D suddenly had more than Eunice to think about on this cool and clear day when he saw the McCray's truck coming. "Doggonnit."

J D and John knew the evening calm had been destrubed when they recognized the old truck approaching the store. This was Friday and those boys were the McCrays and Mac. J D and John knew better than to challenge these idiots in any way what-so-ever. Having a fair relationship with the likes of these crackers was about as likely as a rooster and a fox being good buddies.

"Heah comes de same old stuff." John whispered.

"Ah don pay dem no neva mind." J D whispered back.

J D and John went in the store and started pretending to be busy searching for cold drinks from the bottom of the keg. The poor white trouble-makers followed the colored men. Jennie had grown to know how to handle this kind of problem in her store. She was not the young giggling little gal that she was two years ago.

"Did yu want somethin Mac?"

"Yea, Ah want somethin."

"Yew know wha Ah mean."

Mac didn't like being put in his place in front of coloreds.

"Wha are yu two boys looking fer?" Mac asked J D and John.

Neither of the men answered.

J D felt that familiar fear begin to boil up from the bottom of his being. He could think of nothing that would make that dreadful feeling go away. It looked like every time brighter days lay ahead something always got in the way. Trying to avoid a no-win conflict with the whites here in the deep south was like working with honey bees without getting stung. The colored always had to be one step ahead in order to prevent doing harm to the thin, fragile egos of these dumb white folks. The Negroes weren't much better. Good communication didn't exist between the races in the south during the forties.

"Ah ask y'all ah question." Mac yelled.

Jennie came from behind the counter to stand in front of Mac. "Ah ask yew what did yu want, Mac."

J D heard the sweetest sound that he had heard since he had heard Eunice call his name at church a few Sundays ago. He heard Mr. Britton clear his throat.

"We'll pay fuh de gas and dese drinks in a minute Ms. Jennie." John told Jennie as he followed J D out to the gas pump.

Mr. Britton paid the men and bade them good night. J D was still a bit shaky from the close encounter with the brew drinking Mac. Mac was getting meaner by the day. They say he had failed the army's tests because of something being wrong with his head, or in his head. The word was the man didn't have an ounce of sense. One of Mac's problems was that he drank too much. He didn't work much; He was not smart enough to do white folk's work and was too dumb and proud to do colored folk's works. He was pure white trash.

J D had no problem with people living miserable lives as long as they kept their miseries to themselves. This was never the case with the misfits in Mississippi. They were hell bent to make everybody that they came in contact with just as miserable as they were.

Saturday promised to be a cold and somewhat windy day. J D thought he would drive his family to town and come back to see Eunice. Eunice hardly ever went to town and this Saturday was no exception. The family, and the extended family too, were in town by eleven o'clock a.m. and J D and Willie were on their way back to Eunice's house by eleven a.m. Willie never had any money anyway, so he might as well ride with J D The two bought Eunice a hamburger and a RC cola. Eunice"s house was only four miles from town; it didn't take long to get to where J D felt happy. Bumping down the country road, looking at the dead fields, watching the grazing cattle and men stacking fire wood under the sheds were parts of a kind of life that J D's Mississippi had to offer.

Eunice was busy as usual. She had been shelling peas and beans all day getting them ready for canning next week. The green beans and green peas had been canned back in the summer, now was the time to can a few jars of dry field beans and peas. Unice's mother was not much help now days. The old lady gave up on life when Eunice's father died. The bulk of the house-work fell on Eunice. Women's work on a farm was never finished.

J D didn't like how pale Eunice looked. He knew of the rumors about the curse and the other stories about the family problems, but his faith in the powers of the living God could break the spell. He had to believe in a higher power than the powers of evil. He knew that there had to be something more powerful and just than man and the evils that man casted on each other. He had to trust in something or go crazy.

Eunice thanked him for the cold burger and went to the stove to warm it up. Watching Eunice move about the house doing her chores turned J D's innards to pulp. J D knew that there was no other girl in this world for him. Making this girl happy would be his single mission in life other than his commitment to God. He truly felt this to be an answered prayer and a gift from God.

Mississippi Negroes didn't often ask a girl for her hand in marriage, it was a given. The young men didn't take the young ladies for granted though. It was kind of like the older folks decided the time to get married and to whom. Once young people celebrate their eighteenth birthday the time for courting was over. This was especially true for the young ladies. The men knew if they didn't snag the girl of their choice, some other young man would get her. J D felled right in with the social rules that says that if a young person was not chosen by the time he reached his eighteenth birthday he was not worth the salt that it took to make a pan of cornbread. Country men had to get married or else. There was no place in a hard society for single non-reproducing men. Men without wife and children were at the social level of a castrated hog.

Colored people had a hard time finding rational reasons for living the life of a southerner. If the colored had faith in God, or an equal faith in a wife and children, or maybe both, he could stake a claim on some reasons for his existence. Now, the whites had their own reasons for the existence of colored folks in Mississippi. Their explinations of why the colored people were here did not give the colored much room to be human.

Before J D and Willie left Eunice's house J D promised her he would come over on Wednesday on his way back from town and surprise her. J D hummed to himself as he fired up the truck for the return four miles to town.

"Wha's on yo mind."

"Can't a fella be happy widout somethin bein on his mind?"

"Nawh, not less he be crezier den a bullfrog."

"Well Willie, since yu hafta know, Ah'm thankin 'bout askin her tah marr me."

"Dat's all?' 'Evrybody spects dat yu two will git marred dereckly.' 'Dat ain't no caus ta be dis happy."

"It is if yu hada girl lak Eunice."

The two friends rode on to the county seat without saying another word. Each lost in his own dreams of finding meaning somewhere that will bring some tokens of happiness. Neither of the men knew of anybody being happy. The whites had no more chances for happiness than the colored. The same system that hog-tied the colored also hog-tied the whites. Mississippi was a state where none of its citizens were free to chase dreams of heavenly peace. The Mississippi social system was unforgiving for anybody who dared to challenge the limits of the freedoms that the system allowed. The Mississippi Jim Crowism was the king and both black and white citizen were the king's subjects.

Mississippi had the reputation of being the poorest state in the union and had the dumbest people of all. The state of Mississippi did its cotton picking best to live up to that reputation. The two friends rode into town trying to figure out how to make the best of what they had.

J D and John were at the Britton's Monday morning before the hay-cutter got there. Mr. Britton had hired a local white boy to cut and rake the hay. The boy had a small Ford tractor he used to make beer-drinking money. He went from one farm to the other cutting and racking hay for the small farmers. This white boy was lazier than a 'coon dog at high noon. J and John had no trouble keeping up with this lazy young man.

J D was glad that the season was coming to an end. He would find work in the woods whenever the pulpwood crew went out. This would bring in plenty income to take care of Eunice. He planned to work for the Brittons and do a little farming for himself on the side. Eunice had the house and the few acres of tillable land almost to herself. Nobody in Eunice's family was able to, or wanted to, work in the fields. J planned to live at her place and do a little farming until he could talk Mr. Britton into letting him sharecrop a few acres. He was deep into his planning when he noticed Allen drive up to the store. He and John walked over to visit a minute with Allen and find out what news he had brought, if any.

"Ha Al."

"Howdy y'all." Allen spoke.

"Wha is yu doin hea at dis tiahm uf de day?" J asked.

"Ah jess come back from Mobile County.' 'Ah'm ohn mah way home."

The three men went on in the store together. J D and John didn't want to buy anything, they went in with Allen. They were eager to talk to someone who had been out of the state, even if it was no further than Mobile County.

"We kin finished wid de hayin dis week if it don rain us out." John said.

"Whad yu plan ta do afta dat J?" Allen wanted to know.

"Oh, Ah'll fiahm somethin.' 'Maybe Ah'll work wid de pulpwood crew."

"Why don yu ride wid me when ya ain't busy?"

"Nawh suh. Ah'm gitting marred inna few days."

"So, yu'll need money mo en ever afta yu git marred."

"Ah'll thank bout it."

J D knew one thing for sure; Eunice would never let him haul shine, no sir, not in a million years. A responsible married man would never haul shine across state lines. He not only had Eunice against such notions, the church didn't hold to that kind of devils work either.

They watched Allen disappear down the dusty road. The two hard working hay haulers went back to work.

CHAPTER TWENTY-SIX

▼

J D and Eunice were planning to have a small get-together of close family and friends to share their holy matrimonial celebration. They decided against a church wedding because they could not have the celebration at both churches. Eunice was a member of Sand Field Babtist and J D was at Antioch Baptist church. These communities were never ready to understand the needs of the other. They liked to hoard what they believe to be theirs. The young couple decided on a home marriage where all invitees would be welcome. The relatives on both sides had no objections to the marriage.

Eunice's mother left the entire decision up to Eunice. The old gal had done like many of the older people, given up on accomplishing any successes in this life, if they ever had any dreams of such. The farm country was no place to accomplish dreams of becoming anything other than what one already was. Eunice's mother seemed contented with what was and left the future up to the young. The rest of her family thought that J D was just what the doctor ordered and agreed to the arrangement.

Eunice's family's patch of land had been particially neglected every since the old man died. Her brothers and the one sister thought J D might be a God-sent blessing. With the exception of Eunice, this bunch was lazier than white trash. J D and Eunice had plans for this bunch of good-for-nothings. Her folks hadn't been worth doodley squat in years.

Now J D's folks were a little bit better off than Eunice's folks. The Banks were more ambitious than most people of the community, black or white. The vast majority of the community, both black and white, was about as ambitious as a castrated hog. Poor people had a tough time dealing with the present without being bothered with the future. If they could manage to hang on to the present the future would take care of its self. The Banks were above the average as far as hope was concerned. J D's folks had enough confidence in him to believe that he knew what he was doing.

"Ah neva seed old J D so cranked up.' 'Have y'all?" Asked Joe.

"We know wha he so stirred up ova." Bud attemped to school the rest of the men even though all knew the lessions many times over. "Yep. 'Ah'm gonna git me a sista-in-law.' 'She sho is a purdy little ole thing."

"Ah can't see how dis boy kin be hea wid us whil his purdy thang is ova dar wid dem." Paul added.

"Me nedda" Tommy said with a wink.

"Yep, mah sista-in-law will be de bess lookin gal in Antioch.' Ah don' wan you niguhs lookin at mah sista-in-law, eva."

"Dat goes fuh yu too, Bud." Tommy warned Bud.

The four men usually cut and loaded one load of pulpwood a day and hauled it to town. Nobody was in a hurry to get anywhere. This was the time of the year when farmers did mostly nothing. The only one who wanted to get to town was J D. He was not really interesting in going to town; he was interesting in being dropped off at Eunice's house. The men let J D off at the fork of the road which was no more than a quarter of a mile to her house. The boys didn't want to drive a loaded truck to Eunice's house.

J D had Eunice all to himself which was as close to heaven as he ever got without dying frist.   When he and Eunice were in each other's arms the world was not such a bad place to be in. He could never get enough of the way Eunice made him feel. J D thought to himself while walking up to the front porch,

"Ah'm one blessed po nigguh."

He had to give God the credit for such a blessing. It sure couldn't be from the evil side of the world, he believed.

"Evenin mamma."

"Come ohn in J D" "Eunice is in de kitchen."

"Thanks mamma."

"Hi sugah."

"Howdy yoself, J D"

J D walked up behind Eunice and placed his arms around her waist. These were the only times that he knew he could be a man equal to any man. He had often thought about what kind of a husband that he might be. He also thought about the kind of husband and father that he was ready to become. He had decided to be whatever he had to be to make a happy life for himself and the gal of his dreams. In his arms she felt so small. She would need a strong man to take care of her; he was that man.

J D still felt a sense of sadness deep down within his being. He had no explination for these feelings, but they still came to the surface from time to time. He most often got these dreads when he was around, or was thinking about his life with Eunice. He had no idea what he would do without this pretty little lady.

"Wha yu been doin all day?"

"Ah've got ta ready myself fuh my marrage yu know.' Why don't yu go brin me some stove wood in hea."

"Yessum mam."

J didn't mind doing favors for Eunice but wondered who wouldh've gone for the wood if he had not been here. He had promised her that she will never have to do man's work again once they are married. Nosuh.

"Ah'll brin in nough wood fuh cookin and de fahrplace foe Ah go."

"Dat's nice uf ya."

J worked nearly an hour cutting resin-fat pine and splitting oak wood for the fireplace. The weather was a bit cool for the time of the year. J D made sure there was firewood for the house if he had to haul it from Antioch. Finally he heard the truck coming. He stopped splitting the wood because he didn't want to listen to the shucking and jiving about being henpecked.

J went back in to the kitchen to get one last kiss and hug before the truck got there. This hug will have to last until tomorrow, which will seem like a long time to J D. These Mississippi country boys stored their good common sense in their emotions. Here in the sticks a man could not spend too much time thinking about doing something. He had just enough time to do whatever was on his mind. He held on to her as long as she let him and that was just before the other three boys came in the kitchen.

"Ah hav some cake lef ova fahm Sunday if y'all wan some."

"Yessum we do." Tommy answered before he had time to think about it."

The four men pilled into the cab of the truck and headed down the road.

"If yu don't marr her one uf us will." Bud said. "She sho kin bake a cake."

"Ah bet she's as sweet as dis hea cake is." Paul spoke up for the first time since arriving at Eunice's.

"Too bad yu'll neva know busta." Bud said grinning at J D.

The four men rode home mostly without saying much. Joe had a nice voice for singing and he sung most of the way to where they dropped him off at the road leading cross the field to his house. The night was cool and moonlit. This was possum-hunting weather and the men were getting antious to call out the old dogs and get with it.

"Les's go 'possum huntin lata dis week Joe." Bud hollered to Joe as he went through the gate.

"kay." Came the reply.

The men didn't cut anymore pulpwood for the remainder of the week. They sort of hung around the joint and the Britton store. They still had the church and plenty of sipping whiskey to tide them over until the country side came alive again. In the meantime they sat around gossiping, telling lies, smoking and chewing tobacco. The farmers were not famous for their thinking abilities, but they were known for their reputation for lifting logs, cutting crossties, picking cotton, telling lies, chasing women and drinking whiskey. These woodchoppers would sat around and see who could tell the biggest lie about anything they could get away with. If it was true that lying would guarantee one a seat on the hell-bound train, it sure would be standing room only this time of the year.

J D, Bud, John, Tommy and Joe gathered up their old dogs, including the Bank's old half-dead hound, and headed out for the areas where the 'simmon trees were. Sometimes there would be three or four 'possums in one tree and all the men had to do was shake them out for the dogs to get at. The moon was shinning so bright that the men turned out the carbide light. They could see clearly to the top of the 'simmon trees. The leaves were nearly all off the trees this time of the year. 'Possum hunting was becoming a thing of the past for these young men. They were now looking for something a lot more meaningful in their lives than 'possum hunting. All the fellows kind of knew that this might be the last 'possum hunt they'll ever do together. Two of the young men were planning to get married within months. Supporting a wife, kids and God knows whatever else will take lots of backbreaking work and many things that one would rather not think about. It had always been more than a notion for a Negro to raise a family with dignity in Mississippi. The whites had no easy time of raising a family with dignity either. The whites did have social rights to certain social and moral advantages that the colored could forget about. Uncle Barlow once said that the chances of a colored man living with dignity in Mississippi were less than the chance of lighting a pipe in a winstorm. He said that the colored had to learn to live a good life without universal dignity and respect. These attributes were beyond the reach of the Negroes and possible but not hardly probable for many of the whites. Uncle Barlow was considered the wise colored man in the county, both black and white folks listened to what he had to say. J D wanted Uncle Barlow's thoughts on marriages.

"Evenin Uncle Barlow."

"Howdy young fellow.' Wha brin yo ova ta see me?"

"Ah'm plannin ohn marrin soon n Ah juss waned ta talk ta yu n see wha yu thought bout dis.' 'Ah know yu neva marred agin afta yo wife died lon ago."

"Ah herd 'bout yu n little Eunice gittin marrd.' 'Ah guess yu know bout as much bout wha yu is doin as anyone else."

"It won't be easy makin de kind uf life fuh her dat Ah wan her ta hav."

"Wha kind uf lif do she wan fuh yu?"

"Fuh me?' Ah didn aks her."

"De nex tahm yu see her, aks her wha do she wan fuh de two uf yu.""Yeasuh Ah will."

"Ah ve watched yu fuh a lon taihm n Ah believe Ah know yu purdy good, J D' Yu hav somethin dat will make livin in Mississippi hard fuh ya less yu larn how ta petect yourself.' 'Yu hav to be ver cafful how yu tret de white folks, how you cary yoself when round white folks and how yu tret yo woman n chirren round white folks."

"Wha do ya mean Uncle Barlow?"

"Yu may hav ah few ways bout yu dat Negroes heah in de south don' need ta live de lif uf a southern colored man.' 'Do yu know wha a uppity nigger is?"

"Ah think Ah do."

"Yu go and make plans round wha is possble fuh yu and yo famly heah.' 'Make sense outta wha yu hav ta do heah and wid wha."

Chapter Twenty-seven

▼

J D and Eunice didn't have to make big plans for their being joined in holy matrimony. Large weddings were not part of the colored people's way of getting hitched. The colored wedding pledge was little more than jumping the broom. They planned to live in Eunice's house until a later time, depending on how things worked out and the plans of the good Lord. J D was more a beliver in the influences of the church than Eunice was.

To J D the laws of the church were the foundation on which all humane undertakings should rest upon. J D was, is and may continue to be distrustful of manmade anything. He had no confidence in man's abilities to be fair and square with his fellow man without the good Lord's help. He often thought about the young man over in Alabama who, the rumor has it, tried to run from a mob only to be caught and burned to death or killed and then burned, nobody knows for sure what took place first. The saying is that the young lady that had acused the Negro of violating the rock solid unwritten laws governing contacts between the white women and black men later confessed in church that she lied, so they say. She asked God to forgive her and help ease her quilt.

The white gal had no problem believing that she would be forgiven for what she had done to an innocent man. No member of the white mob that did the murder offered the colored community any apoligies. There were no Sunday sermons preached to the white congregation condemning this barbaric act. J D had to figure out how he and Eunice might make a good God-fearing life out of the little support the Mississippi social relations between the two races offered.

Working around the Britton store was a one-day a week job now that the farming season was over. This would be the case until March when the plowing begins. J D was promised the job as long as he wanted to work for the Brittons. He figured with his patching on the side, growing a garden to help feed the family, they should do pretty good. Raising chickens, a few hogs and milking one or two cows to add to what came out of the garden should be plenty to tide them over.

Jennie had changed somehow, but J D didn't know in what way or why. She often asked J when the marriage was going to be. J D thought at first that maybe Jennie had found someone to offer her more than her daddy's store could. J D noticed the same lost look in others eyes too, especially when they learn about some of their associates getting married, moving north, or leaving for other reasons. These changes in the way his friends and other members of the community treated him and Eunice may be the results of all getting older and coming into their own. Jennie had become a lot less flirtatious with the young men than she once was. J D and Jennie had been friends for a long time, since they were babies. That friendship was based on extreme conditions. This friendship across the great racial divides between the white woman and the black man was nearly an impossibility. This kind of friendship was often one of the most dangerous situations in a colored man's life. J D had known this every since his voice started changing from sounding like a girl's to that of a man's. Jennie's changed attitude toward J might have been for his own safety.

Allen came by the Britton's for gas and to visit with J D whenever J was working around the place. He usually showed up near quitting time so that the two could have a cold drink and some friendly talk. Allen was still in the whiskey-delivering business which gave him plenty of time to drive his shinny car around the country side while most of the locals were either working or spending time at home in front of the fireplace chewing tobacco and spitting into the fire.

"Allen, how's de shin business goin?"

"Good.' 'betta n usual, ya kno."

"Dat don seem lakly.' 'Folks ain't got dat extra money ta buy likker wid."

"Dat's wha yu thank.' 'Des folks got money fuh dey likker when dey don' hav money ta put in de church."

"How many gallons did ya brin back today?"

"Ah didn't go git none today.' 'Ah'll make de run tomor."

"Where is ya comin fahm today?"

"Well, Ah'll tell ya.' 'Ah took Miss Ruby Mae ta Mobile agin.' 'She sho muss be 'specting ta cast a bunch uf spells or sell a bundle uf moojoo bags dis sprin.' 'She bought candles, oils, small bags uf stuff, hey, if ya kin thank uhvit, she bought it."

"Ah believe wha she is doin is interferin wid de Lawd's work.' 'Only de Lawd has de
rahts ta chastise folks fuh dey sins."

"Ah ain't disputin yu J D' 'Ah jes do de drivin fuh a few dollars.' 'She pay me good."

In the deep south all the people claimed to be good Christians. The wife beaters, the drunks, the liars, you name it, they did it but they were all Christians. There was no conflict of any significance with what a man claimed to believe and what the same man practiced. There were no more disagreements about what the spirtual people practicing outside the church than there were disagreements about what they practiced inside the church. The fight to survive here in this poor country left little time for fighting among the Christian folks about true spiritual values. J D often thought the lack of disagreement about religion was more due to the folk's ignorance than to their religious convictions. J sometimes thought that the members of the church didn't have a clue about the real meaning of why the church was even there, He sometimes believed that the people went to church for the same reason they went to a movie, honky-tonk or anyother place where people got together. J thought that maybe the lack of religious differences were due to everybody knowing too much about each other. The good thing about the country was the people lying on each other was not necessary. The people had no private lives at all which meant everybody knew all there was to be known about each other. The only things to lie about were those events and phenomena that nobody knew anything about. J didn't know much about people living outside his area, but he thought that his folks were the biggest lairs in the entire world. Other than each other, they had nothing else to talk about except the unknown and their blind faith.

J D and Allen spent far too much time at the store. Ike McCray and Mac Shelley came rattling up to the gas pump. These men didn't like anybody and didn't anybody like them, especially colored folks.

"Let's make tracks Al."

"Just a minute."

"Darn good looking automobile ya got dar boy."

"It do purdy good." Allen answered without saying Mr. Or sir.

"Purdy good nothing, its a lot better n ours." Mac churned in with his two cent

J D again felt the strong grip of fear on his innards. He didn't think that he would ever get over these panic attacts under these slippery southern racial relationships.

"I should take that thing away from ya." Mac stated as he walked around the car.

"Yeah and Mista. McCray, yo uncle, would take it outta his hide too." J D said calmly.

"My uncle would do that too."

Now that the possible explosive situation had been defused, the men could go their separate ways with no harm being done. Allen's ego might have taken a right hook to the chin, but he would survive. The old truck smoked and rattled on down the road.

"Allen, yu gonna havta avoid aguin wid des silly crackas.' 'Dey can't heah wha yu say."

"Ah don't giva hoot, It do mah good ta set 'em strat."

J D did not feel safe when he was with Allen and white folks, ever. Take an Allen type colored and a Mac kind of cracker and you've got the making of big troubles. J D and Eunice were planning a life filled with happiness. J didn't believe the whites could be happy making trouble for the Negroes any more than Negroes were happy making trouble for the whites…

The Banks family was at home when J D and Allen pulled up. The trees were so naked until the Banks could see the other side of the hill nearly three miles away. During the warm seasons the green canopy of the woods prevented a clear view of the other side of Sugar Bottom. The creek that was the main drain between the two ridges flooded during the heavy rains and left a layer of silk on the bottom land. This bottom land sure was good for growing corn and sugar cane. This was great farming country only if the poor folks would learn to use this rich land.

The valley between the two hilly regions was known as sugar bottom. This name came from who knows where. Some thought that the name fitted the attitudes of the residents who lived on the rich bottom land.

"Evenin folks." Allen spoke to all with one greeting.

"Howdy Allen, how is yo folks?" Mamma asked.

"Doin fairly well, Miss Banks."

Bud, Tommy and John were in the dining room sitting in front of the fireplace chewing cane. Chewing cane was a popular and enjoyable passtime durning the winter months. These country folks were now getting ready for one of the biggest days of the year, even bigger than the big church meeting. Christmas was just around the corner. People didn't make too big a commercial event out of the holiday season, they didn't have the money. The excitement came from having plenty of food and time to eat it. They made sure that those who believed in Old Santa got a few toys and some sweets. The old folks just made sure they had plenty of homebrew and shine. The days between Christmas and New Years were days for over eating, over drinking and walking around looking crazy.

"When is de big day J D?" Asked Grandma Ida.

"Christmas Eve, Grandma."

"She is a purdy little thang.' Ah reckon she is 'bout de purdest gal in dese hea parts."

"Yessum."

"Ah recollect her mamma being even betta lookin."

J D sure didn't have to be told how his future wife looked. He saw her face everywhere he looked. He could hardly wait until the day came when he could hold Eunice as long as he wanted to. He thought maybe he won't be able to get out of bed in the morning and leave for work and leave his heart in bed wit his Eunice.

CHAPTER TWENTY-EIGHT

▼

Allen drove J D and Eunice over to the Britton store to pick up a few last-minute items to use for Christmas baking. Jennie had seen Eunice many times but seemed to always forget her name.

"Hi y'all ' 'Hi Al, J, uh."

"Ah'm Eunice."

Eunice was more into cooking for Christmas than she was concerned about food for the small wedding that they had planned. The guest list for the wedding consisted of a hand full of people. Big Negro weddings were not the thing in Mississippi. The preacher, her mamma, Allen and several others were to be the only guests. The things she was after at the store were the usual spicies and so on. J D and Allen didn't notice Mac and McCray come in until the spring pulled the door shut.

Nobody spoke to anybody. The two white boys did not speak because white boys didn't show respect to young Negro men and women in public. They hardly ever recognize loving relationships between the colored. J D's heart stopped beating the moment he saw Mac looking Eunice up and down, from head to feet.

"That's one good looking nigger gal thar." Mac no more than got the words out before J D was in his face.

J D could not speak right away, he stammered and puffed, the sweat popped upon his forehead. Finally the words poured out.

"If yu lay one finga ohn her Ah'll kill yu white man."

Every moving being in the store stopped dead still. Nobody had ever heard J D threaten anybody before. Mac and McCray were so taken back that even they just stood there with their mouths wide open. Allen and Jennie didn't have a clue of what was coming next. Eunice was the only one who didn't seem to be bothered by what was taking place, "J? J? He didn't mean nothing."

Jennie bagged up the few items, handed them to J D and pushed him toward the door with. "I'll see y'all tomor."

The white homebrew drinkers were standing in the door watching the three colored folks drive away. Mac and McCray were caught completely off guard.

"Well, I be Darn." said Mac. "If that don't beat the hell out uf anythang that I ever heard."

J D kept looking behind for signs of the two white men following. The dusty dirt road was empty.

"Yu aughta ignore dem kind uf folks." Eunice said.

"Ah won't let nobody disrespect yu, Eunice."

"Mista Banks, yu can't change dese white folk.' 'Yu will git yoself kilt if yu try ta make dem respect us colored folks."

"Ah ain't tryin ta, Ah ain't gonna let em mess wid yu…"

"Ah lak ya when ya git mad, J."

"Yu stay outta dis, Allen." Eunice said while giving Allen the don't-you-start-something-eye.

"Don't yu worr 'bout em followin us J.' 'Ah got somethin under dis seat dat'll put some kinks in dose bastas tails."

"Boy, Ah don't wan dat kind uf trouble."

"Me neither, but yu know wha dese mad nuts will do if dey git half a chance."

"Yeah, Ah know.' 'Ah went sho nuf crazy when dat peckerwood said dat 'bout Eunice."

The three rode on in silence. They were thinking about what might have happened back there at the store. Every colored person in Mississippi was well aware of the dangers when these po whites got riled up. When these whites think they have been knocked off their pedestal of assumed superiority by a darkie,

The issue is never settled until some poor darkie put them back upon that pedestal. This restoring the white trash's sense of being untouchable by the colored came from terrorizing a few poor scared blacks.

J D had a strange feeling as if he lived inside a bubble that could and would break at any moment. He was trying to add some stability to the life that he might expect to have in his hometown. He figured that through hard work and trust in the Lord he could have what very few other citizens had, black or white. Fear, as his constant companion, might someday cause him to over react and hurt some of these nuts. After saying good bye to Eunice, J and Allen headed home.

"Allen, wha would you've done in mah place back at de stoe?"

"De same thang dat yu did, if not somethin wurst."

Do yu believe dat de Lawd will eva make thangs betta heah in ar home state?"

"Ah donno.' 'Ah don thank Ah wan dem te change none.' 'Dese crackas kin be fooled ta death, all yu gotta do is play wid em."

"Come ohn Al, yu ain't 'bout ta play dey games n yu knoit.

"Ah'm not talkin 'bout me.' 'Ah kind uf lakit de way it is."

"Dis boy will neva make it ta old age.' 'Dis boy ain't got sense 'nough ta po piss outta a boot wid de direction wrote ohn de side." J mumbled.

"Yu got yo marrage license and all?"

"Yeah, de preacha will be at his house all mornin.' 'We should be dar 'bout twelve o'clock."

"Ah'll pick ya up in plenty uf tiahm.' 'Okay?"

"Okay."

The marriage was so simple until it didn't feel for real to J. He was the same old country boy that he had been before the hitch. It was hard to believe that this was all there was to becoming a husband. This marriage took place at the preacher's house too which added a bit of sacredness to this union .J D hoped from the bottem of his heart that if God was involved in his marriage, happiness was possible. Living according to the biblical teachings and walking with the Lord in everything will give meaning and purpose to his marriage.

The weather turned colder than usual during the Christmas holidays but J D and Eunice didn't mind at all. They were too busy practicing their new freedoms and enjoying the new status marriage and the community gave to them. J D worried about more than just making the marriage one of the best that the community had ever seen; he was a bit worried about Eunice's frail look here lately. He had noticed her limping when she walked and the color of her face early in the morning when she first gets out of bed. The age-old rumor about the evil spell and all poked its head up again, but he refused to believe a single word of the non-sense.

"Ah see yu is a new man now Mrista Banks.

"No Al, Ah'm de same old nigguh dat Ah' wuz all de tiahm.

Nawh, nawh yu ain't neither.' 'Yu got me thankin 'bout jumpin de broom.' 'Ah would too if Ah kin find a gal lak Eunice."

"Yu might neva git marrd den, if findin a girl lak Eunice is wha it'll take."

The friends laughed and continued on toward the Britton store. Neither man had been back to the store since the incident with Mac and McCray. Allen promised to pick up J on the days that J D would be working for the Brittons. Both men were thinking about what they might have to deal with when they meet up with them crackers, but neither spoke about it.

Allen was hoping that when they did, and they will, meet the white men again that he would be there with J D. He knew J was a little hesitant about locking horns with any of the whites, no matter who they were. Al kind of wanted a chance to see if these crackers were as tough as they wanted the colored to believe they were. Allen saw no reason to be afraid of a few peckerwoods that bled like everybody else. Mac and McCray were just two poor whites that belonged to neither side of the racial devide.

"See ya dis evenin J."

"Yep, Ah'll be waitin ova at de barn."

J D didn't see any reason to deliberately push his luck with faith. He thought he'd give them time to think about what happened and maybe come to their senses. It was always hard to figure out what the crackers thought about when dealing with blacks. These people didn't use good sense when they dealt with the colored folks anyway. No sir, they became as nutty as a fruitcake. Now J D never tried to deal with white folks on a rational base. Many of the smart whites lost all common sense when they did business with members of the colored race. They even showed a great deal of stupidity when dealing with anybody not of their particular breed. J figured the less he saw these jokers for right now the better for all involved.

J stopped in at the store for a soda to drink with his lunch. He had never seen the troublemakers here at this time of the day.

"Hey J D' 'It didn't look like you were coming over to say hi."

"Hi Ms. Jennie."

"How is your marriage working out?' 'She sure is tiny and cute."

"Thank yu Ms. Jennie.' 'We had ah good Christmas wid de families.' 'Ah've got two famlies now.

"Yeah I know, but that ain't what I was talking about."

J D had no answer for Jennie and he felt ill at ease talking about these kinds of things with Jennie, or any white woman. Colored men talking to white women about anything sex related is strickly taboo. J and Jennie had been friends for ever, but not long enough for that kind of conversation, because if one of the emotionally sick white men would overhear this kind of talk between a white woman and a colored man his mind would snap. He would lose his religion, his compasion, his love for humanity and all the other characteristics that make him human. The poor man would give up his place in Heaven and give his soul to his bigotry and the devil

"Don't stop coming by just cause you got married J D" Jennie said with a wink.

"Ah won't."

Four o'clock was a long time coming for the newly married J D. This was the first time he had been away from his woman since their marriage. He sure missed that little woman of his. His shoveling horse and cow manure had no negative effects on this happy man. He didn't have his mind on the kind of work that he was doing. A man in love would put up with a lot of stuff except something that threatens the object of his love. The winter work around a farm is not the kind of work one does with dignity. Fixing fences, cutting back bushes from the edges of the fields and hauling manure for the gardens were not the kind of jobs that a young married man bragged about. He'll just have to get use to bathing every night no matter how cold it is.

Finally it was nearly four o'clock and old Allen was a little early as usual. He had no honest work to do so at least he was on time to pick up J D. He also knew Eunice had a dang good supper waiting for J. He would be invited to share their supper. Eunice was accustomed to fixing vittles for a big family. She always had enough to feed extra folks. This was a common habit here in the deep south because you never knew when there would be extra mouths at the table. J was so busy thinking about Eunice until he didn't see the two beer-drinking buddies parked alone the side of the store.

Mac was the first to open his mouth."I guess ya don't know how to talk to white folks, do ya boy?"

J D knew the old devil feeling again boiling up from his stomach into his mouth. He kept trying to remember some verse in the Bible but could not.

"Did you heah me boy?"

"He heard ya Mista Mac." Allen said.

This is when J D knew Allen had a gun in his pocket and would use it.

"Lawd have mercy" is all J could mumble to nobody in particular.

J D had to get Allen out of the area quick. He had never seen that kind of expression on a man's face before. Allen had all the sighs of death written on his face.

"Didja heah me Mista. Mac?' 'I said he head ya!"

McCray was watching Allen with a strange look on his face. He didn't know what to make of this nigger."He heard you Mac.' 'Com on, let's go."

Allen still hadn't moved a muscle, not one. McCray didn't have to be told that this was a dangerous man and if he and Mac wanted to see another day, it was past time to go. "You make sure he heard Mac!" McCray said while pulling Mac through the door.

J D started to breath again only after the white men rode off down the dusty road. He jumped when he heard Jennie say something.

"Those two ain't good fuh business." She said.

J D and Allen rode in silence for a couple of miles before either spoke.

"Yu waned ta kill dem men Allen."

"Only cause dey waned ta kill us."

Do yu thank dey'll fuhgit wha happened?"

"Nawh. Ah won't neither.' 'If ah white man mess wid me fahm hea ohn, he got hell to pay."

J D appreciated what Allen had done, but the nagging thought would not go away. Alled didn't look like he knew J D was there at all. Allen acted as if he hoped Mac did make a move to do something to either him or J D. J saw murder in Allen's eyes. Allen hated Mac with every nerve in his body and would have gladly got everybody killed expressing his hatred for white folks.

J D had to respect Allen more than he respected any colored man in the colored community. The boy had what most of the Negroes wished they had. Allen was one black man who would not go down easily. J often wished that he could overcome his paralyzing fears of his daily encounters with the Jim Crow system here in his hometown. Allen was becoming J D's role model of how to be a man in spite of fear.

Chapter Twenty-nine

▼

The spring rains came early this year which caused the farmers to be late with their plowing and planting. The fields were too wet to plow nearly two weeks into the plowing season. A few of the wise old heads figured this rainy weather was due to the wickiness of the younger generation. "Yes sir, the world was becoming weaker and wiser." Reverend Mayfield was getting older, sicker and harder on these poor souls who had strayed off the path of rightness. The old boy's sermon were more and more leaning toward the hellfire and brimstone sides of his beliefs.

J D and Eunice attended church services every Sunday except when Eunice didn't feel up to going. This hellfire and damnation preaching did not help. J D was not worried about his religious future as much as he was worried about something that he couldn't put his mind to. At times J felt completely helpless when it came to making something positive happen that would help him build a good life for his family. He wanted to show all of his family, both his relatives and his inlaws, how to make life good here in Mississippi with the help of the Lord.

J D's folks would often look at him as if he was a little off his rocker when he talked about the possibility of being happy here in the woods. Happiness was not the main objective of most of these country people. J saw that same lack of hope in the eyes of those who grew up with him. The same hopeless expressions were in the common attitudes of those of the older generation. Even with the sloppy spring and the late start with the farming, J D felt, with the blessings from the Lord, they still had reasons to be thankful.

J D was far from being a community activist trying to change the rules, but he tried to live by the moral rules of the Bible. He thought just to remind the good people of Mississippi of their obligation to their fellowman, dictated by the Bible, would generate enough fairplay to allow everybody to live a relatively happy life. He was still too inocent of the brutal nature of man to understand why his ideal world didn't exist in his beloved state of Mississippi. Fairplay was the last thing these people had on their minds. The only fair play involved in the dealing among neighbors was incidental.

J D continued to work for the Brittons five days a week. Evening and Saturdays were for working his small patch of land there at home. By working for the Brittons during the week and working for himself evenings and Saturdays he could do pretty well. He believed that if he worked hard enough and was honest enough the rest would be easy. In most cases he was right, but there were the few cases where honesty and hard work had little to do with anything at all. The Brittons thought the sun rose and set over J D. The Brittons thought he could be trusted . Mac and McCray disagreed with them. They thought J D was to upity for his own good.

J D was once again taking the truck home with him. He felt safer drivig himself than he did riding with his good friend, Allen. He also made sure he was never in the store alone with Jennie. He would wait for hours if he had to before entering the store when Jennie was the only one there. J was not afraid of what Jennie would do or say to get him in trouble, but was afraid of how some scummy cracker or black might interpret what they see or hear.

Bud and Paul stopped by the store to buy gas and to tell the latest news. J D had been too busy the last few weeks to keep up with what was going on in the community.

"Joe n Steve lef fuh Detroit Sunday, ya know.' 'Dar uncle wrote dem n said de foundry wuz now hirin help." Bud told J.

"Dey always said Dey wuz gonna leave."

"Ms. Ann said Wilma wuz big agin.' 'Her folks sent her ta Mobile ta stay wid an aunty til aftah de baby comes."

"Somebody herd Aunt Sal tell de women in church dat de daddy uf de baby jess might be ah white boy." Paul added

"Dat explains Reverend Mayfield's sermon Sunday.' 'He preached bout livin in sin and layin wid women and men outta de holy union uf wedlock."

Paul had to get Bud back to his planting. They headed back to the Banks' small farm with the seeds and a few bag of fertilizer. Paul having nothing much to do at his house, hung around the Banks with Bud most of the time. J D reckoned these two were planning to pack up and leave Mississippi as soom as the crops were either planted or gathered. The boys leaving and returning with good cars and clothes have taken half the young men back north with them. These returning men came back to marry their longtime girlfriends and take them back to the cities.

Willie went back to his home in Columbia Mississippi. Everybody knew he was leaving as soon as he became of age. He turned twenty years old last fall which was plenty old enough to be on his own. Most of these men and women considered themselves grown before their eighteenth birthday. George had found a job working on a highway gang up in Alabama. The crowd was thinning out fast. The younger generation tends to wish for more than they saw was possible for them on the farm. What the older folks tolerated was out of the question for these young restless whippersnappers.

J D felt the change in his world and didn't like what he thought it meant for the future of his hometown. The winds of change were beginning to blow away all that he had prepared himself for. He sensed a shift in the way the whites acted toward the colored every time a colored drove back into town from up north. The whites resented the big cars these returning Negroes were driving. They didn't like the way these former plowboys talked to the local whites. A few of them boys forgot, or pretended to forget, how to humble down to their social superiors. Yep, fireworks were in the making that will blow the led off this tightly sealed community's ignorance.

J D figured the others could have all the new ideas, new cars, pretty suits and all the rest that went along with being big shots, Eunice was all he needed to be happy. With all the work to be done J didn't have the time for the trouble that was sure to come when these white folks didn't like something. He made up his mind to leave this in the hands of the Lord. Revernd Mayfield had a good point,

"Give ta Ceasa wha belon ta Ceasa."

This kind of advice was sounding better and better to J now days.

Long after Bud and Paul rode off, J D kept thinking about the change he saw coming over the horizon. He conforted himself with the facts that he worked for a good white man and he lived on his own property. Between Eunice's property and his at the banks', he felt pretty confident that with God's mercy everything would be all right.

J D drove home the long way just to have time to look the farms over and let his worries settle down. He had the responsibilities of a husband on his shoulders now. The single men had the freedom to leave or remain, they had a choice. J liked what he had and had no regrets whatsoever. Maybe this year's success will be as green as the trees and smell as good as the honeysuckers blooms, the dogwood and the magnolia blossoms. He even saw a few cardinals and Robbins making ready to raise families. He saw confort and hope in nature.

"How wuz yo day sugah?"

"It's good now dat yu is home.' 'N yos?"

"De same old thang ya know.' 'Bud n Paul stopped by ta talk.

"Yeah, and."

"Joe and Steve left fuh Detroit de weekend.' 'Wilma is in family way agin."

"Agin?"

"Ah fuhget yu don't know much bout de old days.

"Ah'm glad too."

"Ah'm goin out ta de garden fuh ah while.' 'Call me when suppa is ready."

"Ah ain't gonna do no such thang.' 'Ah'm gonna eatit all up."

"Yu will git a whipping too."

"Ah kin do some uf de gardenin while yu is at wok."

J D didn't answer her; he just went to the garden with his hoe to do a little digging. He thought about getting more chickens, turkeys, and one or two pigs to start things off right. He had one cow, but it was not giving milk yet. His folks offered to supply a few chickens and pigs but J knew how it was over there. He could always stop by and get what he needed anyway. One thought kept crossing his mind; he had to convence Eunice to see Doctor Holyfield as soon as possible.

Eunice had never weighed more than ninety pounds and it looked to J D that she may have lost a few of those ninety pounds. When he asked her how she felt she always answered. "Good." He now believes she says she feels good so he wouldn't worry about her. He was beginning to question some assumptions held by the community leaders that didn't add up to plain old good sense. Even Reverend Mayfield never answered J's questions directly. He usually answered the safe way, through the Bible. All the people around the area tended to belive more in the powers of evils than they believed in the teaching of the Bible. He sure would like to know why, and when did this lack of faith in the church come into existence. Maybe this lackadaisical attitude toward living life according to the teaching of the Lord was not new.

Aunt Sal was one of the most faithful church workers in the community, but mothered two kids for the man of God. Now if this kind of shucking and jiving with the Lord was not dangerous, what was? This old gal acted like this kind of serving the Lord was a good Christian thing to do. It was hard to find any person younger than thirty who still believed that a good life was a possibility here in these hills. This held true for both the races. Wholesome living was not part of the goals these folks aspired to. The daily pursuit of these folks, both white and colored, had more to do with alcoholic beverages, chasing other men women, chewing brown mule chewing tobacco, smoking Prince Abbot Tobacco and other totally destructive habits. These habits were killing any chance they may had for making a better life.

It certainly had been a wet season thus far. The dampness was a good thing for many of the crops, and was extremely heathy for grasses for feeding the stock. The Farmers sat around on their porches, or the porches of their folks and friends, looking as if the gods had forsook them. These folks assumed absolutely no responsibility for what came their way through the natural world. They used their idle time to bring harm to themselves or to other community members. It was not uncommon for these people to have children by their own kin, close kin at that. Rainy weather brought out the worst from the flock. Idle minds and hands are the devil's tools for promoting immoral life styles.

There were rumors and convictions floating around to the tune that most of the fever-minded that could never learn to write their names might have been the result of just such a union of hanky-panky going on between kinfolks. J D had some kin that he thought might be the result of serious sinning. He had tried for years to teach one of his older cousins how to put the harness on a mule. That fellow never learned a thing. Small community folks always had to be extra careful because they never were too sure who was their kin and who was not. The young had to pay close attention to the elders that might have a question about their choice of a courting mate. These folk's lives would never look good under rational examining. What they thought and did one moment had nothing to do with what they thought and did in the next moment. Talking about fragmented lives, they had them. Most thought that fever mindedness might just be due to mating within the same ethnic family or caused by something else that was created from these hypocrites' behaviors.

CHAPTER THIRTY

▼

Eunice had been having morning sicknesses for some time before J D learned about them. He happened to go outside near the outhouse early one morning and hear Eunice being sick. His heart almost came to a complete stop when he realized that his wife was sick.

"Eunice! Hey Eunice!!"

"Jess a minute, Ah'll be out in."

"Wha is de matta?"

Eunice didn't answer right away which gave her time to get the words together that wouldn't upset J D any more than was necessary.

"How lon have yu been sick lak dis.?"

"Not too lon J.' 'Ah didn't wan ta wory yu none, especially fore Ah wuz show"

"Show uf wha?"

"Dat yu is gonna be ah daddy."

J D jumped with joy and with a feeling of dread all at the same time. He grabbed Eunice, swung her into the air and gave out one big whoop. J D knew about the responsibilities of being a daddy on a farm. Childern didn't change everyday habits much at all for the man of the house. The looking after of the small children was the job for the women folks. But children were signs of blessings from on high. J D had a few doubts about this commonly held belief.

J D decided to wait until he knew for sure that he was gonna become a daddy before he told his family and his friends. He would wallow in the good feeling and share the good news with no one for awhile. The boys will really have a heyday with this news. This will be the Banks's first grandchild too. J D felt pretty special knowing that God might have picked him to be the daddy of the Banks's first grandchild and Grandma's first great grandchild. J D was not totally sold on the idea that children were blessing from God. There was only one person that J D shared news about the baby with.

"Ms. Jennie ah know somethin n Ah bet yu can't guess wha it is.' 'Not inna million yeas."

"How much you wanno bet?"

"One RC Cola."

"Okaaay, Eunice is going to have a baby."

J D fished out one cold RC Cola for the young lady. What she did next damn near scared him to death. She came around the counter and hung herself around his neck. He thought she was coming after the drink and did not try to avoid her advance. He had never been hugged by a white woman before, not since he could remember. There was one thing for sure; he did not hug her back.

J D was not sure what Jennie's facial expression was a reflection of. He had never seen her look at him like that before. Come to think of it, he had never known her to have a boy friend either.

"Tell Eunice to take good care of herself."

"Yu bet Ah will."

It being Friday and all, J left the Brittons early so he would have time to drive through town and see when Dr. Holyfield could see Eunice. He was surprised to see so many sawmill workers and log cutters and haulers in town on a Friday afternoon. The one hamburger stand had a line at both windows. The white line was short because they were given service first. The colored had to wait until the upper class had been served. Who was in line? Bud and Paul.

"Wha business bought yu two inta town ohn Friday?"

"We wuz 'bout ta ask yu de same thang."

"Ah'm heah ta take care uf a little business, dat's all.

J D walked away from the hambuger line before he could be asked any more questions. The hamburger stand was just behind the doctor's office, in the alley instead of being on the street. The burger stand was in the middle of the alley where most of the farmers parked their wagons and trucks. The coloreds were never allowed to park on the front streets, so the alley was consuder the main street for the colored and a few of the whites.

J D walked in the front of the doctor's house but did not take a seat. The living room was used as a white waiting room. The colored had to stand until they could be waited on, if they could stand, other wise they might be seated on the screened in back porch. Nobody seemed to mind this arrangement because Dr. Holyfield was popular with both white and colored patients. It could be because the next nearst Doctor was sixteen miles farther north. The medical treatment for the folks was the same all over the state anyway.

The Doctor's wife startled J when she seemed to appear out of nowhere.

"What can I do for ya?"

"Ah, aw, Ah wanted ta aks when kin Doctor Holyfield examine mah wif, Eunice?"

"What's ailing her?"

"Ah thank she's in family way."

"She having problems?"

"No mam, Ah jess thank she is weak, she ain't strong lak some folks."

"Can you bring her in Monday morning?' 'We usually don't have any patients Ohm Monday morning."

"Yes mam, thank yu mam."

This was the second time today J D had got himself locked into awkward predicaments. Negro men just didn't discuss anything with sexual overtones with white women here in Mississippi, unless she was older than Methuselah. Now, the next step is to get Eunice down here to be seen by the Doctor.

Negro women going to a doctor for prenatal care was unheard of and this case was no exception.   J D had a sneaking suspicion of something that he just could not bring into focus in his mind. He knew the history of Eunice's family being cursed, according to the rumors. Once his mind is put to rest about those old tales, he will talk to Ms Ann. These midwives did a better job delivering babies than all the doctors in the world could. He had an ace in the hole though, God. If everything else failed, he turned to his faith.

J D took a slow drive through the colored section of town where he saw Doctor Holyfield coming out of the colored owned café. J D pulled off the street and watched from the pickup. He overheard two men whom he knew talking about what had just happened.

"Do ya no wha he stabb him ova?"

"Red Eye said dey got inta it ova a pint uf homebrew."

He had bleed to death long before Doc got there. Nobody tried to help until it was too late.

J D didn't want to hear any more of this insanity.

"Dat place otta be called de graveyard." J said to himself. "A month couldn't pass without some po nigguh shotin or cuttin some otha po nigguh, sometimes fatally."

J D worked twelve hours Saturday in his own garden. The work kind of kept his mind on something other than Monday morning, He was pretty sure nothing out of the ordinary was the matter with his wife. He would get extra assurance by ask the Revernd to say a prayer for her without letting the cat out of the bag.

Talking to himself all day might be a way of asking his God for a little help. He tried to do everything right as he thought God wanted him to. Therefore, God surely was not going to let some curse that was placed on the family a thousand years ago be used against somebody who had never done a wrong thing in her life. Nawh, he had enough faith to offset some little old curse. He did not understand how anybody could live in this world without having lots of faith in God. He didn't think his life would be possible without his church. What was there to trust in this world except God? He kept thinking to himself.

"Heey J!" Come ohn in and wash up fuh suppa."

"Okay!!!"

J D waited until after super before telling Eunice about the doctor's appointment for Monday. At first Eunice said nothing after J told her. She begins crying softly before she admitted being worried about the same thing.

"J Ah'm gonna ta tell ya somethin dat Ah otta told yu fo we got marred.' 'Mah famly got dis notion uf nonsense bout us gitten a spell put ohn us lon fo Ah wuz born."

"Sugah, yu don' need ta tell me 'bout the cuse n stuff.' 'Ah already knowed 'bout de sayin.' 'Ah herd dat ole tale fo we started keepin company.' 'Ah ain't been zactly true wid ya, ya see."

"Yu knoed all dis tahm?' 'Yu knoed n let ohn lak you didn know?"

"Yeah Ah did.' 'Ah wuz too happy n didn' wan anythan ta mess it up."

"J, dah mite be somethin ta dose ole tales, ya kno.' 'Ah've woried 'bout dis thaing fuh most uf mah life.' 'Somtimes Ah can't sleep fuh woryin."

"Sugah?' 'Let's wait n see wha Doctor Holyfield say Monday.' 'Kay?"

J D went to church services alone on Sunday. This was the one of the few time he had gone to church without Eunice since they had been married; it did not feel good.

"Mornin J D. Ain't nothin wrong wid Eunice is it?" Aunt Sal Asked.

"No mam.' 'She is doin purdy good."

J D avoided the questions as much as he possibly could, but some still got to him. He felt that most of the old women had strong notions about what might be the matter with the young wife.

J D snapped out of his personal thoughts when he heard someone clearup his throat.

"Good evenin Uncle Barlow."

"Howdy."

"Ah didn' see ya walk up."

"Yu kno whad youn man, dar is a lot uf thang in dis world dat yu might not unerstand, but dey be heah anyhow.' 'Yu is a good boy, stay dat way, ya hea?"

Uncle Barlow didn't wait for an answer; he just continued walking back to the church.

"Uncle Barlow is de wisest man Ah eva saw, black or white." J mumbled to himself.

Uncle Barlow had a few doubts relative to these young'uns ability to accept the ways of the deep south and make do with what they had and make the best life that could be out of it. He remembered WW1 and saw the small changes throughout the south. He knew that the magnitude of change required to satisfy the colored and the whites would be more than either could handle. He had often thought of leaving the south but he couldn't think of anywhere to go. This was the only place and these were the only people he knew and loved.

J D didn't talk to Ms. Ann about Eunice at all. He knew she would not appreciate them going to see Doctor Holyfield at all let alone going to see Doctor Holyfield first. Midwives and medical doctors often didn't agree on which was the best way to bring babies into the world. J D could see that bringing babies into the world couldn't have been much of a problem because of the number coming in every year. Half the people had more young'uns than they could make a decent living for. Ms. Ann might understand after J D explains why they went to Doctor Holyfield instead of coming to her first.

After Doctor Holyfield finished examining Eunice he told them to come back in a week. He knew of the blood problems that some of Eunice's family had and took lots of blood samples to check out his suspicions.

"I don't think y'all have too much to worry about.' 'You young lady go home and stay off your feet as much as you can until we check this out."

"Thank yu Doctor Holyfield." Eunice said.

"Come on Sugah, Ah'll drive yu home and go back ta work fuh a spell.' Mista Britton said Ah didn't havta come back, but Ah don't wanna axs too much dis early in yo famly way."

"Yes Mista Banks."

J D had to tell somebody about what was on his mind, he told Allen. He felt that Allen already had his doubts relating to Eunice's ability to have children.

"Eunice is in famly way."

"Ah knoed dat fo you said it."

"We went ta see Doctor Holyfield Monday mornin."

"And, Wha did he say

"Nothin yet, he won' kno nothing til de tests com back.

"Then let's don't git our danduff up til we kno somethin ta git jacked otta shape bout."

"Kay, yu right.

Work went on as usual, J D worried as usual and Eunice's morning sickness went on as usual. Farmers know how to do one thing better than any other people know how to do it, and that's to wait. Anybody who depends on nature, or somebody or something outside his own abilities, has to have the patients of Job. Patients were the main highways to success. J D was trying his best to develop these qualities. He just prayed longer prayers and put a few quarters more in the collection plate each week.

J D had the kind of job some called "head nigger" job. That was alright by J D because he didn't pay much attention to these tongue-wagging nitwits anyway. The Brittons hired others to do their plowing, planting, hoeing and so on; J just saw to it that they had the proper tools and transportation and so on. He saw nothing wrong with having a better job than some other folks. These folks were unforgiving no matter which way a man jumped. A man was damned if he did and damned if he didn't. These old, and young, farmers had lived in these cruel conditions so long that they had begun to saintfy getting along just at the lower side of tolerably well.

Monday morning was a long time coming, but it finally drifted in. J D and Eunice went back to see Doctor Holyfield. Mrs. Holyfield told them to wait on the back porch. They sat in the swing for about five minutes before Dr. Holyfield came out.

"Morning!"

"Good mornin Doctor Holyfield." Answered J

"The test shows signs of you being anemic young lady.' 'But I don't think we have much to worry about at the present time.' Now, I'm gonna give you a strick diet and I want you to stick to it.' 'Ya understand?"

"Yessuh"

Doctor Holyfield gave the paper on which the diet was written to J D and suggested that Eunice should start the dieting as soon as possible which was not much different from their normal eating.. They went home with the instruction to come back in if they had any trouble. J D was surprised that the visit had cost only two dollars.

The young married couple talked about everything they knew except the doctor's advice. They had no words for this brand new experience. All they could do was as they were told and pray for the best and have faith that all will end well.

Chapter Thirty-one

▼

The days got long and hot. Everybody at church was praying for rain except J D. He used up all his prayers asking God to take care of Eunice and her unborn child. Many kinds of evil human characteristics boiled to the surface during these scorching hot days. Old long buried grudges appeared out of nowhere and tiptoed their way into good presently-existing relationships. It appeared that at times like these nature brought out the worst in human beings. Rumors thicker than flies around a dead cow were floating throughout the community about a fifteen year-old girl getting in family way and the supposed father refusing to make an honest woman out of her.

The locals made the state of affairs out to be more evil than the situation deserved. The most severe condemnation seemed to always come from those who had at one time or another been guilty of violating the same rule that they were now condemning someone else for bending. The rumor was the girl's father had almore killed the gal and was threatening to kill the accused boy.

Some say the gal had not pointed a single finger at the young man, but he was supposed to be her boyfriend, therefore the social fingers naturally pointed at the poor soul, guilty or not. This game was playing in another arena outside the Antioch community. This was in the Red Creek Church community and didn't give the Antioch area a black eye This made the slandering of the girl's reputation a free for-all for the self-righteous hypocrites of the Antioch community. It became something to talk about during these sizzling days. The gal's daddy was threatening to go and shoot the boy if he didn't come and take the trash, what he called his daughter, out of his house. The boy's daddy and Reverend Ford got together and hatched up a solution to the mess that might save a life or two. These kinds of messes have been known to cause trouble for ten generations down the road.

Reverend Ford got wind of the brewing dilemma while visiting a sister near the young fellow's home. He decided to stop in and get the news straight from the horse's mouth. Mr. Turner and his son, Dan, were sitting on the front porch when Reverend Ford rode up on his black horse. Neither man had to be told the reason the Reverend was crawling out of the saddle in the Turner's yard.

"Good afternoon brotharems."

"Evenin Revern, come ohn in and hava seat."

"Thank yu brotha.' 'Dis heat is gittin ta me and mah hos,"

"Draw de Reverend a bucket uf fresh wadar, son."

The boy did as his father told him which gave the two older men a chance to exchange a few notes. The well was out behind the house near the barn and would take Dan a few minutes to fetch the water.

"Wha brins yu down heah Reverend?' 'Ah hope evrybody is well."

"Nobody is sick, thank de Lawd.' 'Nawh, Ah hea dar is trouble 'tween yu and de Traylors bout yo son bein sponsible fuh his gal's becoming big."

"Mah son says he neva lay a han ohn de gal in dat way.' 'Ah believe em."

"Ah wan yu ta thank bout dis Brotha Turner, Suppose we leav revenge up ta de Lawd and do wha we kin hea ohn oith ta brin dis mess ta a safe end."

"Dis is axin a lot uf mah son.' 'Ah'm willin ta do de bess thang fuh allus."

"Yu n Ah know dis kinda thang been don many a tiahm fo now n will be done many a tiahm mo."

The Reverend knew better than to try and reason with Mr. Traylor. The whole Traylor family had a reputation for being extremely pig-headed. These folks were proud. The Reverend had an idea who the responsible rascal was too. He also knew that to expose this scoudrel would turn the entire community on its head and create a mess of the like nobody had ever heard of. The Reverend sometimes had to pray for forgiveness for some of the means he had to use to accomplish the lesser of several evils. Every state of affairs didn't grant justice to all parties involved. He sure prayed for some other way but had come up with no other way out of this without the unthinkable evils having a feast at his congregation's expenses. Brother Traylor and his family were not in the mood for the truth.

Poor young Dan Turner became another sacrificial lamb in a society where innocence and justice may not be related. . Dan was just one man in a batch of men that had been done grave injustice in the name of peace.It didn't take but the blink of an eye before this coverup of a giant problem was covered up with a smaller problem sprinkled with a dashes of dishonors. Doing the right thing had very little to do with everyday existence. Survival was the game played out in this hard community. Do what bring the least trouble, the least pain, the least killing and so on. Making life endurable required a careful measure of the results of the outcomes of daily action and makes sure that no daily action carrys a lasting negative effect. It took some strange attitudes to maintain stability among these distressed people.

"Yu heah wha hapen down round Red Creek tween Dan Turner and dat Traylor Gal?" J D asked Bud and Allen.

"Yeah.' 'Dat's kinda lak wha hapen ovea in Alabama a few yeas ago.' 'A boy wuz paid ta mar ah gal who wuz goten in famly way by her ohn uncle." Allen responsed.

"Dis kinda doins hav always been wid us.' 'Y'all head uf de white man makin a colored boy mar ah gal that his son got bigged." Bud remembered.

J D was more suspicious of any signs of change in his normal daily activities. Even seeing somebody that he hadn't seen in a while would upset him. He started having strange dreams that would bother him for days, or until other bad dreams crowded out the old ones. J D spent more and more time in church and hanging around the house watching Eunice for signs of her being alright. He was really afraid to leave her at home alone all day. Her mother was there but was of very little help. Everybody in this part of the country either worked or was too old or sick to work. A few were too crazy to work or to be depended on to look after anybody, even themselves. J D found himself taking the long way to town and the long way back to work just to check by home.

One day he found Eunice in bed sick with inflamed joints and suffering agonizing pain. She assured him that it was nothing to worry about and for him to go on back to his work. He went reluctingly back to the Britton's farm. That familiar gut-wrenching fears of what might be coming were back with him as usual. J D had become paranoid and saw the possibilities of threats to his plans for his and Eunice's happiness coming from all directions. He had to talk to somebody whom he had faith in. The Reverend would only offer biblical information, the magic-worker's trade might be outside the blessings of the Good Lord, but a lot of folks bet their lives on the powers of the shaman. J D became more and more interesting in all the powers as long as they work, or might work. He made sure that he offended none of the powers that be. He never wanted to be a pawn between powerful beings.

Allen and J D rode into town Saturday evening to fill the list that Eunice gave to J D. She had been feeling poorly and opts to remain at home. J D had to buy some bug dust for his garden. The garden made the difference between eating like a king and eating like an unfortunate man. There was a few senior whites always hanging around the feed store, but nobody paid much attention to them. They had become too old to be fit for anything else except hanging around the feed store. There was one thing for sure, you could learn a lot about which direction the racial winds were blowing from these old timers. These old southern gentlemen had nothing to do all day but to gauge how long it will take for the old way of life to be just a name on a headstone. J D felt a tinge of pity for these old dying warriors.

"J D, Ah thank yu lak listenin ta dose old fogeys talk 'bout how good it usta be hea in good ole Dixie 'fore dem damn Yankees medle in dey business."

"Allen yu can' blam dese ole usta-bes fuh de way de south is, er wuz."

"Ah kno bettan augn wid yu 'bout yo good white folks.' 'Dat's de reason folks call yu ah house niggah."

"Ah don' cae wha de folks say, Ah don' blam allu de troubles we git on de po old rednecks.' 'Mos uf 'em is wose off den we is n yu know it."

"Ah don't giva shit 'bout who don wha, all Ah know is Ah ain't gonna take no mess offn yo inocent white angels."

"Ah ain't sayin dey's inocent, Ah'm jess sayin we is all Gawd's chillin n we is all guily uf making dis mess dat we is in."

J D and Allen seldom agreed on much of anything when it came to what was important and what was not. J could not think of a thing that Allen thought seriously about, except getting by the best and straightforward way he could. Allen figured every man stood on his own feet and was to be held accountable for whatever he was responsible for. Allen had no problems with holding people to blame for what they did. He was unforgiving when it came to punishment for a wrong done to a fellow man. He thought an eye for an eye was the only fairness that could exist among men of equals.

"Allen, why don't yu come ta church wid Eunice n me Sunday."

"Ah gota church ery Sunday.' 'Yu know dat."

"Ah don't mean juss ta come ta de church yard, but ta actly go in n lisen ta de Preacha's message."

"Ah'll thank ohn it some mo."

"Ah kno why yu go ta church n Gawd kno too.' 'Gawd don' lak ugly."

"Yeah, yea, Ah kno.' 'Let's git a burga n take Eunice one, she migh lak dat."

Allen knew if he mentioned doing something that made Eunice happy J D forgot everything else. Allen had no problems with those who wanted to live within the guiding principles of the biblical teaching. He didn't see himself doing the same thing though. His hauling booze for four or five bootleggers and taxing these voodoo mammas back and forth to buy their magical powers may not set well with the brothers and sisters of the church, but it set well with him. These poor souls needed his services, and usually were his best customers, but they didn't feel too holy sitting next to him in pray meetings. Allen reckoned it was safer to remain behind the line that separated professed religions from the common ideologies of his customers. He presumed that his way of servicing was very much as important to the community as any other community service.

Chapter Thirty-two

▼

J D was working from sun up to after sun down now that Eunice was getting heavy with child. He often had to sit up nights trying to ease the pains in Eunice's swollen joints which have become a daily difficulty for his wife. He even had to skip church a few Sundays because Eunice was too sick for him to leave alone. When he did go for services, he would convence Ms. Ann to come home with him to check on and encourage the expecting mother. Eunice's family history and her physical condition was common knowledge by this time and everybody was saying a prayer for what most thought would not turn out in a good way. The common notions were that Eunice's sickness was nothing but the continuation of the curse.

J D and Allen went to church this particular Sunday more to get the midwife than to hear the preaching and sell shine.

"Howdy youn man, how is Eunice gitting 'lon?"

"Bout de same Ah spec"

"Ah'll go wid yu soon as church is out."

"Yessum."

J D knew something was terribly wrong when he saw his mother-in law coming off the porch to meet them when they pulled into the yard. There were several other close neighbors standing on the porch. J D said nothing; neither did Ms. Ann or Allen. Ms. Ann rushed into the house with remedy bag in hand. The women blocked J D to keep him out of the house.

J D sat on the step and did what he was told without even a whimper. His sense of loss was beginning to over ride any other sensations that he had at the present time. He had no idea how long it was before Ms. Ann came out with the diagnosis.

"She loss de baby, son, and she loss too much blood.' 'Git Allen ta take yu ta git Doctor Holyfield right now.' 'Go ohn now!!"

Allen heard what the midwife said and had the car moving before J D could close the door. Allen was right about how fast his car would go and how good a driver he was. It was a good thing that no other vehicle or animal was on the road that afternoon. Allen ran through all the crossroads without slowing and the one flashing red light once he hit the city limits.

Allen went in to get the doctor who said that he'd be right out as soon as he could get there. J D still had said nothing at all. Allen drove back to the house at breakneck speed.

Everybody had expected this to be the outcome except J D. He lived in denial of most of life's realities, the greatest being in denial about Eunice's health. His folks and friends were afraid of what this might do to him. J D tried hard to simplify a complex life through his dedication to his God and his church.

He and Eunice having children may not be such a good idea, ever, even if she makes a full recovery. Eunice has always been a puny girl. She could work at the house cooking, washing and ironing, but picking cotton, cutting cane and pulling corn were beyond her energy and strength. It took a rough and tough people to make a go of it here on this land.

J D sat in the truck and remains quiet, even after the doctor arrived. He continued his wordless state when Doctor Holyfield came out shaking his head in defeat

"I'll leave it in the hands of God.' 'She has lost too much blood.' 'If she regains consciousness, give her some more of this pain medicine."

Eunice died before regaining consciousness. All had either gone home or was asleep except J D and Allen. The Midwife came out of the bedroom and started praying in a loud voice, the small group of relatives and friends did not have to be told what Ms Ann was telling them. J D had moved to the swing and sat there until he heard Ms. Ann praying. The squeaking swing stopped squeaking. J D went in the bedroom to see Eunice. He kneels down on his knees, kissed his wife and walked back through the house, went off into the cool dark night.

Ms. Ann told Allen."Let em hava cleansin walk.' 'Let em talk wid his Gawd."

"Ah'll wait fuh a while n den pick em up.' 'He sho needs somebody ta be wid em.

"He's going to his mama's and daddy's.' 'You can pick 'em up after a little bit."

"Ah figued as much."

J D hadn't felt anything but gloomy darkness since he knew for sure that Eunice could never live the kind of life that she was attempting to. J had known this from the beginning, but he and Eunice wanted so desperately to find a place for themselves that contained a little slice of what makes life worth the agonies they had to put up with. He realized where he was when he noticed the graveyard at Sand Field Baptist Church. This was the first time that he had no apprehension about being alone near a graveyard at night. He was without sensation, without awareness of the outside world to fear the dead. The terror that was churning in his guts left no room for ordinary misery. He automatically stopped and stood to one side of the dirt road when the car came down the road. J D heard Allen say. "Git in, Ah'll take yu home."

The two friends rode the last few miles to J D's folks place without mumbling a single word.

"See ya in de mornin J D"

"Alright.

J D went to his old bedroom with his brother and cousin the same as he had done for years. It was if he had never left home at all. His people could feel the pain that J was trying to deal with. They had no words that they could think of that might help at a time like this. Rather than taking a chance of saying the wrong thing, they said nothing.

J D remembers very little about the procedures related to the funeral of his wife. The flurry of activities that went on throughout the process didn't penetrate the walls of gloom and grief that had surrounded and overwhelmed him. He could not see how the world may possibly remain the same after this life disturbing event. This mind-shattering truth of his current realities was not testimonial of his previous trust in universial justice. He lingered in a state of distress for the week following the burial.

Allen took it upon himself to go back over to Eunice's mother's house and get J D clothing. All he had could be carried in a pillow case except his one pair of dress shows and his one suit. Allen walked slowly through the house where his best friend had lived hoping to build a good life for himself and a family. Allen wanted to see and maybe make connection to the world where so many of these peoples expected to create a blissful future. Allen had never made such a link to happiness based on the flimsy and narrow bridges between the top and bottom of the social structure. He could see no clear roads from where he was and where he sought after. He saw nothing but what he could make it to be,

Allen was told to take whatever J D may want. He may have any of Eunice"s things that he wanted to keep in memory of his wife. Allen took only the belongings that he knew for sure J D had bought, such as jewelry. He took no clothes. He conveyed to all a farewell for him and J D. He said goodbye for J D because he had a gut feeling that J most likely would never set foot in this house again.

CHAPTER THIRTY-THREE

▼

J D began to experience new dimensions to being that he had never thought about. He had problems saying goodbye to the old and finding new realisms for the future. He began to have misgiving about the assumed certainty that he had always tried to live by. The total foundation upon which he had so carefully built his earthly castle had totally gone kaput. He spent the next few weeks doing absolutely nothing but reshuffling his inner thoughts to be compatible to the new world where he now finds himself in. He had lost his paralyzing fears along with his other losses.

"Did old man Britton pay yu de lass money he owed ya?'

"He don't owe me ah dime.' 'Ah ain't been back since."

"Well, Ah got t hav some gas."

"Yu need som gas money?"

"Nawh."

The two friends hadn't been back to the store since Eunice went away. Ms. Jennie was thankful to see that J D was all right.

"How ya doing J D?"

"Juss fiahn Ms. Jennie."

Jennie noticed some kind of radical change in J's behavior. She saw the hollow brown eyes stairing at her from this crushed man who was once a storm creature. Jennie's heart almost stopped when she saw the old McCray's truck coming sputtering down the road. She prayed that these two rednecks would be nice for once in their lives toward colored.

McCray pulled up to the pump, pumped five gallons of gas, walked by the two colored friends and into the store without saying a word. Neither of the colored men spoke to the white men.

Allen attention was on J D's face which never changed expressions at all. J D's eyes were fixed on the two crackers every second. He noticed something evil about the way J D was gawking at the two men. J D turned and followed the two nigger-haters into the store.

Watching the strange acting J D, Jennie tried to make small talk to the two whites so maybe they wouldn" notice J D standing behind them. "Now that was five gallons of gas, two drinks and what else can I get for you boys?"

Mac started by J D, but J didn't move out of the cracker's path. "Boy, ex." Mac did not get the words out before he knew for sure this was a bad time to get nasty with this stranger.

McCray and Mac climbed in the truck and drove off mumbling to themselves something about J being crazy as a 'coon with rabies since the death of his woman.

"By y'all." Jennie told the two coloreds. Jennie's sixth sense told her that this good bye to the two men was as permanent as death itself. She watched them as they drove away toward the joint over in Alabama.

"Boy, yu alright?" Allen asked.

"Yep, Ah'm Jess fiahn n always will be."

"Yu now might could do wid a good swig uf stump juice, mah boy."

"De soona de betta."

The blues was playing on the juke box when J D and Allen arrived at the hole-in-the-wall. J D never paid much attention to the low-down country blues until now. The music seemed to be talking directly to him. He had never heard the music before, had never felt the music before, and had never liked the blues until he heard it through the fragments of a collapsed world.

The two social rebels hung around the honky tonk drinking coke cola and sipping whiskey all afternoon. Allen had to make a whiskey run early the next day, but the two decided to drive down to Prichard, Alabama later that day. J D rode with Allen every time there was an out-of-town trip to make. Sometimes they took people to see love one in the hospital, sometimes they took folks to funerals. Having the only colored owned car that was in traveling condition filled the need for taxing services that paid more money than working your fool head off in the fields or the woods. This was truer for these two than for anybody else. These mavericks were always ready to ride to anywhere, at anytime and with anybody.

Allen had a light load coming back from Prichard early in the morning. The two men had been up most of the night. They took a short nap while waiting for daylight. Being the only vehicle on the roads before daylight was an invitation to get pulled over by the law. They nodded for a while waiting for the early morning traffic to get on the road. Nearly all the traffic consisted of working trucks and school buses loaded with white kids. Allen drove under the posted speed limits not because of fear of the law, but the fog hung heavy enough to cut with a knife. The danger on highway 17 came from a possible collision with wild deer, or domestic animals more so than with another vehicle. The pockets of the thickest fog lay at the bottom of hills where the deer paths crossed the highway. Allen took care because he didn't want dents in his pride and joy.

"Dey been aksin 'bout ya at church, boy."

"Who?"

"Wilma axs ery Sunday, and some uf de other sistas too."

"AH might go one uf dese days, but now ah can't accep de hopelessness dat dese folks live wid.' 'Ah'm tryin ta cide wha Ah'm gonna do.' 'Ah can't keep ohn ridin wid yu and Ah don' wan ta do wha Ah been doin."

"Ya got tiahm yit."

Allen was glad to hear J D say anything about what he planned to do with what will be his new life. This was the first time J had mentioned thinking about anything since Eunice passing. The men got rid of their cargo and went by the joint again. It was actually too early for anything to be going on, so they just sat around drinking cokes and eating cheese and cookies.

"Al, do we sit around and drank cold drinks fuh eva?"

"Lak Ah told ya a lon tiahm ago.' 'I'm saving money ta git mah black butt outta heah."

"Ah gotta few dollas saved but not nea 'nough ta leav ohn."

"Ah wan ta pay fuh mah caw fo Ah leav.' 'Ah don't lak ta thank 'bout leavin momma, but ah kin send fuh her latta, ef she'll com."

"Al, wha would yu do ef yu wuz me?"

"Ah donno, Ah jess might catch de furst thang smokin dat's goin mah way.' 'Ah don blieve yu kin fihn wha yu is lookin fuh heah in Missippi."

J D was beginning to realize that things here in his loving Mississippi were a lot worst for everybody than he had ever dreamed of. He could not imagine working on a farm or doing public work in Mississippi for the rest of his life. It was getting hard for him to think about hanging in the area one more day. His family was the only reason he was still here. J D wanted a reason for being, a reason for putting up with a bunch of Jim Crow chicken shit, a possibility to make something out of his years on earth. Nothing seemed worth a damn anymore to him.

J D's family was extra nice to him since the dreadful days and he loved them for it. He recognized they might not be so nice if they could read his mind. J D had no desire to work, live or do anything else here in his hometown. Everywhere, everybody and everything here were reminders to him of a dream that could never be.

"Let's git a good nights sleep tonight old boy, we hav ah lon ride ahead tomor, J D"

"Whar is dis lon jouney to?"

"Down to New Orlean, de city uf cities."

Early the next morning Allen and J D picked up the hoodoo queen and headed down the U.S. highway toward New Orlean. Allen and the old lady had made plenty trips down this old road. Al felt eerie along certain areas of this road. Gray moss hung from the oak trees creating a dark and forbidden woodland that seemed to hide evils beyond belief. Al had never been afraid of things he could see and defend himself against, but this weird stuff was another matter. He appreciated J D's company.

"Purdy contry, huh?"

"Ah sho wouldn wan ta be walkin down hea at night by maself.' 'Dat's fuh sho."

"De towns alon de Gulf uf Mexico is purdy."

J D didn't care much for the city of New Orlean. The people were in worst shapes than those back at his home. It might have been the part of town they went to, but what a mess. He had never seen so many people sitting around doing nothing but drinking and nodding. The heat was nearly unbearable and the flies and roaches were even more awful. New Orlean was not one of J D's possible destinations when he makes his escape out of Mississippi.

Allen parked in a vacant lot in full view of what looked like a rooming house to wait for the mojo lady to take care of her business. The trash was everywhere on the streets.

"How in hell duh dese folks live lak dis?" J D asked nobody in particular.

"Yu'll git useta it if yu stayed heah ah while.' "Yu couldn' pull dese po bastads outta heah wid a par uf good mules."

"How lon do it take her ta do wha she com ta do?' 'She been in dah fuh ah spell now."

"Depends, depends ohn how many wan magic bags, ah cuses cast ohn sombody."

"Allen yu believe in dat mess?"

"Ah don' even thank bout dis.' 'Ah do de drivin, dat's all." J D was now realizing just how many crazy things that folks did trying to solve their problems. He was slowly grasping the notion that all was for nothing. These folks had nothing to be afraid of simply because they had nothing to lose. They conducted themselves as if they had everything to lose. J D was in the same stage of life with nothing to lose and nothing to be afraid of, not anymore.

CHAPTER THIRTY-FOUR

▼

The crop growing season had come to a close and the country folks were gearing up for the crop harvesting time. The winter's supply of vituals for the animals and the people will be decided by the kind of crops produced from a long hot and sweaty growing season. Gathering in these critical foods becomes everybody's jobs during harvesting time, except men like Allen and J D. These men were paying more attention to the gathering of cash crops.

J D had lost much of his concerns for balancing the right and wrong of things from a moral point of view, but he was slowly drifting toward the stuff that worked. He had sense enough to know that his new approach to problems solving was a guaranteed short-life expectancy here in the south. J D had become another Allen who thought if he could not have the kind of future that he wanted, he rather not have a future at all here in his place of birth. With his new attitude running at full speed, J saw terrible measures waiting for him and Allen if they continued in the direction they were headed. J D had lost his way.

Returning country boys from the far north brought signs of success and tales of plenty more where that came from. Just about all the young men, and a few of the brave older men as well, talked about was when they will be leaving their hometowns and escaping to the land of milk and honey. A few of these country folks didn't believe all the reports of good times to be had up north. J D had a big problem with the rumors that answered all the Negroes' prayers. The promised land lay a few miles north of Mississippi, so the sayings went. white folks were white folks no matter where they were. J.D wanted a little more than food, clothing, house and a used car to feel like a whole person.

"Ah heah Genal Motors is hirin help lak foty goin nawth."

"Bud, yu don' believ all ya hea do yu?"

"Ah'm tellin ya wha Ah herd, J."

"Ah'll be ohn mah way as quick as Ah kin save 'nough money fuh mah bus fare." John added.

"Ah don' kno if Ah lak de ida uf workin in a factry all day and half de night fuh som Yanky." Allen declared deafeningly

"Com ohn Allen, let's go." J D growled

J D became harder to get alone with by the day. The old fears that used to get in his way were now replaced by anger and frustration. He began to think that men like him and Allen had no place in the here and now. Allen's fast driving didn't bother J now days, which testified to the changed man.

They had to wait at the little country store for the whiskey to be brought to them. The two buddies had no problem with waiting except the brand new deputy saw an opportunity to put into practice his recently learned policing skills They watched the deputy drive up, park, get slowly out of the car and mosey over to where they sat sipping their cold drinks.

"Yew boys waitin fuh somethin?"

"Yeah." J D answered too quickly.

The deputy turned directly toward J D and asked the question again. "Yew boys waitin fuh somethin in particlar?"

J D never took his eyes off the deputy's sun-shade covered eyes. "Yeah, we is."

"We is hea waitin fuh Mista Clark." Allen plugged in.

"Be right with you boys." Mr. Clark yelled from the rear of the store. "It's alright deputy.' 'These boys work for me."

J D and the deputy kept on eyeballing each other until the deputy turned slowly and climbed back in his shinny police car and sprayed gravels all over the yard getting back onto the highway.

"Don' wory 'bout dat stupid depedy. He won' mess wid us so lon as we is haulin Mista. Clark's likker."

"Ah ain't worred 'bout dat cracka none.' 'Ah kinda hope he would try somethin out hea ohn de road whar dah is nobody ta see wha hapen."

"Boy, Ah thought Ah wuz nuts, but yu beat all."

"Dat peckawood betta fiahn sombody else ta mess wid.' 'Ah'll make em wish he neva saw a colored man befo."

"Ah kno how yu feel boy.' 'Ah've wanted ta kick a cracka's butt fuh as lon as Ah kin member." Allen had hated white folks every since he saw them damn near beat his uncle to death. He promised himself that it would never happen to him without some of them getting hurt too.

"Natures makes it hoid nough ta liv ah good life widout, de folks, black n white, being busy makin life even mo hoid."

These idiotic country folks never get enough of eating chitlins, coons, 'possums and collard greens and slaving to the whims of the white folks. Allen was thinking of all the times he had wondered how such ways of existing were born. He still had no satisfactory answer.

"Boy! dis old pile uf nut n bolts will run."

"Ah don told ya a lon tiahm ago dat nothin could out run dis heap."

"Dat cracka back dar won' forgit us disrespectin em, yu know." J D said with a sly smile.

"Who give ah do-do."

Allen was pretty sure that if he had to he would have no trouble outrunning the deputy's hunk of junk. He knew once they hit the back country that would be all she wrote for the deputy and his shinny car that he couldn't drive worth a shit.

J D and Allen were picking up pretty good money with their hauling and selling the devil's brew. This was the cash season and everybody had a few dollars to spend to make themselves feel and look better. Allen's customers were not in the habit of saving money for a rainy day. They either didn't have enough to save or nowhere to save it. Anyway, these poor old plowboys spent, or gave away, their money before it hit their pockets. There was not too much left after the pencil-pushing dishonest good old boys got through cheating them out of most of the cash. Monies left after the white predators got their shares were up for grabs for the colored predators. Between the preachers and the whiskey peddlers colored people's money disappeared like magic.

Allen and J D made sure they were somewhere on the receiving end of the money pipeline.

Allen usually made the Joint in Alabama his last whiskey stop. This was where the Antioch boys hung out.

"How bout a sip uf mah good stuff?" Allen asked J before they got out of the car.

"Ah reckon one won't kill me.

"Look boy, dis is sealed sippin whiskey, dis ain't rotgut."

J D saw Maggie sitting on the narrow porch drinking a cold drink. He remembered taking his first drink of rotgut right here at the hole-in-the-wall. He had become a regular member in the last few months. He saw no change in the place or its customers. The sip of whiskey lifted his spirit and pushed the depression to the back of his mind. Despair had been with him more and more here lately and the whiskey was the only relief he had. Maggie was her old self which was about the best looking woman in this neck of the woods. He had never thought much about the reasons that Maggie might be the way she was.

"Howdy Mista Banks!" Maggie spoke with an all-knowing look in her eyes.

"How is ya?" J D returned the greeting with a sharp edge to his tone of voice.

J D sort of resented what he assumed was the attitudes other folks had about him and his change in life-styles. He especially didn't go for these know-it-alls who figured he had returned to his right mind and the real world. This real world was nothing but a make-believe thing that allowed losers to get alone with less than what they deserve. He thought about the bunch of gutless people leaning on the artificial spirits found in a bottle of moonshine, in the church or in somebody's arms having sex just to get through the days. None of these tricks fulfilled the basic requirements for being all that God had intended for a man to be. J D resolved right then and there to never let himself become adrift on the river to nowhere.

"Hey fellow, want nother sip?"

"Not yit Al, maybe latta."

J D had known folks like Mr. Dan, Uncle Author, Grandma Ida and too many others to count, who made it through the day with a swig or two of stump juice. The poor and ignorant of both races were too locked in to an unbending social structure with its unworkable rules for the lives of all involved. He could see hope for a person who wanted to make the best that he could with what he had. All hopes, expectations, ambitions and plans for a higher level of existence were destined to crash on the reefs of Jim Crow laws. J D had no trust in his motherland and its conditions and relationships among its citizens.

"Al, how lon is we gonna do wha we do eryday?"

"Til we kin do betta, dat's all."

"Dat mite be a smart spell off."

"Ah've been thinkin 'bout maybe movin ta Mobile.' 'Ah could still do wha Ah'm doin n live down dar whah de action is."

"Wha good jobs is in Mobile 'cept riverfront work?

"No, No Ah'm sayin Ah mite do wha Ah'm doin now."

J D felt that Allen came closer to being a whole human being than anybody he knew except for maybe Mr. Barlow. Allen played by no rules, he just did what the moment called for. J D kind of agreed with Al's style. He couldn't think of a single rule that was true all the time. It was simply a make-the-rules to fit the situation that you found yourself in at any particular time. Not being legal citizens, there were no legal laws that applied to the lower classes in J's home town. The Negroes did not legally exist in the south as full citizens with full citizen's rights. The Negroes, and the poor whites, were counterfeit humans to a degree that erased them out of the human race. They could never be for real under such a fictitious tradition as Jim-crow rules.

CHAPTER THIRTY-FIVE

▼

The backbreaking farm work continued all the way through the long scorching summer days. The wagons and trucks lined the narrow dirt road with their load of harvested crops. The cotton went to the gin the melons to the roadside markets and the not-for-sale produce went to the farmer's barns. The old folks were predicting a very good and blessed year for the devoted Christians of the area. Even the hogs were getting enough to eat for them to be ready for fall butchering.

"Yep, Gawd has laid his hands ohn dis community." Reverend Mayfield preached.

Folks were too busy this time of the year to be aggressive toward each other, most were that is. The only hostile goings-on came from a less obvious source than direct physical assaults. The magic workers were busier than usual for this time of the year. Allen and J D were making more trips to get voo-doo supplies than they were for whiskey. There was no scarcity of homebrew because the farmers had plenty summer produce to make their own beverages with. The voo-doo queens were busy casting spells on some poor cotton picking gal or man because they were suspected of violating some social customs regarding the relationships between man and woman. The Sunday services were about giving thanks to the good spirits for blessing the community with an abundance of foods to last through the winter. The voodoo workers were busy petitioning the evil spirits to rain a flood of bad luck on some of the church members for reasons only the devil knew. J D and Allen added their part to the mix of total misunderstood attempts to control others; they always had the loco oils that made being a good, or a bad, person as easy as falling off a log.

"We gotta make a run ealy in de mornin, ya kno."

"Look Al, jess com ohn by, Ah'll be up.' 'Ah hav ta git up cause daddy gits erybody up fo daylight."

"We'll drive down fo de sun heat up de ar to much.' 'We kin be dah and back lon 'fo one ah'clock."

"Ya mite if dat depudy don git us.' 'Dat's one mean Alabama redneck."

"See ya in de mornin."

"See ya."

J D kept his money in his pocket becaust there was no safe place to stash the few dollars. He had managed to save pretty good since he and Allen had been making these runs. Tonight he had looked at his family and felt a profoundly sorrow for them and what their chances were of realizing any significant change for the better in their oppressed existence. He planned to send for them if he could get relocated and get a good paying job.

"Mamma, Ah want yu ta keep dis fuh me.' 'If yu need some uf it, take wha you need."

"Wha do yu thank yu is goin?

"Nowhah in partcular."

Allen showed up in time for breakfast. That boy sure loved syrup and biscuits with a little meat greese poured over the syrup. Fatback, syrup, butter, biscuits and sometimes an egg made the usual country folks energy-loaded for the long days work. Most of these skinny country boys could eat an unlimited number of these heavy biscuits at one setting. Mamma Gains sure knew how to cook biscuits.

The two friends moved off into the slight foggy morning to make their run. At least they didn't have to spend the whole day standing on their heads in the blistering sun picking cotton for nothing.

The cotton picking starts early before the sun rises so they could grab a sack full of dew-wet cotton to weigh up. The damp cotton weighes more than dry cotton. This cheating was common practice when the pickers were picking for hire. Those early birds took the only chance they had to load up the scales. The counterbalance on the scales was usually loaded with an extra dab of lead just to be unfair to the sweaty cotton pickers which was also a common practice for the boss. These poor folks were swindled in every way one could imagine.

"Al, don' yu thank you is goin way too fas?"

"Don't wory, Ah got dis old bucket uf bolts."

J D laid back and let Allen do his thing. He knew Allen had a great love for speed. The slinder Alabama pines became a blur as the sedan clawed its way down the narrow dirt road. They eintered the highway without slowing except enough to maintain control. Now Al pushed the chevy to its limits.

"Ah got ta git some gas." Allen pulled into the station.

"Moning boys, how much you want?"

"Fill up."

The attendant paused for a moment and thought better of the question that he wanted to ask and went on to fill the tank. This boy didn't get orders like this much at all, not even from the white folks, much less the colored customers.

Allen paid with a ten dollar bill which was another unusal here in southern Alabama. The two men pulled out of the station the same way they came in, in a cloud of dust.

"We'll be at de waterin hole in bout fifteen minutes." Al said.

"Yeah, we mite."

Allen and J D had been buying their gasoline at the country store located about three miles after entering the main highway leading to Mobile County. They didn't buy their gas where they picked up the devil's juice. It was not a good idea to hang around the pickup station any longer than absolutely necessary. Al slowed down to the posted speed limits when he entered Mobile County.

"Ah see yu hav sense 'nough ta watch out fuh dat crazy depudy."

"Dat bastad don' need much of a excuse ta start trouble.' ' Dis cracka is tryin ta prove somethin."

"All dese peckewoods is out ta make de colored folks less den wha Gawd had in mind when he created all dem.' 'Slow down Al, yu see wha Ah see?"

"Dat's dat scoundel.' 'He picked dis tiahm cause we don' hav de old man's booze in de car."

"Ain't we had nough uf dis chicken shit Al?"

The deputy had half the highway blocked with his cruser and was standing in the middle of the other lane. He had picked a good spot, right in front of a house where he had eyes looking on. Allen veered to the other lane of the highway, blew his horn and speeded up. The deputy jumped out of the path of the crazy boy's car. Al knew he would. The chase was on for less than one mile.

"Ah'm gonna pull ova J D' 'Let's see wha dis silly white trash wan wid us.' 'We ain't done nothin ta be runnin fuh."

J D was experiencing a brand new self at the moment. He felt no anxiety one way or the other. The old dread and alarm were no more. He was feeling like a man in charge of his future for the first time in his life.

"Pull dis buggy ova Al.' It's two uf us and only one uf him."

"Alright yew damn boys, git out of the car.' Both of yew is under arrest for tryan to run down a lawman."

"Ah wuzn't drivin de cotton picking car.' 'Why rest me?"

"Yew heah me, git over by the trunk of mah car, right now!' 'Yu two niggers come down heah disregarding the Alabama law like yew owned the place."

The deputy made the misstake of pushing J D up against the car with enough force to cause J to loose his footing. That's when J heard Al say." Yu damn redneck…"

Allen attacked the deputy from behind and grabbed the revolver and at the same time pushing the deputy down the hill toward the small creek. Both colored men went after the skinny white boy with all they had. Allen had to stop J D from beating the poor bastard to death.

"We ain't gonna kill em J.' 'Come ohn man, we got ta git outta heah now!"

The cautious one of the two friends had changed. Allen was the one to call a stop before they went too far.

With the words from Allen, J D kicked the white boy into the shallow creek and followed Allen up the hill to the cars. J D retrieved the deputy's revolver from the ground and got the shotgun from the deputy's car.

"Let's git J D"

"Not 'fo we push dis damn buggy inta de creek wid dat fool down dar.' 'We can't leav em wid a car so he kin run fuh help.' 'We need some tiahm ta git outta dis nex uh de woods."

"Boy, Ah reckon we done gone and done it, Huh?"

"I wand yew ta member dis fo the rest of yo life cracker.' 'Yu got yo ass kicked by two niguhs." J D had to imprint this message on the brain of the deputy.

The deputy's car was easy to move because it was on a hill. The boys just had to put the shift in neutral and let gravity do the rest. The deputy had to scramble to get out of the path of his own free-rolling vehicle.

"Yu said yu could drive, now is de tiahm ta prove it."

The men didn't have to be told what kind of trouble they were in. They knew the penalty for assaulting a deputy or any white man for that matter. That's what the charges will be even though the two men have done nothing more than stood up for their right to be. Justice in the Alabama courts did not exist for colored in situations such as this. The two outlaws were not too troubled by their new places in the southern social structure. They were the kind of men who had no future in the south as it applied to the colored people anyway. Instead of worrying about the dangers they were facing, these two jokers never felt as alive as they did after they kicked the daylights out of the smart-ass deputy. This high on the fact of being fully alive, feeling no obligation to appreciate a system that shows no mercy for them, was something new to them. They were in charge of themselves for the first time in their lives. They felt like men. They no longer had to play the victim's role of being racially responsible for all the hardships nature placed on the shoulders of man. They were free from the straitjackets of fear.

"Ease up Al.' 'We don' need ta have ta kick anotta lawman's ass today."

"One ain't nough man!"

"Jess drive ohn inta de city.' 'Ah guess yu already figued out we can't go back home."

"Yeah, wha is we gonna do fahm heah ohn, J D?"

"Ah gotta few dollars and Ah know yu hava few dollas too.' 'Yu still hav de money de Sheriff gave yu ta pay de licker bill, don't ya?"

"Ah had complete fuhgot dat damn money.' 'Ah gotta dollars uf mah own in de trunk."

"We betta drive ohn down ta New Orleans tonight fuh sho.' 'den we kin figue somethin out.' 'Wha do ya thank?"

"Let's ride."

The news about what the men had done, or at least what they were alleged to have done, spreaded like wildfire in a winstorm. The Mississippi Sheriff and his deputies were out to the Bank's house in no time flat. Their being out there told the colored folks that they had not caught the two escapees.

"Wha do yu thank Bud?" Daddy Banks asked Bud.

"Dem two ain't crazy nough ta come nowhar nea dis place soon.' 'Dem white folks thank allus niggas is crazy as mad dogs."

CHAPTER THIRTY-SIX

▼

J D and Allen were relieved when they crossed the Louisiana state line. They pulled over at the first roadside store they came to. They figured the small country stories would be the last place the news would hit, if it got that far West. The men stocked up on cheese, crackers, sardines, candy and moon pies. Two colored men riding around in a four-year old car was not too unusal in the state of Louisiana, the two men hardly drew a second glance. After the supply stop, they drove on to New Orleans.

"Damn dese skeetes.' 'We got skeetes at home but nothin lak dese killas."

"Hey Al, Keep de winder rolled up.' 'De heat is rough, but de skeetes is much wose."

The men thought that morning would never come. They sure were glad to see daybreak. The mosquitors must have gone to bed because they left.

"Al, we havta figure out whar we is goin.' 'We can't go back home yit, maybe fuh a lon tiahm ta come.' 'Yu know how dem rednecks thanks bout nigguhs lak us."

"It don't matta non whar we go, as lon as we git outta de south."

"We gotta go somwhea, and dat's fo sho."

"Dang dese hot drinks.' 'Yu reckon we gotta stay outta sight heah in de big city?"

"Nawh, nobody pay much 'tention ta two mo colored boys mixed in wid all dese.' 'Ya kno wha dey say, we all is jess niggahs."

J D and Allen remained in the city of New Orleans for two days before making the decision to drive north. They had not made contack with their families since they had become men. They knew their folks knew they were alright. The news would be big if they had been caught, if for no other reason than to teach the other darkies a lesson. Yes suh, they were still foot-loose and fancy free.

"Look Al, we havta decide whah we is headed fuh fo ar money runs out.' 'Ah'm thankin uf goin ta Detroit whah mah uncle is.' 'It'll be good if we went togetha.' 'wha do yu say?"

"Lak Ah say, Ah don' cae whah we go, so lon as we go back through by home fuh ah spell."

"Hav yu loss de little sense dat yu had?'

"It's rite ohn de way.' 'We'll be in and out fo dem dumb crackas know which way we went."

The idea didn't sound as crazy as J D thought when he heard Allen say it. He enjoyed the thought so much until he laughed out loud.

"Wha's so foot-stompin funny?"

"Ah wuz jess thankin 'bout wha yu said 'bout goin by home when we head nawth.' 'Yu set ohn doin wha ya said?"

"Ah sho do."

"Den let's git hopin."

The two outlaws serviced the car before crossing the Mississippi line from Louisiana. They made sure the oil, tires, gas and anything thing else they could think of was in good condition. They bought extra oil, tire kit in case of a flat, brake fluid and fan a belt.

"Let's stay in Mobile til afta midnight, den drive de back way as much as we kin.' 'We'll be at home at fust light 'fo mose uf dem folks git up."

"Ah still got some sipin whiskey in de trunk, ya wanta sip?"

"Maybe lata, we still hav de depudy's pistol back dar too."

Allen knew the back roads as well as he knew the main highway through the Alabama and Mississippi woods. The only living critters that were out and about before daylight were the night creatures. The Chevy purred through the still night illuminating the tunnel through the tree-lined roads and mirroring the green eyes of the cattle resting along the fenced grazing lands. The cool air, the peaceful night critters, the dark homes and the sleeping businesses made it hard to believe the evils that would come with the rising sun. The two men pulled their car in behind the Banks' house so it could not be seen from the road.

"Now Ah know yu boys is silly as dey git.' 'We thought yu'd be somewhar in de nawth by now."

"We couldn leave 'fo sayin bye ta y'all." J D told his daddy.

"Y'all betta hury up and be ohn yo way." Bud was concerned for their escape out of Mississippi and Alabama. "Ah sho wish Ah could go wid y'all."

Bud was about to make up his mind to go until mamma Banks spoke up.

"We need yu heah fuh de summer; we got ta git de crops in."

Mamma had a box of food ready in no time. She had jars of peaches, jelly, tomatoes and other foods that she thought they might need on their way up north. "Come ohn ya two, git ohn dat road." Mamma advised the men.

"Ah won't go by mah house, y'all kin tell mamma whar we went.' 'Tell her Ah'll writ as soon as we git ta Detroit." Al thought going by his house might be risking to much.

J D felt the keen sense of loss again when he looked back at the people and the home he had known all his life. The meaning of the moment was as clear as the breaking of day and just as brand new. This was the end of all he had and the beginning of what he never had, a chance to start a new life

"Les go de turner bridge road.' 'Nobody lives in dem woods." J instructed.

"We be gittin buddy."

The two men were lost in their individual thoughts about what lay behind and what might lay ahead on the road to the future. What they were leaving behind was nothing to be smug about, but it was all they knew.

"Gawd dawg!" Allen howled as he applied the brakes.

"Ah see Dem and dey done seen us." J D answered without being asked.

The only thing that Allen could do was to drive onto the side road behind the crackers's truck and block them from leaving.

"Let's make sho dat dar hunk of junk don't run fuh a tiahm." Allen told J D.

Allen was reaching under the seat for the thirty-eight revolver before he opened the door. "Git de pistel outta de trunk J D.' 'I'll keep em busy ."

"Yeah suh."

"Mornin y'all!' "Y'all goin fishin,?"

The two white buddies had not noticed that Allen was holding a gun and started to talk too much for their own good.

"Yu niggers done gone and done it now.' Smart-ass niggers like y'all will git what you deserve behind what you done." Mac said with that stupid grin on his face.

J D walked from behind the Chevy with the gun in his hand. "Is dat a fac?"

McCray saw the gun before Mac did.

"Y'all is in 'nough trouble already without you gittin in mo"

J D started to let the air out of the tires, but Mac didn't like that at all. Mac turned redder than a beet and came at J D on a dead run. J D tried to split his head wide open with the barrell of the thirty-eight. Blood squrited from Mac's busted forehead. When Mac went down, J D was on top of him like a rooster on a hen.

"Dis will be a ass-kickin dat yu won' neva forgit.' 'Go back and tell yo cracka friends how you got your butt beat."

In the meantime Allen had clobbered McCray over the head when he tried to go and assist Mac. McCray helded his bleeding head in his hands crying for mercy. He actually thought that the two colored men were going to kill them. "Please don't do no mo to us y'all.' 'We won't tell until y'all git far away."

The two black men were beginning to know the pleasures of having absolute power over other men, especially white men. They were beginning to understand how the whites felt when they dealt with coloreds.

"Dat's 'nough J.' 'We don't want ta kill de lowdown bastad." Allen yield.

After cutting the tires on the truck and throwing the battery into the creek, the two men went on their way leaving the bleeding white boys lying on the grass near their useless truck. The northward bound men were well aware that traffic hardly ever came through this road. Nobody lived on this end of the road and the county did very little to maintain it.

They rode in silence for most of the day. The two felt safer once they crossed over into the state of Tennessee.

"How fuh is Detroit J D?"

"Ah don't zactly know and Ah don't zactly cae."

The two friends rode on toward their future without looking in the rearview mirror.

J D had never gone back to the house that he and Eunice shared for their short lovely marriage. He had never gone back to visit the grave where his wife lay at rest. He might return someday. He may some day be able to visit his wife's and his baby's graves, some day.